José Saramago, award-winning author and the most celebrated of contemporary Portuguese novelists, began his career with an extraordinary little book which set the agenda for all that followed.

The last years of Salazar's dictatorship provide a backdrop for *Manual of Painting and Calligraphy*. The story is told by H, a second-rate artist commissioned by a wealthy client to paint a family portrait. As he works, he reflects on his struggle to survive in a bourgeois world obsessed with status and affluence. His portrait focuses animosity, his sitters are left uncomfortably exposed. The novel explores wider issues: the functions of art and literature; the critic's role; and, in H's tour of Italian galleries, a meditation on the influences shaping western culture. Back in Portugal, H is embroiled in political fear and mistrust when a friend is arrested by the secret police. He falls in love, too, and by the end of the story defines his objectives and achieves an inner freedom. This coincides with the Portuguese Revolution of 1974 and Salazar's overthrow.

Cover based on part of a self-portrait by JOÃO HOGAN (1914-1988) Collection: Augusto Capelas Reimão

Manual of Painting & Calligraphy : A Novel

JOSÉ SARAMAGO

Manual of Painting & Calligraphy:

A Novel

Translated from the Portuguese by
GIOVANNI PONTIERO

CARCANET

in association with
CALOUSTE GULBENKIAN FOUNDATION
INSTITUTO DA BIBLIOTECA NACIONAL E DO LIVRO
INSTITUTO CAMÕES

INSTITUTO
CAMÕES

This translation first published in 1994,
and this edition first published in 1995, by
Carcanet Press Limited
402-406 Corn Exchange Buildings
Manchester M4 3BY

Manual de Pintura e Caligrifia was first published in 1976
© Editorial Caminho, SARL, Lisbon, 1983
Published in Great Britain by arrangement with Dr Ray-Gude Martin,
Literarische Agentur, Bad Homberg, Germany.

This translation from the Portuguese
Copyright © Giovanni Pontiero 1994

Cover design and calligraphy by Kim Taylor

This book belongs to the series *From the Portuguese*,
published in Great Britain by Carcanet Press
in association with the Calouste Gulbenkian Foundation
and with the collaboration of the Anglo-Portuguese Foundation.
Series Editors: Eugénio Lisboa, Michael Schmidt, L.C. Taylor

A CIP catalogue record for this book is available from the British Library.
ISBN 1 85754 203 7

The publisher acknowledges financial assistance
from the Arts Council of England
Set in 11/13.5pt Photina by XL Publishing Services, Nairn
Printed and bound in England by SRP Ltd, Exeter

TRANSLATOR'S FOREWORD

'Each book I write is a conversation with my reader.'
J.S.

José Saramago first began to attract attention outside his native Portugal in the early 1980s with a steady output of substantial novels. The author was already sixty when he published *Memorial do Convento* (*Baltasar and Blimunda*, 1982), a passionate and compelling narrative set in the eighteenth century, which won critical acclaim and several prestigious literary prizes. His books were soon being translated into more than twenty languages. Further explorations of Portugal's cultural heritage followed: *O Ano da Morte de Ricardo Reis* (*The Year of the Death of Ricardo Reis*, 1984); *A Jangada de Pedra* (*The Stone Raft*, 1986); *A Historia do Cerco de Lisboa* (*The Story of the Siege of Lisbon*, 1989); and his most controversial work to date, *O Evangelho segundo Jesus Cristo* (*The Gospel according to Jesus Christ*, 1991).

Self-taught, Saramago did various manual jobs before turning to journalism, editing and translation. In the late 1960s he published a book of verse and this was followed by collections of essays and short stories and a play. Then in 1980, he published a political novel, *Levantado do Chão* (*Raised from the Ground*), which was much praised in Portuguese literary circles. This was encouraging, in so far as his first novel, the *Manual de Pintura y Caligrafia* (*Manual of Painting and Calligraphy*) had aroused little interest when it first appeared some three years earlier. Critics might have been misled by the title into thinking this was some kind of handbook for art students. When the novel was reprinted in 1983, critics came to realize, however, that this was the matrix of the more capacious books that were to bring Saramago fame.

The *Manual* is narrated in the first person by H., a portrait-painter of no great merit who, like all the main characters in the novel, goes unidentified for, as the author warns the reader: 'names are not persons'.

There are striking similarities between H.'s quest for self-awareness and Saramago's own reflections on the function of art. By the end of the novel, both author and protagonist have defined their objectives, and the sense of inner freedom they achieve coincides symbolically with the Portuguese Revolution of April 1974 and the overthrow of Salazar's dictatorial regime. The tense atmosphere in which this novel was written cannot be underestimated. Dogged by poverty and ignorance, Portugal was controlled by a backward-looking oligarchy. The rich and powerful thrived while the rest of the nation stagnated.

The influential industrialist referred to as S. who commissions a portrait, is a typical *nouveau riche* of the Salazar era. Formidable and arrogant, he demands a portrait in keeping with the canons of bourgeois taste, namely, an acceptable and flattering resemblance. H., on the other hand, is in search of an 'inner reality' capable of exposing the real person behind the mask. From the outset, relations between the painter and client are awkward and strained, and a clash of wills becomes inevitable.

Convinced that anyone who paints portraits portrays himself, H. would argue that the finished picture is only worth as much as the painter himself. Painfully aware that he is no Rembrandt or Van Gogh, H. nevertheless feels that his portraits could be more expressive and truthful. Accurate observation, alas, is not enough. The real test is to transform *seeing* into *knowing*. Here the protagonist speaks for Saramago, who in several interviews has insisted that: 'Each of us sees with the eyes we possess and our eyes see what they can ... Besides, the human beings we see around us are not one but multiple.'

H. eventually turns to writing in the hope of transcending the limitations of pictorial representation. Lines and colours on the canvas can only convey so much. Certain ambiguities are beyond the painter's powers but might prove to be less elusive if written. H. sees painting and writing as 'two skills so closely related that they are interdependent', but writing offers the greater freedom because, unlike the painting of a picture, a narrative can be prolonged indefinitely and the written word teaches us to listen to the human voice. He believes the important books of antiquity reveal a close resemblance to paintings and altarpieces and the most lucid and concise of those texts have been written with an eye for visual detail. A quotation from Quintilianus' treatise on *Rhetoric* reminds us that 'the orator (or writer) should not simply master the distribution of words but in his own hand he should be able to trace out the pattern ... that is why great artists are referred to as men of letters'. These words refer us back to one of the novel's central themes, namely, that: 'Biography is to be found in everything we do and say, in our every gesture, in the way we sit, the way we talk and stare, the way we turn our head or pick up an object from the floor. And that is what the painter (or narrator) must try to capture. Everything in life that is lived, painted and written adds some new link to our prehistory.' Confronting the empty canvas or blank sheet of paper, H. must reflect and fill the void waiting to be inhabited, and this is the crucial test for any artist.

The details we glean of H.'s past also suggest a close affinity between author and protagonist. Both experienced a childhood of poverty when sacrifices had to be made to acquire any kind of formal training. Both confess to being timid and somewhat insecure, introspective and sceptical by nature. Like Saramago himself, H. is a compulsive reader and thinker, a creature of habit, disciplined in his working habits and with few interests outside his studio apart from dinner with friends or visits to the cinema. He shares the author's fascination with women. Both feel irresistibly drawn to 'the sphinx and her mysteries', and H.'s amorous adventures persuade him that there are uncanny similarities between making love and the artist's tense struggle with paints and words.

Both as a man and artist, H. feels diminished and jaded. His relentless musings about the meaning and validity of art develop into a subtle debate about cognition. Images are fleeting and the creative process whereby they are captured is so very fragile. H. wryly concludes: 'It is a mistake to confuse art with life.' The distinction between reality and artifice is often imperceptible and as he goes on laboriously copying from the works of old masters and the writings of famous authors, he begins to suspect that ultimately 'all truth is fiction'.

A tour of Italy's museums and galleries, starting in Bergamo and progressing south to Naples and Pompeii, confirms H.'s intuitions about the cultural influences which have shaped western civilization, but the artistic legacy of successive generations is somehow incomplete. This gives no cause for pessimism but is simply an invitation to find the links in the chain and divine new paths for artistic creativity.

Overwhelmed by the art treasures of Italy and exhilarated by the welcoming 'voice and smile of Siena', by 'gentle Ferrara', by 'seductive Bologna' and Naples, 'a gymkhana of placid madmen', H. is no less sensitive to the political and social tensions which continue to plague a nation still contaminated by Fascism. Filing past the canvases and statues keeping vigil in those museums, H. becomes increasingly aware that works of art somehow withhold as much as they reveal, however patient or experienced the observer.

Once back in Portugal, H. abandons portrait painting and turns to scenes from everyday life for fresh inspiration. The sudden news of a friend's arrest by Salazar's secret police brings him into confrontation with the fear and mistrust which has gripped the entire country. Ironically enough, it is in this grim climate of repression that H. finally falls in love. M. helps him to discover that 'perfection exists' and she provides the reassurance so propitious for an artist's work.

Under the guise of a painter's odyssey, Saramago is already mapping out the itinerary of subsequent novels. His fictional works emphasize the importance of harmonizing aesthetics with ethics, ideals with social and political realities. As in all his novels, the most commonplace detail in the *Manual* throws new light on the complexities of life and death, love and conflict, fact and circumstance. Serious and mocking in turn, Saramago invites the reader to re-examine values and objectives. Self-questioning must precede any process of renewal. Like Marguerite Yourcenar's Hadrian, H. reacts against an existence which seems 'less vast than our projects and duller than our dreams'. Like the Roman Emperor, H. studies self, his fellow-men and books in order to investigate 'those intermediate regions where the soul and flesh intermingle, where dreams echo reality, where life and death exchange attributes and masks'. Opposed to the concept of an absent, impartial narrator who limits himself to registering impressions without reacting to them, Saramago defines art as a magical operation capable of evoking a lost countenance for the author, his characters and his readers. Reflection is the hallmark of all Saramago's writings and his *Manual of Painting and Calligraphy* convincingly demonstrates how paintings and literature can teach us the art of living and dispel fear of death.

Manchester, January 1994   GIOVANNI PONTIERO

Manual of Painting & Calligraphy : A Novel

On revient de loin. La formation bourgeoise, l'orgueil intellectuel.

La nécessité de se réviser à tout moment. Les liens qui subsistent.

La sentimentalité.

L'empoisonnement de la culture orientée.

Paul Vaillant-Couturier

I shall go on painting the second picture but I know it will never be finished. I have tried without success and there is no clearer proof of my failure and frustration than this sheet of paper on which I am starting to write. Sooner or later I shall move from the first picture to the second and then turn to my writing, or I shall skip the intermediate stage or stop in the middle of a word to apply another brushstroke to the portrait commissioned by S. or to that other portrait alongside it which S. will never see. When that day comes I shall know no more than I know today (namely, that both pictures are worthless). But I shall be able to decide whether I was right to allow myself to be tempted by a form of expression which is not mine, although this same temptation may mean in the end that the form of expression I have been using as carefully as if I were following the fixed rules of some manual was not mine either. For the moment I prefer not to think about what I shall do if this writing comes to nothing, if, from now on, my white canvases and blank sheets of paper become a world orbiting thousands of light-years away where I shall not be able to leave the slightest trace. If, in a word, it were dishonest to pick up a brush or pen or if, once more in a word (the first time I did not succeed), I must deny myself the right to communicate or express myself, because I shall have tried and failed and there will be no further opportunities.

My clients appreciate me as a painter. No one else. The critics used to say (during the brief period many years ago when they still discussed my work) that I am at least fifty years behind the times which, strictly speaking, means that I am in that larval state between conception and birth: a fragile and precarious human hypothesis, a bitter and ironic interrogation as to what awaits me. 'Unborn.' I have sometimes paused to reflect on this situation which, transitory for most people, has become definitive in my case, and to my surprise I find it painful yet stimulating and agreeable, the blade of a knife one handles cautiously while the thrill of this challenge makes us press the living flesh of our fingers against the certainty of that cutting edge. This is what I vaguely feel (without either blade or living flesh) when I start on a new picture. The smooth, white canvas waiting to be prepared, a birth certificate to be filled in, where I (the clerk of a civil register without archives) believe I can write in new dates and different relationships which might spare me once and for all, or at least for an hour, this incongruity of not being born. I wet my brush and bring it close to the canvas, torn between the reassuring rules learned from the manual and my hesitation as to what I shall choose in order to be. Then, certainly confused, firmly trapped in the condition of being who I am (not being) for so many years, I apply the first brushstroke and at that very moment I am incriminated in my own eyes. As in that celebrated drawing by Bruegel (Pieter), there appears behind me a profile carved out with a cutting tool, and I can hear a voice telling me once more that I am not yet born. Thinking it over carefully, I am honest enough to dispense with the opinions of critics, experts and connoisseurs. As I meticulously transpose the proportions of the model onto the canvas, I can hear an inner voice insisting that painting bears no relationship whatsoever to what I am doing. As I change my brush and take two steps backwards in order to focus more clearly and work out the distinctive features of this face I am about 'to portray', I reply inwardly: 'I know', and carry on reconstituting an indispensable blue, some landscape or other, white strokes to provide the light I shall never be able to capture. None of this gives me any satisfaction because I am merely observing the rules, protected by the indifference which critics have used like a cordon sanitaire to isolate me; protected, too, by the oblivion into which I have gradually fallen, and because I know that this picture will never be exhibited in any gallery. It will pass directly from the easel into the hands of the buyer, for this is how I do business, by playing safe and demanding payment in cash. There is no lack of

JOSÉ SARAMAGO

work. I paint the portraits of people who have enough self-esteem to commission them and hang them in the foyer, office, lounge or boardroom. I can guarantee durability; I do not guarantee art, nor do they ask for it even if I were able to oblige. A flattering resemblance is as much as they expect. And since we are in agreement here, no one is disappointed. But what I am doing cannot be called painting.

Yet, prepared as I am to confess to these deficiencies, I have always known that no portrait is ever faithful. I would go further: I have always thought myself capable (a secondary symptom of schizophrenia) of painting a true portrait but always forced myself to remain silent (or assumed that I was forcing myself to remain silent, thus deluding myself and becoming an accomplice) before the defenceless model who patiently sat there, feeling nervous or pretending to be relaxed, certain only of the money he would pay me, but foolishly intimidated by the invisible forces which slowly swirled between the surface of the canvas and my eyes. I alone knew that the picture was already finished before the first sitting and that my task would be to conceal what could not be shown. As for the eyes, they were blind. The painter and his model always look terrified and ridiculous when confronted with a white canvas, the one because he is frightened of being incriminated, the other because he knows himself incapable of making any accusation, or, worse still, tells himself – with the presumption of the castrated demiurge who boasts of his virility – that he will refrain from doing so only out of indifference or compassion for the model.

There are moments when I manage to persuade myself that I am the only portrait-painter left and that once I am gone no one will waste any more time on tiresome sittings or trying in vain to achieve some resemblance when photography, which has now become an art-form by means of filters and emulsions, seems to be much more successful at penetrating the surface and revealing the first inner layer of a human being. It amuses me to think that I am pursuing an extinct art, thanks to which, because of my fallibility, people believe they can capture a somewhat pleasing image of themselves, organized in terms of certainty, of an eternity which does not only begin when the portrait is finished, but was there before, forever, like something that has always existed simply because it exists now, an eternity counted back to zero. In fact, if the client were able or willing to analyse the viscous and amorphous density of his emotions and then find ordinary words to clarify his thoughts and actions, we would know that for the sitter it is as if that portrait of him had always existed, another him, truer than his former self because the latter is no longer visible, whereas the portrait is. This explains why clients are often anxious to resemble the portrait, if it has captured them at a moment when they like and accept themselves. The painter exists to capture that fleeting glance, the sitter lives for that moment which will be the one and only pillar of support for the two branches of an eternity which is forever passing and which human folly (Erasmus) sometimes believes it can mark with the tiniest of knots, an outgrowth capable of scratching this gigantic finger with which time obliterates all traces. I repeat that the best portraits give the impression of always having existed, even though my commonsense may tell me, as it is telling me even now, that *The Man with Grey Eyes* (Titian) is inseparable from that Titian who painted the portrait at a given moment in his own lifetime. For if there is something which participates in eternity at this moment, it is the picture rather than the painter.

Unfortunately for the painter, or to put it more precisely, all the worse for the painter who is trying to paint a portrait only to discover that everything is wrong, the lines are awkward, the colours wild, and the blotches on the canvas capture a likeness which may satisfy the sitter but certainly not the painter. I believe this happens in the majority of cases but because the resemblance is flattering and justifies the fee, the client carries home that presumably ideal image of himself and the painter sighs with relief, freed from the mocking spectre which has been haunting him night and day. When the finished portrait remains there, waiting to be collected, it is as if it were revolving on its vertical axis and turning accusing eyes on the painter: one might almost call it an apparition, had it not already been described as a spectre. On the whole, any painter who really knows his craft recognizes that he is moving in the wrong direction right from the initial sketch. But given the difficulty of explaining his mistake to the sitter, and because most clients are pleased with what they see from the outset, afraid that another angle or perspective might show them in a less favourable light, or, on the contrary, turn them inside out, like the finger of a glove (the thing they fear most of all), the painting of the portrait goes on, increasingly superfluous. As I said earlier (in different words), it is as if the painter and his model were both intent on destroying the portrait. They have put their boots on back to front and the path they have covered, which appears to go forward because of the footprints left on the ground, in this case the canvas, is in fact a hasty retreat after a defeat sought and accepted by the two warring factions. When death removes the painter and his model from this world, and the flames, by some happy coincidence, reduce the portrait to ashes, they will erase some of the deception and make room for some new adventure or dance, some new *pas de deux* which others will inevitably recommence.

On starting to paint the portrait of S. I also realized that my method of division (a picture, according to my academic approach, is also an arithmetical operation of division, the fourth and most acrobatic of operations) was wrong. I knew it even before drawing a line on the canvas. Yet I made no attempt to correct anything or start again. I accepted that the toes of the boots should be pointing north while I was allowing myself to be dragged south towards a treacherous sea where ships are lost, to an encounter with the Flying Dutchman. But I soon realized that the sitter on this occasion would not be deceived or would only be prepared to be deceived the moment I showed any awareness of being at his disposal and therfore allowed myself to be humiliated. A portrait that should embody a certain circumstantial solemnity, of the kind that expects no more from one's eyes than a fleeting glance, and then blindness, came to be marked (is being marked even now) by an ironic crease which was not my doing, which may not even exist on S.'s face, yet deforms the canvas, as if someone were twisting it simultaneously in opposite directions, just as irregular or faulty mirrors distort images. When I look at the picture on my own, I can see myself as a child at a window in one of the many houses where I lived, and I can see those elliptical bubbles in the glass panes of poor quality found in such houses, or that impression like an adolescent nipple sometimes formed in glass, and that distorted world outside which was all askew whenever I looked away from the window-pane in either direction. The portrait on the canvas stretched over the frame ripples before my eyes, undulates and escapes, and it is I who am forced to admit defeat and avert my gaze and not the painting, which opens up once understood.

I do not tell myself that the work is not ruined, as I have done on other occasions in order to go on painting, anaesthetized and remote. The portrait is as far from being completed as I would wish or as close to being finished as I had hoped. A couple of brush-strokes would finish it, two thousand would not give me sufficient time. Until yesterday, I still believed I could complete the second portrait in time, I felt confident I could finish both pictures on the same day. S. would collect the first portrait and leave the second one with me, proof of a victory I alone would relish, but that would be my revenge against the irony of that distorted image S. would hang on his wall. But today, precisely because I am sitting in front of this paper, I know that my labours have only just begun. I have two portraits on two different easels, each in its own room, the first portrait there for all to see, the second locked up in the secrecy of my abortive attempt, and these sheets of paper represent a further attempt I shall make empty-handed, without the assistance of paints and brushes, simply with this calligraphy, this black thread that coils and uncoils, comes to a halt with full-stops and commas, draws breath within tiny white spaces and then advances sinuously as if crossing the labyrinth of Crete or the intestines of S. (How odd: this comparison surfaced quite unexpectedly and without any provocation. While the first is no more than a commonplace image from classical mythology, the second is so unusual that it gives me some hope.

JOSÉ SARAMAGO

Frankly, it would be meaningless if I were to say that I am trying to probe the spirit, soul, heart and mind of S.: the intestines form another kind of secret.) And as I said at the outset, I shall go from room to room, from easel to easel, only to return to this little table, to this lamp, to this calligraphy, to this thread which is constantly breaking and has to be tied beneath my pen, yet is my only hope of salvation and knowledge.

What is the word 'salvation' doing here? Nothing could be more rhetorical under the circumstances, and I loathe rhetoric although it is my profession, for every portrait is rhetorical. Here is one of the meanings of rhetoric: 'Everything we use in discourse to impress others and win over our audience.' Knowledge is preferable, because to desire and strive for it always commands respect, although everyone knows how easy it is to slip from sincerity into the most awful pedantry. All too often knowledge entrenches itself within the most solid bastions of ignorance and contempt. It is just a matter of using the word unwittingly or without paying too much attention, so that the simple combination of its sounds will occupy the place or space (inside the air pocket where the word lodges and mingles) of what should be, if truly understood and practised, a work to the exclusion of everything else. Have I now made myself understood? Have I myself understood? Cognition is the act of knowing: this is the simplest definition with which I must be satisfied, for it is essential that I should be able to simplify everything in order to proceed. It was never exactly a question of knowing in the portraits I have painted. Enough has already been said about the counterfeit money in my change and I have nothing more to add. But if on this occasion I was unable to simply mess up the canvas in accordance with the desires and money of the sitter, if for the first time I secretly began to paint a second portrait of the same sitter and if, also for the first time, I am repeating, attempting, drawing a portrait in words which definitely eluded me through the medium of painting, this can be attributed to knowledge. When I applied the first stroke to the canvas, I should have put my brush down, and, with all the apologies of which I am capable in order to disguise the extravagance of my gesture, I should have accompanied S. to the door and calmly watched him go down the stairs, or taken a deep breath in order to recover my composure with the unexpected relief of someone who has just had a narrow escape. Then there would have been no second portrait, I should not have bought these sheets of paper or be struggling with words more awkward than brushes, more similar in colour than these paints which refuse to dry in there. I would not be this triple man who for the third time is going to try and say what he has unsuccessfully tried to say twice before.

That is how it turned out. The first picture was a complete failure and I could not give up. If S. eluded me, or I failed to capture him and he realized it, then the only solution would be a second portrait painted in his absence. I tried this. The sitter became the first portrait and the invisible one I was pursuing. I could never be satisfied with a mere likeness, nor even with the psychological probing within the grasp of any apprentice, based on precepts as banal as those which give form to the most naturalistic and superficial of portraits. The moment S. entered my studio I realized I had to know everything if I wanted to dissect that self-assurance, that impassiveness, that smug expression of being handsome and healthy, that insolence cultivated day by day so that it might strike where it hurt most. I demanded a higher fee than usual and he agreed, paying me a deposit there and then. But I should have put my brush aside at the very first sitting when I found myself humiliated without quite knowing why, without so much as a word having been spoken. One glance was enough and I found myself asking: 'Who is this man?' This is precisely the question no painter should ask himself, yet there I was doing just that. As risky as asking a psychoanalyst to take his interest in a patient just a little bit further, which could lead him to the edge of the precipice and his inevitable downfall. Every painting should be executed on this side of the precipice and in my opinion the same is true of psychoanalysis. And it was precisely in order to keep myself on this side that I began the second portrait. This double game was my salvation, I had a trump card which allowed me to hover over the abyss while to all intents and purposes appearing to founder, suffering the humiliation of someone who has tried and failed in his own eyes as well as in the eyes of others. But the game became complicated and now I am a painter who has erred twice, who persists in error because he cannot escape and turns to writing without knowing its secrets. However inappropriate or apt the comparison, I am about to try to decipher an enigma with a code unknown to me.

This very day I decided to attempt a definitive portrait of S. in words. I do not believe that at any time during the last two months (it was exactly two months yesterday that I began the first portrait) the idea would have occurred to me. Yet strange to relate, it came naturally, without taking me by surprise, without my questioning it in the name of my literary ineptitude, and the first action it provoked was the purchase of this paper, as naturally as if I were buying tubes of paint or a set of new brushes. I was out for the rest of the day (having made no appointments for any sittings). I drove out of the city with a ream of paper on the seat beside me, as if parading my latest conquest, the kind of conquest for which the seat of a car is as good as a couch. I dined alone. And when I returned home I made straight for the studio, uncovered the portrait, applied several brush-strokes at random, and once more covered the canvas. Then I went into the spare room where I keep my suitcases and old paintings, I added the same brush-strokes to the second portrait with the automatic concentration of someone performing his thousandth exorcism and then seated myself here in this tiny room of mine, part library, part refuge, where women have never felt at their ease.

What do I want? Firstly, not to be defeated. Then, if possible, to succeed. And no matter where these two portraits lead me, to succeed will be to discover the truth about S. without arousing his suspicion, since his presence and images bear witness to my proven inability to give satisfaction while satisfying myself. I cannot say what steps I shall take, what kind of truth I am pursuing. All I can say is that I have found it intolerable not to know. I am almost fifty and have reached the age when wrinkles no longer accentuate one's features but give expression to the next phase, that of encroaching old age, and suddenly, I repeat, I have found it intolerable to lose, not to know, to go on making gestures in the dark, to be a robot which dreams night after night of escaping from the punched tape of its programme, from the tapeworm existence between the circuits and transistors. Were you to ask me whether I should take the same decision even if S. were not to appear, I should be at a loss for an answer. I think I would but cannot swear to it. Meanwhile, now that I have started to write, I feel as if I had never done anything else and that I was actually born to write.

I observe myself writing as I have never observed myself painting, and discover what is fascinating about this craft. There always comes a moment in painting when the picture cannot take another brush-stroke (bad or good, it can only make the picture worse) while these lines can go on forever, aligning the numbers of a sum that will never be achieved but whose alignment is already something perfect, a definitive achievement because known. I find the idea of infinite prolongation particularly fascinating. I shall be able to go on writing for the rest of my life, whereas pictures are locked into themselves and repel. Tyrannic and aloof, they are trapped inside their own skin.

I ask myself why I wrote that S. is handsome. Neither of the two portraits shows him to be so, and the first one should try to present him in a favourable light or, at least, give a real likeness with all the flattering ingredients of a portrait that will be well rewarded. To be frank, S. is not handsome. But he has that self-assurance I have always envied, a face with regular features in the right proportions which confers that solid look which men who are physically as weak as I am cannot help but envy. He moves at his ease, sits in a chair without so much as looking at it and is comfortably seated at once, without any need for further adjustments which betray embarrassment and timidity. One might think he had been born with all his battles won or that he has others to do his fighting for him, invisible warriors who quietly perish without fanfare or speech, preparing the way as if they were simply the bristles of a broom. I do not believe S. is a millionaire by current standards but he is not short of money. This is something one can tell just from the way in which he lights a cigarette or looks around him. The rich man never sees or notices, he simply looks and lights a cigarette with the air of someone expecting it to arrive already lit. The rich man lights the offended cigarette, that is to say, the rich man is offended as he lights the cigarette because there is no one there to do it for him. I am sure S. would have found it perfectly natural if I had rushed forward or showed signs of doing so. But I do not smoke and I have always kept a sharp eye for a chance to deflate and subvert this affected gesture – from the moment a flame is released from a lighter and then extinguished, the opening and closing of a circular movement, according to circumstances, can be a sign of adulation, of subservience, of complicity, a subtle or crude invitation to go to bed. S. would have liked me to acknowledge the wealth and power I perceive there. Artists, however, traditionally enjoy some privileges which, even when they do not exploit them, or only exploit them as a last resort, maintain a romantic aura of irreverence which confirms the client in his (provisional) state of subordination and in his individual superiority. In this somewhat farcical relationship, the artist and the client each plays his respective role. Deep down, S. would have despised me had I had attempted to light his cigarette but worse still, he would have achieved what he wanted had I done so. There were no surprises on either side and everything passed off as expected.

S. is of medium height, robust, in good physical shape (as far as I can tell) for a man who appears to be in his forties. He has enough grey hairs at the temples to add a touch of distinction and he would be the perfect model for advertising luxury products associated with country life, such as brier pipes, hunting-rifles, Scottish tweeds, powerful cars, holidays in the Alps or in the Carmargue. In short, the kind of face most men desire because promoted by the American cinema and associated with a certain type of woman with long hair, but probably not worth keeping (I mean the face, not the woman) for any longer than it takes to photograph: in real life men are more commonplace, sallow, unshaven, have bad breath and often suffer from body odour. Perhaps S.'s face – his eyes, mouth, chin, nose, hair roots and hair, eyebrows, skin-tone, wrinkles, expression – perhaps all this is to blame for the untidy mess I have transferred onto the canvas and which is no clearer even in the second portrait. Not that it bears no likeness or that the first portrait is not the faithful image I charitably set out to achieve, not that the second portrait could not pass for an exercise in psychological analysis expressed through painting. In both cases, I alone know that both canvases remain white, virginal, if you prefer that word, ruined, if truth be told. Yet I come back to asking myself why (since the S. I have described is so loathsome) I feel this obsessive need to understand and get to know him better, when much more interesting men and women whom I have portrayed during all these years of mediocre painting have passed through my eyes and hands. I can

JOSÉ SARAMAGO

find no explanation other than being middle-aged, the humiliation of suddenly discovering that I do not match up to expectations and this other and more burning humiliation of being looked down on, of not being able to respond to S.'s contempt with indifference or sarcasm. I tried to destroy this man when I painted him, only to discover that I am incapable of destruction. Writing is not another attempt to destroy but rather an attempt to reconstruct everything from within, measuring and weighing all the friction gears, the cogwheels, checking the axles millimetre by millimetre, examining the silent oscillation of the springs and the rhythmic vibration of the molecules inside the metal parts. Besides, I cannot prevent myself from hating S. for that cold glance he cast over my studio the first time he came here, for that disdainful sniff, for the disagreeable manner in which he thrust his hand into mine. I know very well who I am, an artist of no importance who knows his craft but lacks genius, even talent, who has nothing more to offer than a nurtured skill and who is forever treading the same paths or stopping at the same door, an ox drawing a cart on its daily rounds, yet before, when I approached this window, I used to enjoy watching the sky and the river as Giotto, Rembrandt or Cézanne might have done. For me differences were unimportant. When a cloud slowly passed, there was no difference and when I later held my brush to the unfinished canvas anything could have happened, even the discovery of a genius entirely my own. My peace of mind was assured, all that could happen now was more peace or, who knows, the excitement of a masterpiece. Not this gentle but determined rancour, not this burrowing inside a statue, not this sharp and persistent gnawing, like a dog biting its lead while looking anxiously round, fearful that whoever tied it up may suddenly reappear.

It would be pointless to gather more details about S.'s general appearance. The two portraits are there and they reveal as much as is necessary for what matters least of all. In other words, they do not tell me enough but satisfy those who only care about appearances. My task is now something else: to discover everything I can about S.'s life and put it in writing, to differentiate between inner truth and outer skin, between substance and shell, between the manicured nail and the clippings from the same nail, between the pale, blue pupil and the dry matter which that glance in the mirror each morning reveals in the corner of my eye. To separate, divide, confront and understand. To perceive. Precisely what I could never attain while painting.

If revealing a man's profession tells us something we ought to know about him, and if running a business empire is a job in addition to all the advantages such a role implies, then I hereby affirm that S. is managing director of the Senatus Populusque Romanus. What is the Senatus Populusque Romanus? As used here, it is a disguise and another example of my penchant for anachronisms (the best history of mankind would be the one which gathers up all the ears of grain from the ground in one fell swoop and then raises the different phases of time to the heavens or to our eyes, ripe grains all of them, yet still far from being bread). I am not, however, disguising everything because SPQR are the actual initials of the firm where S. is in control. I am associating the Senate and the Roman People with capitalism and confirm that, at heart, there is only one senate and few differences in the people. I have another reason, a somewhat muddled reason, perhaps simply a tortuous expedient for not writing out the names in full: in my profession (which is that of painting) we start by applying the colours just as they come in the tubes and which bear names that appear to have been established for ever and ever. But once mixed on the palette or canvas, the slightest overlapping modifies them, or the light, and a colour is still what it was, as well as being the colour next to it and a combination of the two, and any new colour or colours that result enter into the permanently unstable spectrum in order to repeat the process, at once multiplier and multiplying.

While alive, the same is true of man (once dead it is no longer possible to know who he was): to give him a name is to capture him at a given moment in his earthly journey, to immobilize him, perhaps off-balance, to present him disfigured. A simple initial leaves him indeterminate, but determining himself in movement. I concede that I am being whimsical here, the fantasy perhaps of someone who has learned to play chess and thinks he can suddenly exhaust all the possible combinations (writing, or the calligraphy which precedes it, is my new form of chess) or it could be nothing more than the short-sighted man's bad habit of peering at things, whereby he comes to discover, and for no other reason, what can only be seen up close. S. is an empty initial which I alone can fill out with what I shall know and invent, just as I invented the Senate and the Roman People, but in the case of S. the line will not be drawn that separates the known from the invented. Any name that starts with that initial could be S.'s name. They are all known and invented, but no name will be given to S.: the fact that all of them are possible makes it impossible to choose any one of them. I know what I am talking about and can prove it. One need only play on the sounds of the following names in order to appreciate the emptiness of a name once completed. Can I choose any of these for S(es)?: Sá Saavedra Sabino Sacadura Salazar Saldanha Salema Solomon Salust Sampaio Sancho Santo Saraiva Saramago Saul Seabra Sebastian Secundus Seleucus Sempronius Sena Seneca Sepúlveda Serafim Sergius Serzedelo Sidonius Sigismund Silvério Silvino Silva Sílvio Sisenando Sisyphus Soares Sobral Socrates Soeiro Sophocles Soliman Soropita Sousa Souto Suetonius Suleiman Sulpicius. Of course I can, but in choosing a name I would already be classifying and putting him into a specific category. If I were to say Solomon, he immediately becomes a man: if I were to say Saul, he becomes another man; I kill him at birth if I should opt for Seleucus or Seneca. No Seneca is capable of administering the SPQR today (Seneca, Lucius Annaeus Seneca [4BC–65AD] born in Cordova, Latin philosopher, was one of Nero's preceptors; later he fell into disgrace and was ordered to commit suicide by opening his veins. Treatises: *De tranquillitate animi, De brevitate vitae, Naturales Quaestiones, Epistulae Morales.*) The name is important yet is of no importance whatsoever when I read off once more without pausing all the names I have written: by the second line I lose my patience and by the third I am completely satisfied with the initial. This is another reason why I myself intend to be a simple H. and nothing more. A blank space, were it possible to differentiate it from the margins, would suffice to say all that can be said about me. I shall be the most secretive of all and, therefore, the one who will say most about himself (give most of himself). (Give of himself: take from himself, waver.) Other people here will have a name: they are not important. Adelina, for example, I shall name. I only sleep with her. I neither know nor desire (to know) her. But I shall strip her of that name, just as I strip her of her clothes or ask her to strip, the day I find that name becoming the colour of the paint inside the tube or a bubble on the window-pane. Then I shall call her A.

Had S. not been managing director of the Senatus Populusque Romanus, he would not have sought me out to paint his portrait. He had the ironic courtesy to tell me this, with the negligent air of someone who excuses himself of some little foible, attributing it to alien motives which one only respects or tolerates out of disdainful forbearance. But in telling me he was also confessing to the first crack in his shell, before I had even considered a second portrait. In the boardroom of the SPQR there are three portraits of former directors and it was the board which decided (to avoid the absurdity of commissioning once again a portrait taken from a photograph, as happened when S.'s father died and the painter was called Henrique Medina) that the present managing director should have his portrait painted while still alive and that it be put in the fourth frame hanging to the right as one entered. S. agreed to having his funeral pyramid erected and I was chosen (now that Medina had retired) to open and seal the secret chambers. Using different words, S. told me these things (except for those I discovered later) in case I should hear about them in some other manner, and I charitably began mixing the colours on my palette as I listened. I could see the absurdity but absurdity cannot bear being watched, nor is it necessary in order to feel greater hatred and contempt. S. showed himself to be detestable: one more turn of the screw. As for me, next day I mounted a fresh canvas on the easel in the storeroom and made a start on the second portrait.

Were it not for my meticulous craftsmanship, which substitutes minute detail for talent and close observation for rapid intuition, I should be unable to describe this exterior of the SPQR which extends inside like a thermos flask, concealing the machinery, chemistry, or who knows what, which constitutes the core of any large business concern. Let me try to explain. When I went to the SPQR to study the chamber, the light, the ambience where I would hang my painting (and I could have spared myself the time and effort had it not been for my professional scruples), I first looked at the façade of the building, which I barely remembered, and once inside I felt as if I were moving round an inner façade which extended into walls, furniture, the faces of employees, carpets, black telephones, clear varnish, an even temperature, the clean smell of polished wood, a surface as opaque as a tiled façade rising on three floors in a square which looks almost provincial. It was also like entering the mouth of a sleeping giant, sliding along the walls of his gullet, passing through his stomach and re-emerging simply through the orifice of a body, through mucous membranes successively transformed, as remote from the circulation of blood-vessels and the functioning of glands as something about to be rejected through the elasticity of the epidermis. I should therefore add that being able to speak of what I saw, I do not know what I saw, I have not transformed it into knowledge. Not yet.

I hate saying *azulejo*, not to mention having to write the word here. As far as I can see (I am not referring to what I have achieved, for I am merely an academic painter), there are no more colours to be invented. Combining two, I produce a thousand, combining three a million, combining seven the infinite, and if I were to mix the infinite, I should regain the primordial colour in order to make a fresh start. No matter that these colours have no name and cannot be given a name: they exist and multiply. But I detest this word (shall I learn to detest others?) glued to things which do not correspond: *azulejo* suggests blue, made of blue, bluish, blueness, bearing no resemblance to these tiles which have no blue, these squares of painted clay which form an overlay in gold, orange, red and ochre, with an imponderable silver dust which might be in the glaze, on the façade of the SPQR. At certain times of the day this façade is visible and invisible, the sun beating down at a certain angle transforms the multiplied flower into a single mirror; an hour later the outlines are restored, the colours regain their purity as if the glaze had caught and retained only as much light as was needed for human eyes that do not want to see less but must not see too much, at the risk of no longer seeing what they wanted, but only seeing what they preferred not to see. There is a friendly rapport between the eye and the skin which the eye sees. And perhaps blindness would be preferable to the keen vision of the falcon lodged in human orbs? How does Juliet's skin appear to the falcon's eyes? What did Oedipus see when he blinded himself with his own nails?

SPQR also has one of those revolving doors which I regard as the bourgeois version of that boulder covering the entrance to the cave of the Forty Thieves. It is not called sesame (a plant yielding gingili-oil) and it represents the supreme contradiction of a door that is simultaneously always open and always closed. It is the giant's glottis, swallowing and spitting out, ingesting and vomiting. One enters in fear and emerges with relief. And there is a moment of anguish when, in the middle of a movement, we find we are no longer outside yet still not inside: we are travelling in a cylinder as though penetrating a wall of air, viscous as slime in a well or as solid and compressed as the base of an obelisk. I can recall moments of suffocation in my childhood, certain monstrous or simply black images (a black man would describe them as white) seated in my heart, and this shining drum brings back those primitive terrors. To leave, in this instance, is truly to issue forth, to emerge, to erupt from this dense atmosphere into fresh air one can breathe.

But I am now inside and crossing the vast foyer with its long, ornate counter from behind which employees raise their heads and start turning them slowly as if their faces, too, were a revolving door with larvae and cobwebs inside. No one recognizes me. Through an opening at the far end there is a broad stairway ('Go straight up to the first floor and ask for me'), with wooden bannisters in the Ionic

The Manual of Painting and Calligraphy   21

style (explanation: a cross-section would reveal the two lateral volutes of the Ionic capital) and a functional runner made of coarse fibre, held in position with brass stair-rods. I am surprised by these old-fashioned surroundings. The stair-well ends up in a rectangular gallery confined on three sides by a balustrade formed by an extension of the handrail. A porter in a blue uniform gets to his feet as I approach. 'I'd like to speak (I use the discreet conditional tense instead of the more forceful present indicative: I wish) to Mr S.' 'Whom should I announce?' I give my name. For this man I am no more than a name when he shows me into the waiting-room, yet he did open the door for me and leave me alone with the upholstered chairs, the carpet, English engravings of hunting scenes, the heavy crystal ash-tray. To get this far any name will do. From now on only another name will get me any further: the name or the person? Or neither the name nor the person, but S.'s secretary, for example, a privileged entity like S.'s glove or the knot in his tie? I remain standing. I hate sitting down in waiting-rooms when there is not much waiting to be done. No sooner has one settled on the sofa or perhaps not even settled because still trying to find a comfortable position for one's shoulders or to steady one leg before crossing the other one, naturally with that false air of self-assurance which is soon belied when the crossed leg uncrosses itself and takes the place of the other one which, in its turn, attempts the same abortive movement if the waiting drags on – no sooner has one settled or started to settle than the door opens abruptly, if it is S. himself arriving, or tentatively if it is some subordinate, whereupon we have to jump from the sofa, hampered by the crossed leg, almost trapped inside the springs which maliciously detain us. And if it is S. himself who enters with outstretched hand, we have no hand to extend, occupied as we are in trying to recover some sort of balance so that everything should seem natural and betray no hint of absurdity or anguish in this first scene of the first act. These things never happen to me. I went up to the only window in the room, which looked onto an inner patio with greyish walls, and on the floor below I could see another window which, I assumed from the lay-out, must look onto the large

JOSÉ SARAMAGO

foyer I had crossed earlier. All I could make out was a man seated at a desk with a pile of green papers before him (I said a pile of papers but let me correct myself: a neat pile) and to the left, forming an angle of forty-five degrees with the edge of the desk, stood a filing cabinet which the man was rifling through (not the edge) with his left hand, while holding a rubber stamp, seal or signet, bearing who knows what characters, in his right hand. And just as the man was in this position with outstretched arms, it looked as if he were embracing the emptiness before him, empty simply because I could see nothing beyond him. Then his left hand extracted a yellow filing card while his right hand, armed with some mysterious instrument, landed on the green paper and, coming down brusquely, left a black mark which from a distance was simply a blot. The same hand then grabbed a pencil with which he wrote something on the filing card, then his left hand returned to the cabinet to replace one card and remove another at the same time as his right hand put down the pencil and secured the black handle of the stamp only to go back to the beginning and repeat the same broad gesture of someone embracing emptiness. Seventeen times this operation was repeated and it was only when I heard the door open behind me that I focused my eyes on the image of the man who was working like this: he looked tall and bent, and he suddenly reminded me of a photograph someone once took of me in which I have my back turned, firmly turned, as remote from me as that man in the moon carrying a bundle of wood on his shoulders whom my grandmother used to point out to me and in whom I devoutly believed for a time. It is a photograph I often glance at (I have it hanging in my studio), filled with curiosity as if I were looking at a stranger. I never recognize myself at that height, with that curved back and those protruding ears, at least in the photograph. Which is the real me?

On turning round I catch the secretary, Olga (this is how I shall refer to her from now on), coming towards me. I am finally seated because I trip over another ash-tray on a tall stand and find myself obliged to make some futile but unavoidable gestures in order to meet up with the secretary Olga by raising my hand to hers as she begins to speak. I listen to what she is telling me as I dance on the tightrope of the unexpected, that Mr S. is not available, that he had to leave on urgent business, that he naturally sends his apologies and that she, Olga, his secretary, will accompany me to the board-room and try to answer any queries. I shake her hand, which as one would expect is soft and perfumed, and assure her 'that is fine and any questions will only take a minute'. Although looking straight at me, Olga the secretary makes no attempt to conceal her curiosity. Neither does she hide or presume to hide her disappoint-ment. I suppose she had another image of painters. She does not realize that I am simply an academic painter (will she have heard of such painters?) who dresses quite normally and that he/I could just as easily be sitting there with arms outstretched embracing empti-ness, looking up a filing card with the left hand while clutching an ash-tray in the right hand, just to be that little bit different. Like a couple of magpies we both try imitating the human voice as we leave the waiting-room and walk along the wide corridor on the other side where three huge, varnished doors on the left lead into the directors' boardroom, as I soon discover when Olga the secre-tary with a graceful turn of the wrist and swaying of her shoulders, turns the handle of the second door and goes in. I pause for a frac-tion of a second in the doorway, as we all do to prove that we are not ill-bred (good breeding is often simply a question of a fraction of a second, sometimes even less), and I enter discreetly while Olga the secretary switches on all the lights as if she were doing the honours in her own home. I approve. Strictly speaking, nothing is our prop-erty, but it is fitting that we should be seen to be self-confident and relaxed when we use something which belongs more to others than to ourselves, for there is always someone who owns even less. If I go to the cinema, the theatre or a concert, I know that the seat in which I am sitting does not belong to me but I behave as if it were my right-ful place in this world, a place for which I have fought and worked so hard.

The table is the first thing to attract my attention (nothing else attracts me but once having set eyes on the table I imagined there would be other objects of interest). The table is enormous, polished, dark as basalt, and looks like a vast swimming-pool filled with black water or mercury. There is nothing lying on top: not so much as a briefcase, inkstand or writing-paper, not even a symbolic blotting-pad. The chairs, eleven of them, are all alike except for the one at the head of the table, on the left, which is about ten inches taller than the others. The chairs are upholstered in red (expensive fabric) with lots of tiny brass studs. Perhaps dissatisfied with the lighting or disturbed by my silence, Olga the secretary ostentatiously drew back some curtains. I stopped gazing at the table and stared at her (a verb which means virtually the same thing but avoids that tiresome repetition reputed to damage style). This Olga the secretary is quite good-looking: much too tall for my taste (but what has my taste got to do with it?). She is also rather bony but smart in appearance. She treads the ground firmly and there is that untranslatable curve in her leg and thigh which the French call *galbe*. I watch her advance, suddenly aware that I am examining her swinging her breasts and tossing her head just once, so that her loose hair settles on her shoulders just where the mirror prescribed. Frankly, I have to smile because of what I am seeing, the rather nervous smile of someone who, being as fond of women as I am, always fears them to begin with, but I modify my smile with words and they come out constricted by that rectangular room and not free like those breasts and swaying hips.

She motions me to the far end of the room opposite the president's chair. I follow her, amusing myself, sniffing her out but hating her for those swaying hips which will never dispel or placate this black cloud forming deep inside my body and which I recognize as sexual desire. I pause at her side. 'Here is the frame,' she tells me as she stands there, staring at the empty space as if inviting me to join her in contemplation. It is clear that the portrait alongside the frame is that of S.'s father and those further along of his uncle and the company's founder. I go up to one of the windows: surprisingly, it looks onto a garden, suddenly green and luminous. I take another look around me, ask Olga the secretary to turn out the lights and open all the windows, to close all the windows and turn on all the lights, to turn off some and switch on others, to turn on others and put some out. I amuse myself a little, perform my little role as sorcerer and perturb Olga the secretary, make her nervous, cause her to breathe with greater anxiety, I am a kind of hypnotist, capable of laying her on top of the table with a simple gesture in order to possess her at my leisure while thinking about something else, perhaps about the green garden, perhaps about that mysterious fringe of light which has settled on the edge of the frame. And as I withdraw I shall be careless enough to leave behind on the mirrored surface of the table a trickle of sperm, like a protruding white scar wherein my frustrated children stir restlessly.

Olga the secretary is right beside me, composed, a little stiff, as if I had actually tried to rape her, and she, out of respect for her employers, were anxious to avoid any scenes. I give another smile and inquire about the dimensions of the frame. She blushes and tells me she does not know. I ask her to telephone me at home the following day once she has checked the measurements since I need to buy a canvas to fit the frame. She understands but is blushing again and as I go up to the window to take another look at the garden, she deliberately heads for the door, makes it clear that there is nothing more to discuss and it is time I left. As I walk along the corridor to the top of the stairs, she starts talking about S., informs me he is expected back in the office next day and that she will be in touch to make an appointment for the first sitting. I make some suitable reply and we bid each other a dry farewell. Somewhat puzzled, I recognize this same dryness in myself as I descend the stairs and start to see the revolving door flashing ahead of me. I look round the foyer for the man with all those papers. There he is, opening and closing his arms as though he were methodically drowning amidst yellow filing cards and green papers, while a magpie chatters before him and tries to speak.

I left the Senatus Populusque Romanus and went home. I sat in front of the empty easel and began reading. I had deliberately chosen the writings of Leonardo da Vinci. And passing from precept to precept I came across something which had often crossed my mind: 'Painter, look closely at the ugliest part of your own body and put all your efforts into improving yourself. For if you are brutish, your figures will also look brutish and have no soul; and in this way all the good and bad in you will somehow show in your drawings.' Meanwhile, it was time for dinner. I rested the book on the open palm of a St Antony who had lost the Child Jesus and made my departure. I cherish the firm belief that this saint never loses any opportunity I give him to improve his knowledge by reading the works of posterity: I discovered this when I saw him looking nervous and bashful one day after I had given him a book which was much too risqué for his pure mind. Today he had something better to read. Having died, according to historians, in 1231, it probably never occurred to St Antony that anyone could become as great a sinner as Leonardo da Vinci. Nor as absurdly human.

The first sitting took place three days later. Everything had been arranged through (or more appropriately by means of) Olga the secretary because, contrary to what she had told me, S. did not go to the SPQR the following day or, if he did, he had more important things to do than waste time on me. Having no maid, secretary or apprentice, I opened the door myself when he rang the bell. My clients usually find it 'most interesting' that I myself should open the door without any formality and wearing this overall of sorts, which is a compromise between a baggy shirt and the traditional 'artist's smock'. As a rule, they are cretins who know nothing about art and think they are about to discover it here just because they see canvases lying around, pictures and drawings stuck haphazardly on the walls and a certain amount of disorder kept within strict limits, which offers an additional attraction to the startled eyes of someone who has never seen any other art nor any other way of living art. My life is a discreetly organized imposture. Since I never allow myself to be tempted by exaggeration, there is always a safe margin of retreat, an indeterminate zone where I can easily appear to be distracted, inattentive and, above all, anything but calculating. I am holding all the cards even when I fail to recognize the trump. It is true that my winnings are small when I win, but my losses are also minimal. There are no great or dramatic happenings in my life.

I showed S. into the studio. He seemed relaxed, as if familiar with every nook and cranny (he had been here only once before, to commission the portrait), and immediately asked me, perhaps with excessive haste, where I should like him to sit. I sensed a hint of tension. Could Olga the secretary have told him about my magical way of playing with windows and lights in the boardroom? Could he be such an imbecile as to allow himself to be intimidated by my

JOSÉ SARAMAGO

antics, especially when described by a third party? Or was he simply trying to keep his distance, to show the substantial difference between his time and mine? Could he be trying to emphasize that a company director and artist-cum-painter have nothing in common, other than the face one lends X by the hour (with the one clear distinction that in this case the one doing the lending is paying for what he loans)?

I pointed out the large upright chair used on these occasions, which I take the trouble to modify from portrait to portrait so that at least the chairs are not repeated, for I am quite sure that my clients would not tolerate any such repetition. They would sooner accept looking like each other than seeing themselves seated in the same chair. Uncertain, perhaps suspecting that he was sitting down far too quickly, S. settled into the chair and waited. He crossed one leg, a gesture with which I am all too familiar, and then uncrossed it at once. I told him to relax and not to worry about striking a pose. For the moment, I simply wanted to make a few quick sketches in charcoal in order to familiarize myself with his face, the movements of his eyes, the twitching of his nostrils, the curves of his mouth, the weight of his chin. I prefer not to talk while I am working but I have to adjust myself to the client who is paying, become almost like putty in his hands while painting his portrait. Therefore I force myself to speak but rarely succeed in sounding natural. I refuse to discuss the weather and try to avoid asking questions that are indiscreet, although I have sometimes asked them inadvertently, and with experience I have learned to open these conversations on the same note, tactfully inquiring if this is the first portrait. I do not insist, even less so if they answer: No, this is not the first portrait. One might easily lapse into or wilfully indulge in disparaging remarks whereby, once the moment of mutual agreement had (perhaps) passed, I would naturally end up betraying myself in public as a disloyal fellow-artist. In the case of S. I knew I was risking nothing. Had he already had his portrait painted, Olga the secretary would certainly have told me, either to annoy or flatter me. Even without this reassurance, there was no risk. S. was not the type of man who seeks the trite satisfaction of a portrait in oils. Sporting a nice, even tan, which bore no resemblance to the wretched appearance of the man in the street whose skin begins to peel after being exposed to the first rays of the sun, S. overcame his initial nervousness now that I had assumed my role as craftsman and started tracing on paper what his features dictated. I do not believe I thought about this at the time. But on reflection (I now have to reflect on everything before giving my hand a free rein to write without interruption) I discover the reasons for S.'s sudden complacency: our relationship had defined itself after some initial uncertainty and the world had been restored to order. He did not answer my question but raised another, to give the impression that he was sufficiently interested, in the precise terms of a paternalism he had exercised on other occasions: Had I been painting for long? As far back as I can remember, I replied. I don't believe I have ever done anything else, I added. Of course it was a lie, but it is an interesting phrase which flatters the person saying it and pleases the person who is listening. It can be a pretext for engaging in a lively discussion about the controversial issue of vocations (Is one born an artist or does one become an artist? Is art an ineffable mystery or a question of rigorous training? Are the revolutionaries of art truly mad? Did Van Gogh really cut off his ear? Is the naïve painter terrified of the void? And what about El Greco? Did El Greco have some visual defect? Picasso, on the other hand, had a constant and *implacable* lucidity, would I not agree? And what did I think about the painter Columbano?), but S. pretended not to be listening and asked me if he could see the sketches. Naturally the patron wished to inspect the work of his employee. I passed him the sheets of paper which he quickly scanned, nodding his head with greater force than the situation warranted, and then handed them back to me. I punished him somewhat for his impertinence by keeping the drawings in my hand without looking at them or at him, thus showing that there had been some mistake, that the rules of a cordial relationship between painter and client had been infringed. Did he not realize that a drawing is something sacred? Was he not aware that it cannot be seen without permission and sometimes not

JOSÉ SARAMAGO

even with permission? Putting the sheets of paper on one side, I told him that was all I needed for the moment. I also suggested it might be a good idea to arrange the next session right away rather than waste time trying to contact him through an intermediary. I spoke these words on a somewhat aggressive note, I accentuated the word *intermediary.* At that moment I felt certain (mindful of thousands of illustrated anecdotes worldwide) that S. was having or had had a sexual relationship with Olga the secretary, and by sexual relationship I mean everything that happens in bed or somewhere else in the absence of a bed between persons of a different or the same sex who decide to investigate a partner's sexuality with some parts of their body. S. was equally brusque as he suggested a date for the next session and I softened my tone, reassured and confident (by his very brusqueness) that there was no longer any (sexual) relationship with Olga the secretary. I accompanied him to the door. We tacitly avoided shaking hands as we said goodbye. I heard him quickly descend the steep staircase and within minutes start up the engine of his powerful car and drive off. There was no need to go to the window to know that the message vibrating in the atmosphere was from him. Still annoyed? Or being sarcastic? Had my reign ended so soon? Had my prestige, aura, see-how-different-I-am waned so quickly? What would he have to say, what sour comments would he cynically make while dictating letters to Olga the secretary? When talking about me, would they refer to H. or to that artist fellow? How do others actually talk about us? How do others see us? How do we see ourselves?

I picked up the drawings again, examined them with indifference, laid them aside. This was a face that would cause me no problems: as regular and commonplace as any well-designed advertisement. A mouth which would look good with a pipe, eyes one could show half-closed against the sea-breeze, hair for the same wind to tousle or for feminine fingers with long, lacquered nails to stroke with knowing and calculating sensuality. Looking through the window I saw the white evening sky and felt I was all alone. Holding a gin and tonic, iced and aromatic, in one hand, I leaned back on the well-worn studio divan and sipped at my leisure. I had left the kitchen light on but made no attempt to get up and switch it off. Had I closed the fridge door? The clock chimed (I never use a wristwatch when I am working) and I thought Adelina might already be at home. I got up from the divan, went into the bedroom where I keep the telephone and when she answered I immediately invited her to dinner and suggested we could go to the cinema afterwards. She accepted without a moment's hesitation. She never refuses.

At this time, I had only known Adelina a little over six months. That is to say: I had known her for at least two years, but had only been going to bed with her (to have sex, of course) for little more than six months. We had started this affair in the usual way: some friends who had called for a chat after dinner brought Adelina with them, a long-standing friend, the hours passed, eventually everyone left except Adelina, her idea or my silent insistence, and once we were alone we discovered we had been interested in each other for a while, and things being what they are, she stayed and slept what was left of the night after we had made love. She lives with her widowed mother who does not ask too many questions if Adelina returns home in the early hours, but to stay out all night looks bad. And Adelina tells me she tries not to upset the old girl. I pray in silence that her dear old mother will not change her mind, but to keep the fire burning I periodically throw a tantrum. Poor Adelina, torn between a false lover and a mother who has relinquished all her authority except for this nightly vigil. So far, this triangular situation has worked to perfection.

Anxious to speak about S., since the objective of this inquiry is to find out what has been lost between the first and the second portrait, or what was already lost forever (what had been forever lost in me), I must probe the meaning of this complacency which brings me to discuss Adelina when it has nothing to do with Adelina. But perhaps there is no point in drawing up an inventory of someone's strengths and weaknesses in order to fight them, or to record statistics without first examining our own strengths and weaknesses. Any such examination will make it impossible for us to ignore those which weigh on us like lead pellets revolving inside a cylinder moved by some other force, within whose movement those same lead pellets are activated without affecting the cylinder or the effective force. Poor Adelina, as I jokingly think of her, is much less 'poor' than I have suggested. She comes into my bed, consents and demands that I enter her (this ingenious transposition results in total obscenity because entering her literally means that I have reduced myself to minute proportions in order to be able to press [or should I say regress] inside her or, on the contrary, that this same interior has become as big as a cathedral, the Basilica of St Peter, the Church of Notre Dame, the greenish-gold grotto of Aracena through which I pass [penetrate] in my natural size, splashing about amidst humours and secretions, resting on swollen mucous membranes, and ever advancing towards the secret of the universe, towards the laboratory of the ovaries, the stentorian cry of [mute] Fallopian tubes, inhaling the earth's primordial odours stored there in all female sexual organs, no longer obscene because sex is not obscene, as I have come to know). And because I am entering her and she is, however involuntarily, a part of this life in which she and I participate and where we are both on the same ledge, on the same narrow ridge of Chartres, I can neither say 'Poor Adelina' nor forget her. Inside her I am forever spilling millions of spermatozoa already condemned to death, trapped in a viscous fluid which pours from me as I lie there panting, and even though I do not love her nor she love me, neither of us escapes the fleeting moment when our weary and sated bodies rest, mine nearly always on top of hers, hers sometimes on top of mine, and as we lie, the one on top of the other, our united bodies support each other. At the end of the sexual act (also known as making love) the body underneath weighs on the one on top, and anyone who has failed to discover this possesses neither body nor sex nor self-awareness. The force of gravity is, therefore, exercised twice, not in order to annul itself but to ensure complete prostration. For the levitation of bodies is impossible when the male organ is still deeply anchored inside a woman's body, spilling or having spilled the white secretion from the testicles and is washing itself between the red or rosy inflamed walls at the same time as the remote sadness of copulation enshrouds the mind in veils and pulverises those abandoned limbs one by one.

Adelina and I both know that one day we shall terminate this relationship: only our inertia keeps it going. Needless to say, I am not the first man in her life; she has had various men, some of whom I know and who speak to her as friends, for they never loved her nor did she love them, just as I shall speak to her as a friend when we come to experience the brief sorrow of parting. And perhaps she will call at my house when some other Adelina is there who will spend the night with me when all the others have gone, perhaps she will leave with another man and spend the night with him, and far away from each other we shall make gestures we both know on other bodies, our past forgotten and so absorbed or distracted by this new encounter that there is no common memory, and even if there were, it would be pure thought, something from another existence or even relating to someone else. That is why I am so convinced of this simple truth of mine: the I at this moment is fundamentally different from what it was a moment ago, sometimes the opposite, but certainly always different. So I am convinced the past is dead (it would not be enough simply to say it is over). The women I have had so far are dead and the more I loved them the more dead they are. Yet I loved none of them sufficiently for part of me to die with them.

Relationships such as this one are remarkably serene. They work as long as the need to be mutually faithful does not become a burden, and they have already terminated once this tacit agreement has been infringed. Nothing is lost or complicated so long as the game is honest: only bourgeois couples betray each other, only marriage certificates become the cages of frenzied madmen, a wild jungle inhabited by mindless dinosaurs. If Adelina leaves me or I should ask her to go, or we both suddenly look at each other with indifference, one hour of time will settle quietly on another hour of time, and the world will prepare itself for rebirth. And if we should separate here in my flat, I shall be listening out for her footsteps descending the echoing staircase, increasingly less distinct, increasingly further away, and perhaps one of my women neighbours who knows her and thinks our affair is permanent will greet her: 'Good evening, see you tomorrow', and I alone will know and Adelina, too, that there will be no tomorrow. As for the evening, if we look closely we can see that it is as pleasant as any other. Both of us also aware that we shall say in our turn, 'Good evening, see you tomorrow', when we meet again, with scarcely any sexual attraction unless suddenly aroused by an incautious glance, some fortuitous contact, or a little too much alcohol which has gone to the head. By then everything will be dead with no resentment on our part. There is no other difference.

Adelina is eighteen years younger than me. She has a good body, an exquisite belly inside and out, a wonderful fornicating machine, and she has the kind of intelligence I admire. She's not very bright, my friends remark, but then she is no fool either. She manages or owns a boutique (I have never really found out which) and earns a good living. She does not live at my expense, I am glad to say. She seems to be satisfied with our arrangement, somewhat independent and detached, but always willing to go out with me and I suspect she would not be averse to a closer relationship. I use my work as an excuse, and she has the decency to consider it a profession like any other, for she knows enough about the arts to make the distinction. Thanks to her good taste and common sense and to the esteem in which she obviously holds me, we can discuss painting without referring to my work, as naturally as we might discuss astronautics without my being Laika or her being von Braun or vice-versa. Yet I find this silence somewhat annoying: nothing I do matters to her; neither my pictures, which she does not like, nor my money, which she does not need. To be frank, the only place where we can honestly meet is in bed: there I am not a painter nor she the owner of a boutique; as for intelligence, that of the sexual organs suffices and they know what they are doing.

It was not until fifteen days later that S. explained why he wanted this portrait, so much at variance with his nature and outlook as a man of his time. I never ask my clients in this blunt manner why they decided to have their portrait painted. Were I to do so, I should give the impression of having little esteem for the work which provides me with a living. I must proceed (as I have always done) as if a portrait in oils were the confirmation of a life, its culmination and moment of triumph, and therefore accept the inevitable fact that success is the prerogative of the chosen few. To ask would be to question the right of these chosen souls to have their portrait painted, when this privilege is clearly theirs by right and because of the large sum of money they are paying and the sumptuous surroundings in which they display the finished work, which they alone appreciate according to how they value themselves. I have often thought about the care with which spotlights are installed to enhance these portraits, like tiny suns created exclusively to illuminate a single planet from a certain angle: a diffused light contemplating the entire surface, a soft, crepuscular glow which obscures nothing yet highlights nothing, and there is that preferred light which encircles faces and illumines them in search of an imaginary spirit or a real one covered with impenetrable layers of paint. Confronted by pictures lit up in this way, one is obliged to stop. We are as bereft of ideas as the painting is of meaning, everything sharing in the same complicity, in the same connivance, in the same hypocrisy. On these occasions I am truly ashamed of my profession: to live a lie, to exploit it as if it were truth and justify it with the indisputable name of art, can sometimes become intolerable. The one who least deserves to be despised is the person having a portrait painted, who can be forgiven, after all, for being so ingenuous. I am speaking about the portrait I am painting, about the portraits I see which could have been signed by me; I am not referring, for example, to the portrait of Federico da Montefeltro painted by Piero della Francesca, which can be seen in Florence. At this very moment I can get up from my chair, search among my books and once more gaze at that profile of a middle-aged man who knows he is ugly but is unperturbed, his nose shaped like an easel, and in the background an imponderable landscape which I know to be the real Tuscany. And having looked (or not wishing to look now), my fingers grow numb with that severe chill known as despondency, remorse and defeat, and where an infinite and nameless expanse of ice still remains. I transfer this reflection to the names of the model and the painter and begin savouring them, separating them between my teeth into tiny morsels, translating them into my native Portuguese in order to know them better or lose them forevermore: Frederico de Montefeltro, almost unchanged, and Pedro da Francisca or dos Franciscos, the son of a shoemaker, poor devil, whose mother might have been called Francesca, and who as an old, blind man allowed himself to be led around by a boy named Marco di Longaro, who appears to have been born just for this because all he left behind were the lanterns he went on to make in order to earn his living. And I, who will leave no lanterns behind and have never learned to guide myself, ask what purpose eyes serve.

When S. told me, smiling, that his portrait was being painted at the request of the Board of Directors and to please his mother, I froze as I stood there at my easel with one arm poised in mid-air, my eye fixed on the tip of my brush where the paint slowly trickled, liquid viscera abruptly cut off at the root, but still throbbing, like a lizard's tail or the surviving half of a blindworm. I hated S. for making me feel so unhappy, so positively useless, so very much the painter without any painting, and the brushstroke which I finally applied to the canvas was, in fact, the first brushstroke of the second canvas. We have all dreamt at some time or other of saving someone from drowning, and after having used my arms as best I could, I found myself holding a plastic doll with a derisive smile on its face and a mechanism inside which produced the sound of laughter. It was only later that I learned the story of the portrait of S.'s father: the sheer absurdity of it all would have dissuaded him from saying anything. Nor is it true, as I said earlier, that I remained charitably mixing the colours on my palette as I listened: that came later, and not charitably, or simply with the unconscious charity of someone aware of seeking revenge by some means or other. As a painter, only the techniques of painting were within my grasp, and that was how the second portrait came about. Perhaps my silence may have offended S. and turned against him a weapon which was not being handled by me. His patronizing disdain soon turned to a hostility he made no attempt to conceal. This was clearly why the sessions became less frequent. The first portrait made little progress, as if awaiting the second one painted in different colours, with different gestures and no respect, because determined by wrath, because money could not paralyse it. Even at that point I believed the craft of painting would be enough to achieve the modest victory of coming to terms with myself.

After all, how important is the story of the portrait of S.'s father? Let the portrait painter who has never copied from a photograph cast the first stone, and I shall not be stoned because no one will ever remember my having been involved in anything like that. What is the difference between a silent photograph and a vacant face that leers and grimaces in pursuit of some impossible and sublime expression? The painter Henrique Medina was wise enough to earn his money without being obliged to speak to his foreign clients. And what would this one say to him if he were to speak? What does S. say to me as I paint his portrait? What ties exist beyond our common fear and mutual dishonesty? At least Olga the secretary, so reserved in the great boardroom, so secretive as she guided me along corridors, spoke as much as I allowed her, so nervous and absurdly flustered, so bourgeois after all, and almost endearing in her sudden desire to be esteemed by the middle-aged painter who was listening to her message, somewhat distracted, but converting that same distraction into the invisible cloak of rapt attention. S.

could not keep his appointment and she had called to tell me since my telephone was out of order, something of which I myself was as yet not aware. I invited Olga the secretary to enter, as she stood there trying to recover her breath after climbing four flights of stairs in the absence of any lift. I noticed that she had come prepared to linger, curious to probe a world of which she knew nothing and undoubtedly adorned in her imagination with all those picturesque details one finds in certain second-rate films. I also noticed (but not on this particular day) that S. had spoken about me in formal terms, not out of any respect (I assume) but because to have treated me disrespectfully would have shown a lack of self-respect, once he had resigned himself to sitting quite still while I examined him like a surgeon, fabricating a double without flesh or blood but with a threatening illusion of reality. Olga the secretary arrived exuding confidence, as she thought, but inquisitive and flustered and, therefore, at risk. Well, perhaps not: after all, she was not falling into the hands of a sadistic assassin, so there was no danger and there might, in fact, be much to gain. As there turned out to be for both of us and on two occasions.

I asked her if she would like a drink and she accepted a whisky. She wanted to know if she could be of any assistance and I said no thank you, mine was a bachelor establishment, rarely tidy or clean, and my domestic skills did not go beyond removing ice from the fridge. She found that amusing although it was not my intention. Now I really was distracted, without knowing how to make conversation. As we drank, I reminded her of the offhand manner in which she had received me at SPQR. She could not remember, she could not remember at all, she assured me. Perhaps she had been worried about something at work, letters waiting to be typed, behind with her filing. That was obviously the explanation, I agreed. Then it was her turn to ask if she could see her employer's portrait. From where she was sitting one could only see the back of the canvas. I held her by the elbow as she got to her feet and squeezed it a little more tightly than was necessary. She did not react and allowed herself to be led in this manner. We both looked at the portrait, with me right behind her as she stood there quivering with excitement and curiosity. She found a remarkable likeness and asked how much longer it would take to finish the portrait. 'That depends,' I told her. 'If your boss goes on missing appointments, it could take some time.' Ever the loyal secretary, she embarked on some garbled explanation about S. being so busy, not to mention his golf and the factory, his bridge and the new factory under construction. I sat her in the chair reserved for my clients and I perched on a high stool. I could see quite clearly that she was ready for a sudden affair and sensed it in her every movement, as if the unfinished portrait of S. were inciting some kind of incestuous passion. Or perhaps she, too, had some wrong to redress in order to be able to live in peace. Human behaviour resides in a world of hypotheses. If, in Eça de Queirós' novel, Padre Amaro dressed Amelia in the Virgin's mantle, why should Olga the secretary not make love to me before the portrait of her employer (patron, father, sugar-daddy) who had started an affair with her and then lost interest?

I never cease to be amazed at the freedom women enjoy. We men regard them as inferior beings, we are amused by their little foibles, we sneer when they get things wrong, yet every one of them is capable of surprising us, laying before us vast territories of freedom, as if in the depths of their servitude, with an obedience which gives the impression of being in pursuit of itself, they were putting up the defences of a harsh independence without restraints. Confronted by these defences, we men, who think we know everything about this lesser being we have been taming or thought we had tamed, find ourselves disarmed, powerless and terrified; the lap-dog which was so endearingly wriggling on its back and showing its tummy, suddenly jumps to its feet, its limbs trembling with rage, its eyes full of mistrust, irony and indifference. When Romantic poets compared (or still compare) woman to a sphinx, how right they were, bless them. Woman is a sphinx who had to exist because man appropriated science, knowledge and power. But such is the fatuousness of men that women were content to put up the defences of their final refusal in silence, so that man, resting in the shade as if stretched out

JOSÉ SARAMAGO

under the penumbra of submissive eyelids, could say with conviction: 'There is nothing beyond this wall.'

A grim miscalculation from which we are still trying to recover. Olga the secretary made love to me, but not out of obedience to the male or because used to submission, much less because she found me attractive. She accepted me because she chose to and had prepared herself for any eventuality. And if it is true that the half-hour which elapsed between her arrival and the moment when she crossed her arms and pulled her blouse over her head was taken up with the same old gestures and foreplay of weary seduction, this was due to that little ritual couples must observe rather than upset the sequence. This also explains our interest in the ups and downs in the life of the prostitute with whom we have just entered a rented room. She might even be offended or we might feel we had offended her if we were not to ply her with questions.

Within the half-hour Olga the secretary finished drinking the first whisky and started on a second. Within the half-hour I made a rapid sketch of her, but a good likeness and, in order to show it to her and examine it together, I sat beside her on the divan. Sitting slightly further back, I was able to lean over her shoulder and brush my face against her hair. Familiar ruses giving the appearance of being distracted and at the same time denying it, whereby the equivocation becomes extreme in this tacit game in which both sides play with their own and each other's cards while pretending to be mere spectators. It was at some point within this half-hour that she asked me if she could keep the sketch and I began insisting that I wanted her to have it. Then, next minute, I was pulling her towards me by the shoulders and turning her towards me, began putting my lips to hers. And believe me, if she drew her face away it was only so that everything should not be confined to that moment, which already had its surfeit of pleasure given and accepted, and might therefore be considered incomplete although essential for any pleasure to follow. I am playing with words as if I were using colours and still mixing them on my palette. I am playing with these events while searching for words, however tentative, to describe them. But I must confess that no drawing or painting of mine could ever convey what I have just ventured to express in writing. The mouth of Olga the secretary put itself within reach of mine as the black cloud from the centre of my body, which is my sex and much more than simply sex, became charged with the rapid currents of a nameless fluid which draws my blood to secret caverns. I then knew that this was precisely what Olga the secretary had planned the moment S. asked her to call in person to cancel his appointment, or shortly afterwards, and that all I had to do was to assist in this purification, first and foremost the involuntary agent of her revenge, already its agent before Olga the secretary even reached my flat and my sex was quiescent, hers unmistakably quivering with desire. We kissed like two adults who know all about kissing. We kissed, knowing how to get our lips into a comfortable position, how to prepare that first meeting of tongues, how to control our breathing. And we both knew exactly when I should lean over her and she should bend over me until we found ourselves half-lying on the sofa, in possession of this new intimacy of bodies pressed up against each other as our mouths went on provoking from afar our sexual organs which were already stimulated. The most difficult moment of all is when mouths separate: the least word can be excessive. Knowing this, I reached out to hold her breasts and appearing to avoid me she crossed her arms and pulled her blouse right over her head. Half-dressed, we had no difficulty in making love. Driven by thoughts I could sense, she soon caught up and overtook me, allowing me to witness her orgasm in the motionless centre of my black cloud until it was my turn to lose self-control and enter the maelstrom. As first acts go, it had been excellent. No words were spoken and I was frightened because I was dependent on her for any serenity afterwards or that common and ill-disguised vexation which can so easily ensue in these situations. I could see from the position we were in that I must be pressing on her leg and I asked her if it was painful. 'A little,' she replied and these were the first words exchanged and the movement that followed was facilitated by the same physical discomfort as we began getting dressed and I calmly helped her into her blouse,

JOSÉ SARAMAGO

an old married couple for whom there are no more surprises. But when I caught her looking at S.'s portrait, when I saw that mocking smile, I asked her abruptly if she had been S.'s mistress. I was taken aback by my own question but she was certainly expecting me to ask her sooner or later, for she simply turned and replied, 'Of course', starting to speak while still gazing at the painted face of S. and finishing as she looked at me, or perhaps not looking at me, not looking at this face already lined with wrinkles, at this vague blotch that often passes for a face, not looking at me at all, but at some endless desert stretching behind or inside me. And this secretary Olga, whose importance consists of being a secretary and having an exceptionally generous orgasm, allowed a breach to open in her defences for one brief moment so that I might experience once again my former vertigo when confronted with what I choose to call the fundamental freedom of woman. By mutual consent, she was taking her revenge on me.

Within minutes, she resumed her subordinate role. Smiling flirtatiously, she came up to me, put her arms around my neck and pressed cool lips to mine. We were playing a different game and clearly with marked cards, but this was our only possibility of appearing natural. This was why we could ask each other in jest: 'How did this happen?' and I could ask, as was expected of me, 'When can we get together again?' to which she naturally replied: 'Who knows, I really can't say, this was utter madness.' We made playful gestures with our hands, trying not to appear distracted, and kissed each other deliberately but without too much insistence. In both of us the tide was ebbing like life taking its farewell. She gave me another kiss as we said goodbye on the landing, a kiss which gathered up what little passion remained. She did not cast so much as another glance at S.'s portrait.

I slowly closed the door, returned to the studio, feeling physically tired, mentally distracted, torn between the modest triumph of easy conquest and the irony of having to confess to myself that I had made no conquest whatsoever. Of the two of us, she alone had got what she wanted, she alone had been free. As for me, I had passively played an active role (a contradictory and redundant statement) in a farce, the silent servant who delivers the letter whereby the plot unfolds. I shook my St Antony by the hand (the position of the right arm allows for this) and stroked his friar's tonsure. No one can dissuade me from believing that the pitchers this saint shattered were a subtle disguise for the hymens he penetrated. But St Antony was so conciliatory towards the world, so friendly towards women, that the pitchers were miraculously restored, but not those virginities, and just as well. Repeating these witticisms of a somewhat unimaginative heretic, I went off to run a bath. Waiting for the bath to fill, I stood there watching the hot water gushing from the tap and listening to the hissing of the heater in the kitchen next door. Perhaps I was feeling a little lonely. Night was starting to fall. When I finally turned off the tap, all I could hear at first was total silence, but as I began undressing I could hear the (discreet) sound of singing coming from my neighbour's radio. I could barely make out the words in French, let alone identify the voice which might have been that of Leo Ferré or Serge Reggiani. Both middle-aged, one step away from what they do not want, one step away from that last remaining phase which they fear might be all too short: the time it takes to get into a warm bath and lie there, as the building settles down for the night, as the body cools down and the water with it, only the dripping tap persisting as one waits to see if someone will notice before the water overflows and floods the flat below. On an impulse which I made no attempt to restrain, I pulled out the plug. The water quickly disappeared right down to the final gurgle coming from that antiquated plumbing. Then, saved from death, I turned on the shower and washed myself. Quickly. And within minutes, half-dried and wrapped in a dressing-gown, I looked through one of the studio windows at the night sky and the lights on the river. Darkness everywhere. 'What's happening?' I asked myself.

JOSÉ SARAMAGO

Twenty-three days have passed since I wrote: 'I shall go on painting the second picture', and today I ask myself: 'Should I carry on?' In between (separating us) is the distance covered in these pages and I never imagined I should be able to write so easily. At this stage, many things which seemed important have undoubtedly lost any value or meaning, especially the second portrait. As the painter mentioned in the opening pages, I can now see that this picture is a mistake: no one can be and not be at the same time. I cannot be the painter capable of achieving his objective in the second portrait, if I have gone on, submissive and salaried, painting the first one. As a portrait painter, I am and will remain simply the painter of the first portrait: I am not allowed a second portrait. So when I admitted that the attempt had failed, I was also admitting that I could nevertheless carry on with it, as if at heart I felt incapable of giving up the possibility, however remote, of becoming the painter who is real because hidden. I would relish my triumph on my own, finally rid of that vulgar portrait I had sold, engaged in dialogue with the portrait in reserve which no amount of money could ever buy. Now I know it will never happen. Using a spray-gun, I covered the second portrait with black paint. I banished the colours of error and the false gestures which put them there into a superficial but eternal night. Covered in black paint, the canvas is still mounted on the easel and consigned to the shadows of the storeroom, like a blind man fumbling in the dark to retrieve the black hat he removed an hour ago. I can visualize the canvas from here, invisible, black over black, fettered to the skeleton of the easel like a condemned man to the gallows. And between the true image I attempted of S. and the world of light (or the passing darkness of these nocturnal hours) there is a membrane formed by millions of tiny drops, hard and resistant as a black mirror. I did all this as if I were carefully dissecting a limb, gently cutting into the fibre of the muscular tissue, tying up veins and arteries with the dry, meticulous gestures of someone tightening a garrotte or like the skilful executioner who knows precisely how much force to exert in order to dislocate the vertebrae and sever the spinal cord. There is only one portrait of S., the only one I am capable of painting, which conforms not to what I am but to what is expected of me, although it might be truer to say that I am precisely what is expected of me and nothing else. If these words are true and I am not mistaken, then I exist merely within the dimensions of the picture they buy from me. I am the object bought and fully satisfy the client's needs. Once the natural buyers (assuming it is natural to buy such things) have departed this world, who else is likely to want such pictures? Who else will commission them? Once there is no longer any public for this art, what am I to do with art or myself? In the storeroom the second portrait gives me one half of the answer: the attempt to sell something else has started to fail and is now simply an attempt which has ended in frustration. I certainly did not erase it from myself but withdrew it from the time of others. It is a sign of prohibition which only I can see: but it closes a path I thought I was opening to the world.

These sheets of paper remain. This new method of drawing remains, coming to life without my having memorised it. At each moment, even when I break off, it offers me the emerging scroll, and demonstrates with every pause the probability of never ending. When I place the nib of my pen on the interrupted curve of a letter, word or phrase, when I carry on two millimetres beyond a full stop or comma, I limit myself to carrying on a movement already under way: this design is both the code and its deciphering. But the code and deciphering of what? Of S.'s personal details or of mine? When I undertook this task I thought I was doing it (at this distance it is no longer easy to be sure, even if one checks the proposal in the text: besides, any checking will only give me the immediate outer layer of a proposal formulated in words, not the words I am writing today, but those I wrote at the time) in order to discover the truth

JOSÉ SARAMAGO

about S. Now, what do I know about this, about the so-called truth about S.? Who is this S.? What is truth? asked Pilate. What is, I repeat, the truth about S.? And what kind of truth or thing which can be defined, described or classified as such? biological truth? mental? affective? economic? cultural? social? administrative? that of the temporary lover and protector of little Olga, his fifth secretary? or conjugal truth? that of the unfaithful husband or of the husband betrayed in turn? that of the man who plays bridge or golf? that of the man who votes for fascist governments? that of the after-shave he uses? that of the brand-names of his three cars? that of the water in his swimming-pool? that of his sexual obsessions? that of a gesture I would describe as self-conscious when he slowly scratches his chin? that of the vertical wrinkles between his eyebrows? The truth of the shadow he casts? of the urine he passes? of the voice which once dismissed thirty-four workers from his first factory because he was building a second one? The truth of the new machines which have already dispensed with thirty-four workers and tomorrow will dispense with another thirty-four? What truth, secretary Olga?

I did not ask her any one of these questions but all of them and countless others weighed on my body as my body weighed on that of Olga the secretary three days after our first (sexual) encounter. What made her come back? I do not believe it was simply the pleasure of repeating her blissful orgasm. These things (events, sensations, pleasures) count less than one imagines: the memory does not pin down pleasure but registers it as an attribute rather than a virtue. But Olga the secretary came back and had not just one but two orgasms, and she called out during the second one while I, lying on top of her, liberated myself in silence. Could she have come because of S., to carry on with her little act of revenge, to commit her little sacrilege, incest without any consequences, the modest depravity with which she challenged the system which (in)dignifies her from nine in the morning until six in the evening and during all the other hours of night and day, outside and within the Senatus Populusque Romanus.

The Manual of Painting and Calligraphy

Olga the secretary came to my house straight from the SPQR and lay down at once. Without even going to take a look at S.'s portrait, she lay down at once, not on the uncomfortable divan but on top of the bed, stripped to her bra and panties which I would later remove. This is how these things must be done. We felt very much at ease because Adelina (her photograph is on the bookshelf in the bedroom amongst other bric-à-brac) carefully avoids coming here on days when she is menstruating. I suspect she is responding to some obscure, unconscious conviction that she is in a state of impurity. On days such as these she is the most punctual daughter in the world. After closing the boutique, she drives straight home in her little car and there the two women remain, mother and daughter, the one dried-up, the other moist, confiding nothing yet sharing the same destiny. These are days of rest for me, even as I lie here having been run over by Olga the secretary, who gets out of bed and goes to the telephone to warn them at home that she is working late at the office, an urgent job her boss needs first thing in the morning, she will not be back for dinner and expects to be very late. Out of curiosity I eventually ask her who she was talking to. She had been speaking to her mother, mothers are always mixed up in these situations whether they know it or not, and it is left to them to explain their daughter's delay and absence in a convincing manner so that minds are put at rest and bourgeois honour preserved. At least Olga the secretary is not married nor does she appear to have a steady boyfriend. She awaits good fortune in some form or other and knows she has not found it here. She came because she wanted to and because she had a score to settle with the portrait in the studio. Sitting on the bed, now completely undressed, her skin glistening with perspiration (I probably forgot to mention it is summer and I have always noticed how scrupulously novelists describe the cycle of the seasons), she asks me if we can dine at home. There is no need for her to rush home, as I have just heard, so we might as well take advantage. She enjoys going to bed with me, I know how to make love to a woman and give her satisfaction and although she realizes this is only a casual affair, it still feels good. She tells me all

JOSÉ SARAMAGO

this in a manner which sounds uncouth but is simply natural. I reply in keeping with the precepts of male modesty to the closing words of her little speech and lead her into the kitchen: dinner consists of eggs and bacon, bread and wine. And there are some tinned peaches for dessert and reasonable coffee. Life is extremely simple.

After dinner we made love for a second time. Were I given to such things, I should have set up a tape-recorder in the room to register such different reactions, the words spoken before, during and after sex, the sighs and moans when there are any, words of a tenderness in search of someone to whom it might offer itself and which reveals itself there and then, obscenities which fire the blood and brain, verbal assent regarding gestures and positions. In this way I could have recorded the whole story of life in the Senatus Populusque Romanus, the details about S., an explanation of the relationship (sentimental, sensual, amorous, erotic or social?) between boss and female employee, the confirmation of the circumstances in which the portrait of S.'s father was painted, something about the unbearable and provocative tyranny of S.'s mother, also some of the comments made about the behaviour of S.'s wife, and the way in which the plot was hatched and carried out to liquidate a rival company, with only Olga the secretary as witness, as a trustworthy employee and private secretary to the managing director. I listened to all this without paying much attention (I had not yet started writing this), treating her long speech as if it were a confession, a declaration of faith in that universal goodness which sometimes comes to us (I mean faith, not goodness) after having generously made love, especially if the orgasms are simultaneous and our bodies then abandon themselves to a vague feeling akin to gratitude. I found myself comparing all of this to those leisurely conversations in bed in some brothel when the prostitute is not in a hurry and the Madame is in a good mood (either because the client is new or because he is never away from the place), although there in my own bed, my brain muddled, I was unable to work the roles out properly, that is to say, I could not tell which of us, she or I, was playing the part of the prostitute. It was almost midnight when Adelina telephoned me. She was already in bed and prepared for yet another painful night, and I kept up a relaxed and normal conversation while trying not to feel those insistent fingers investigating my body. Adelina rang off saying 'See you tomorrow', to which I replied 'See you tomorrow', while Olga the secretary, suddenly losing interest, got up and began looking for her clothes.

I felt much too weary to try and understand. I just lay there, stretched out on top of the sheets because I like being naked and know that mine is not one of those bodies that inevitably clutters space. Age has not ravaged everything. Olga the secretary (why do I refuse to separate her name from her profession? the name of her profession?) finished dressing and at that moment the picture we presented became incongruous, just like the *Fête Champêtre* (Giorgione) or its nineteenth-century counterpart *Déjeuner sur l'herbe* (Manet) or the lunar pictures of Delvaux, with the one difference that here it was the gentleman (or monsieur) who was naked. The incongruity of the picture (my picture) and of the pictures (Giorgione, Manet, Delvaux) was, in my perception, the same incongruity which assembled the umbrella and sewing-machine on top of the dissecting table (Lautréamont). I asked Olga the secretary if she had heard of Lautréamont and she simply said no, without even bothering to inquire why I had raised the question. In return, she asked me the time because her watch had stopped, and I replied that there inside that room it was ten to one but as for outside, I really could not say, no doubt it was much later since my clock was (often) slow. She wanted to know the difference and I replied smiling: 'Had you been outside, you would probably have left by now, but inside this room you are still here.' Tempering my impudence at the last moment, I hastened to add, and just as well, 'so that I might enjoy your company a little longer.' She made a vague gesture like a conditioned reflex, not (entirely) conscious, the gesture of someone about to start removing her clothes again with weary resignation. Then she appeared to change her mind (perhaps even unconsciously), lifted the supper tray from the floor and carried it into the kitchen. She called through and asked if she should wash up, but I

JOSÉ SARAMAGO

told her not to bother: there was no need for her to wash either the dishes or the soiled sheets. I kept these last words to myself and began to feel sleepy, longing to escape this world. I could hear Olga the secretary in the bathroom, probably applying her make-up, and I wished she would go, descend the steep spiral of my staircase, drawn by the weight of the sewing-machine which was working rapidly and sewing the steps while the umbrella, rolled up and sinister, pierced the eyes of the people in the pictures hanging on the wall of the staircase and forming another spiral, while I, still lying there stark naked on the dissecting table, awaited the inevitable. I awoke from my dream and saw Olga the secretary in the doorway of the bedroom, ready to leave. She told me: 'I'm going now: you can adjust your clock.' I made as if to get up and detain her but she waved good-bye without coming near me, disappeared into the narrow corridor, opened the door and closed it quietly behind her as she must have learnt from her mother. Then I could hear her heels tapping on the steps like the needle of a sewing-machine. Would the neighbours think it was Adelina leaving? I dialled fifteen (the speaking-clock) and then rang Adelina to tell her how much I loved her (she was already asleep). Next day my cleaner would change the sheets. I got up to look for a book to read before falling asleep and chanced upon the *Roman Dialogue* by that ingenuous, good-natured fellow Francisco de Holanda, which he wrote in honour of the fatherland (not this fatherland which is fast asleep). I opened the book at random and began reading until I came to that passage in the second dialogue when Messer Lactantio Tollomei answers Michelangelo: 'I am satisfied,' replied Lactantio, 'and now understand more clearly the powerful influence of painting which, as you have observed, can be recognized in all the achievements of the ancients as well as in their prose and verse. And perhaps with your great works you will not have probed as deeply as I have the affinity between writing and painting (but almost certainly between painting and writing) or observed how these two sciences are so closely related that they are interdependent, although at present they somehow appear to have become separate. Yet every man, however wise and experienced in whatever field of learning, will discover that in all his works he is forever emulating the skilful painter who carefully touches up his pictures until he achieves the right effect. Now, on examining the books of antiquity, there are few really famous texts which do not resemble paintings and altarpieces. And without question, the most ponderous and muddled of these texts are by authors without any feeling for design or sense of structure, while the clearest and most concise are by writers with an eye for visual detail. And even Quintilianus in his admirable books of *Rhetoric* affirms that the orator should not simply master the distribution of words but in his own hand he should be able to trace out their pattern. And that is why, Signor Michelangelo, you are often described as being a great scholar and preacher and a skilful painter, and why great artists are referred to as men of letters. And anyone who takes the trouble to study antiquity will discover that painting and sculpture were simply called painting and that in the time of Demosthenes they were called antigraphy, which means to draw or write, a term common to both of these sciences, so that the writings of Agatharcus may be referred to as the paintings of Agatharcus. And I believe that the Egyptians also knew how to paint and if they had to write or express something, the hieroglyphics they used were painted animals and birds, as we can see here in this city on certain obelisks which were brought from Egypt.' Next day I could not remember having read any further, nor can I be sure whether I suddenly fell asleep at the end of the paragraph or if I sat there for a while, gazing at this extract from Lactantio's lengthy discourse. I fell asleep and had no dreams except perhaps for those undulations which seemed liquid and slowly swirled, written or sketched, and passed before my eyes for who knows how many hours of sleep.

I spent the morning working on the second portrait. I had woken up determined (what had provoked this resolve during my sleep?) or had determined at some point while awake (but when and for what reason?) to persevere with the portrait. Not that it was not making good progress, but unlike the first one, obedient to a set plan of methods and procedures (naturally subject to the introduction of

JOSÉ SARAMAGO

factors and variants peculiar to each model), the second one allowed for and demanded a different freedom, further changes in accordance with new elements I had or thought I had at my disposal as I tried to discover the true S. For the first time I transferred the picture from the storeroom into the studio without removing it from the easel and placed it alongside the first portrait. There was scarcely any resemblance except for that one finds between one man and another, both belonging to a species characterized and distinguished from others by certain forms. Even I was not aware of having painted them so differently, although deep down I knew that they were the same person. Yet there was something else I had to clarify. Was this the same person because just as meaningless (what I am doing here is not painting), or the same person because finally captured in the second portrait and an essentially different image? As far as likeness goes, the first portrait is a portrait of S.: his own mother (mothers are never deceived) confirmed as much the only time she ever came with her son to the studio. But the second portrait, which even his own mother would not recognize, is just as good a likeness in my eyes although quite different from the first one, just as one drop of water differs from another. Who would see this second portrait as a true likeness? In other words: at what moment in life has S. been or is ever likely to be this portrait? As I looked from one picture to another, I thought how interesting it would be to show the portrait from the storeroom to Olga the secretary without telling her who it was supposed to be (Ah, this business of writing can be so ambiguous). Having known him in bed, would Olga the secretary be capable of recognizing S. once disfigured? Am I trying to say this knowledge is disfiguring? That it is comparable with this other disfigurement I have achieved in the picture, both of them presupposing knowledge or its pursuit? And why is the pursuit itself not disfigured? What was I to Adelina when, even though we knew each other, I still had not been to bed with her? What am I to her in my own eyes, knowing that I have been to bed with Olga the secretary without Adelina knowing?

I drank a large cup of coffee without anything to eat. My cleaner arrived mid-morning. She has been coming here for three years yet I cannot say I know much about her. She looks older than me but is probably younger. Formidable, sharp and taciturn, she works with the efficiency of a machine. She washed up the dishes, changed the sheets (she must find it painful if it reminds her of the moments of pleasure she experienced before being widowed), she cleaned the rest of the flat without touching the studio and departed. She asked no questions, knows that I always lunch out and that she is paid weekly. But what does my cleaner Adelaide really think of me? What first and second portrait would she paint of me if she were a (bad) painter like me? I can hear the shuffling of her slippers as she descends the stairs and discover (to be frank: rediscover) that I am interested in the noise people make when they descend the stairs, I store them in a useless but seemingly indispensable archive, like some harmless yet obsessive foible. Once more I find myself alone in the silence of my studio, the forgotten street beneath my windows and the other rooms recovering their interrupted solitude while objects which have been moved, suddenly transferred or ever so slightly adjusted, either become accustomed to their new position by spreading out with sheer relief, like fresh bed-linen, or trying to come to terms with the outrage, just like those soiled sheets rolled up in the laundry bag and smelling of cold sweat.

Seen from a distance, I have the gestures of Rembrandt. Like him, I mix the colours on my palette, like him I extend a steady arm and apply firm brushstrokes. But the paint does not settle in the same way, there is a slight turning of the wrist, a greater or lesser pressure exerted by the bristles of my brush, unless Rembrandt used some other kind of brush which might explain the difference? If I were to take a microscopic photograph of a tiny section from one of Rembrandt's pictures, surely this would confirm the difference? And would that difference not be precisely what separates genius (Rembrandt) from mediocrity (me)? (Between parentheses: I put Rembrandt and me between parentheses to avoid writing 'genius from mediocrity', an absurdity which not even a writer as inexperienced as myself would let slip.) But since all the painters of my generation use brushes similar to mine, there must be other differences to make critics praise them and not me, so that although they are different among themselves, they are all considered to be better than me and I am judged as being worst of all. A question of how one holds the brush? A question of what then? I can remember words by Klee: 'A naked man should be painted in such a way that the viewer admires the anatomy of the picture rather than that of the man.' If this is the case, what is wrong with the anatomy of these faces I am painting, if they fail to arouse any admiration for the anatomy of the pictures themselves? Even though I know perfectly well that a microscopic photograph of a painting by Rembrandt would look nothing like a similar photograph taken of a painting by Klee.

I work slowly on the background of the second portrait of S., with brownish whorls probably recovered from my dream. They gradually cover the naturalist features with which I had earlier tried to express industrial and financial power: factory chimneys, serrated rooftops, a cloud in the form of a large escudo sign lying on its side. As I fill in this new background, I notice how S.'s face (or this image which I alone call S.) seems to be covered in ash, a dead face starting to turn blue and decompose. I avoid touching his head with my brush. I work only on the background, applying one colour over another, now adding some darker tints which leave traces untranslatable into any other language, and the thickness of the paint creates a kind of foreground which transforms the plane of the head and trunk into a collage which looks as if it might have been added later, using the palm of my hand and the tips of my fingers to smooth down the outline where the wet paint gathers. At this moment, but without stopping to think about it, I have my first intuition of this picture's final destiny. I have buried S. in excrement.

Two days later I began writing and during this time both pictures progressed to their inevitable end: the second to that black cloud which isolated it from the world, the first to the boardroom of the Senatus Populusque Romanus. Today is really today. There is no truth to look for, nothing to be construed within its appearance. The only remaining portrait of S. will be collected tomorrow. The paint is dry, the portrait is good, technically speaking, and guaranteed to last. In these matters I am the best painter in town. But in this city I am also the greatest failure alive. I have never successfully completed any of my projects and not even these sheets of paper have increased in volume since I started writing from scratch. It is over and done with. I tried, I failed, and there will be no further opportunities.

JOSÉ SARAMAGO

Writing can no longer do anything for me, but I have decided to salvage at least the embers of these last four months. Olga the secretary came to collect the portrait, accompanied by a messenger (for the first time I noticed on the lapel of the man's jacket the initials SPQR and here I was thinking I had invented the anachronism), and she was in every way the efficient and solicitous employee with that touch of authority (by contamination and contrast) who had accompanied me to examine the portraits in the boardroom. She handed me the cheque, put the receipt I had written, stamped and signed, into a folder and politely said goodbye, without being hostile or aloof, simply neutral. I stood there listening to the clicking of her footsteps descending the stairs and other footsteps, those of the man, heavy and cautious, contrasting sounds, loud and soft, which diminished in unison, while keeping up the counterpoint, getting further and deeper into the spiral until they vanished into silence, the noise of the street, before resurging, transformed into the banging of car doors and the throbbing of an engine being started up before tailing off into the perspective of the road ahead and finally dying away.

Who would have thought that on this divan, no matter how uncomfortable, Olga the secretary had made love to me, that on this bed, fully stretched out and stark naked, she had made love for a second time, had come twice, and called out the second time. Who would have thought that on both occasions she carried away inside her part of my body, its secretion, that incredible fluid wherein these aspirants to a peculiar parasitism hover and swim by the million. Who would have thought, watching us engaged in the simple act of giving and receiving, that there were other accounts between us, not pending, but settled so recently that I am not even sure whether the wet stain we both left on the sheet had completely dried. I believe I have already written that life is extremely simple. I had one more reason for thinking so. And if this philosophy is not worth much, it has, in recompense, the advantage of setting its limits the moment it defines itself, like dying before birth, like that butterfly which survives for no longer than a day and has already perished by nightfall. I feel myself to be in some kind of night without having really known day, merely clinging to the simple affirmation that life is simple. Today, as I always do when I sell a picture (and this one was sold at a good price), I shall organize a little party (a reunion to be more precise) in the studio. I usually serve drinks, a trinity of nuts – pine-seeds – raisins, canapés, things one can buy already prepared and which I suspect are all made from the same basic ingredients although presented under various guises. Naturally Adelina will be there and several friends whom I have invited. But I ask myself why anyone should be interested in these details.

What obstacle finally detained me on the road I indicated on the first page of this manuscript, for there it remains, still questioning me? On that same page I confessed that the attempt to paint a second portrait had failed; on that same page, or shortly afterwards, I clearly stated what I as a painter think of my painting, of which that first portrait is truly representative. It would not be through painting that I should discover something (I no longer call it the truth) about a sitter, however much the latter might think he knew about himself on recognizing himself in the picture. By resorting to writing I knew that I was simply turning my back on a problem: I was not ignoring it, I knew it was just as daunting, but it was as if the novelty of the instrument (everything for me had to be real invention and not merely an imitation of earlier experiences) was sufficient in itself to bring me close to my objective. It was as if (having convinced S. of my talent as a painter) I had taken him by surprise. If there was anything S. felt he ought to mistrust, these were surely my brushes, my paints, my gestures of blessing and excommunication over that portrait which gradually acquired definition; not some sheets of paper he could not see or a picture that was not only hidden from him. But by what route should I travel in order to arrive at this unprotected place, exposed, one might even say innocent, where I should at last know and finally come to understand S.? What I learned about him I found out through Olga the secretary and even then involuntarily. She succumbed without any conquest on my part. I lost time in digressions which (as I now see all too clearly) led me to other parts where I discovered more about myself than about anyone else. How disappointed Vasco da Gama would have felt if, on sailing to the Indies, he had finished up at the mouth of the Tagus. Things were different for Magellan who, had he survived the voyage, would have made it a point of honour to land at the very spot from whence he had set sail, who knows how long ago. But I had no desire to go on a trip round the world, and not even this calligraphy would be capable of carrying me all that way. All I wanted (a man with only one profession) was to give my work some *raison d'être*, even though cheating by using the tools of another craft and other hands. Confronted with the outcome of this experience, I should like to know where I went wrong, at which point I deviated and moved further and further away from my objective, thus depriving myself of any assistance from Olga the secretary who could have been so useful. I want to believe that I somehow knew it would be hopeless. Olga the secretary would have given me (and she did give me something) her image of S., just as the man who serves him by annotating files and stamping papers would have provided me with another image. Not forgetting the image given by the messenger who came to collect the portrait and who probably descended the stairs quivering with excitement at the great honour of being allowed to carry that precious object in his arms, perhaps shaking with rage at being asked to do it, perhaps resigned to obeying orders, perhaps proud and capable of deep hatred. Just as I would offer my image of him were I to take the trouble of capturing it, after discovering where to look for it. But it would always be an image, never the truth. And this was probably my biggest mistake: to think that the truth could be captured externally and simply with one's eyes, to imagine a truth exists which can be grasped at once and thereafter remain still and at peace, just like a statue, a truth which contracts and expands depending on the temperature, a truth which eventually erodes, modifying not only the surrounding space but subtly altering the composition of the ground on which it stands, shedding minute particles of marble, just as we shed hairs, nail clippings, saliva and the words we speak. Even if I had been apprenticed to Sherlock Holmes or to one of those modern detectives who use their brains as well as their muscles and weapons, I should end up a frustrated wreck to whom the wholesome S. would say with a smile: 'Elementary, my dear Watson, such is life.' Frankly, what questions could I ask and of whom in order to discover the truth? Go to bed (since that is where fate decreed it should begin) with all the women S. has slept with, including his wife? Plant spies in the SPQR, install microphones and hidden cameras and put compromising documents on microfilm? Disguise myself as a golf caddy? A bartender? Aim a gun at him as he turns the corner and threaten him: 'The truth or your life', while recognizing there and then that life is not truth? With considerable effort I would get to know the history of the Senatus Populusque Romanus and the family who owns the firm, I would discover S.'s date of birth and all the other important dates in his life so far, I would be able to investigate his friends and enemies, I would have as many images of him as I have facts, dates, names of his friends and enemies, but even after collecting everything possible the ultimate question would remain unanswered: how to put all these facts into a portrait, or indeed a manuscript? My art, in the final analysis, is worthless; and what is the use of this calligraphy?

Anyone who paints portraits, portrays himself. Therefore, the important thing is not the model but the painter and the portrait is only worth as much as the painter himself and not a groat more. The Dr Gachet painted by Van Gogh is Van Gogh and not Gachet, and the thousand different costumes (velvets, plumes, gold necklaces) in which Rembrandt painted himself are more expedients to give the impression that he was painting other people while painting himself in some other guise. I said I do not like my painting. That is because I do not like myself and I am obliged to look at myself in every portrait I paint, futile, weary, disheartened and lost, because I am neither Rembrandt nor Van Gogh. Which goes without saying.

But the person writing? Is he also writing himself? What is Tolstoy in *War and Peace*? What is Stendhal in *The Charterhouse of Parma*? Is *War and Peace* the whole Tolstoy? Is *The Charterhouse of Parma* the whole Stendhal? When they finished writing their books, did they find themselves in them? Or did they believe they had written nothing other than a work of fiction? And in what sense fiction, since some of the threads in their plots are historical? What was Stendhal before writing *The Charterhouse of Parma*? What did he end up being after writing it? And for how long? I only started writing a month ago and it seems to me that I am no longer the same person. Because I have added another thirty days to my life? No. Because I have been writing. But what are these differences? Apart from knowing what they consist of, have they reconciled me to myself? As someone who dislikes seeing himself portrayed in the portraits I paint of others, would I like to see myself in this manuscript, an alternative portrait in which I have ended up portraying myself rather than someone else? Does this mean that I get closer to myself by means of writing rather than through painting? And this raises another question: will this manuscript go on even after I assume it to be finished? If the straits of the Tagus are located where I hoped to find India, will I be obliged to relinquish the name Vasco and call myself Ferdinand? Heaven forbid that I should die *en route*, as always happens to the man who fails to find what he is searching for in life. The man who took the wrong route and chose the wrong name.

One often mistakenly describes oneself as a friend, or the name itself is misleading, and in this way and no other the word came into being. I am not criticizing my friends but the role we tacitly accept of looking after each other, of showing a solicitude the other person may not need yet expects to be shown, of exploiting presence and absence and complaining or not complaining of both according to our own best interests which ignore those of our friends. Because of this bad conscience (remorse, moral disquiet or gentle rebuke from our so-called conscience), a planned reunion of friends is rather like a meeting of twin souls: everyone has abandoned whatever cannot be shared amongst those present, everyone becomes impoverished and diminished (for better or for worse) in order to become what is expected of them. For this reason, anyone who is anxious to keep up friendships lives in constant fear of losing them and is forever adapting to them just as the pupil of the eye responds to the light it receives. But the efforts made by groups of friends to adapt to each other (how would the pupil of the eye adapt to simultaneous lights of varying intensity if it could separate them and react to them one by one?) cannot last for any longer than the ability of each guest to raise or lower his or her own personality to a level agreed by all. It is always advisable, therefore, to curtail reunions before they reach breaking point and each of those tiny planets feels an irresistible urge to form another constellation elsewhere or simply to drop from sheer exhaustion into black, empty space.

Besides Adelina, who acted as hostess, eight friends of both sexes gathered in my flat. There were several steady couples amongst them, although I had my doubts about one couple (they were not together last time) and they had the same casual look Adelina and I were beginning to take on. But while they are still glowing (a banal expression which aptly conveys that aura of intense passion invisibly surrounding recent couples), we move about in a gentle glow and know it. Who are these friends of mine and what do they do? Several of them work in advertising, one is an architect, there is a doctor with his wife, an interior decorator who is really Adelina's friend, a publisher, widowed and older than me (nice to know I am not the oldest person here), who is infatuated with the interior decorator but resigns himself to looking on as she flirts right and left. What distinguishes this group, apart from its ability to smoke, chat and drink at the same time (just like any other group), is their friendship towards me, which I reciprocate as best I can, know how to (or choose). If we were to try to find an explanation for this relationship, I am sure we would not find one: nevertheless we go on being friends because of our inertia nourished by fear of that momentary solitude which we selfishly shun. What finally keeps us in that group is knowing that it will continue even after we have withdrawn. By continuing to take part, we can go on believing we are indispensable. It is a question of pride.

The same pride or fear of being inferior when compared with others provokes unspoken resentments and conflicts under the supreme justification of friendship and results in an unpunishable form of aggression for which the occasional or habitual victims are expected to appear grateful. This aggression is so blatant that even in a group such as ours, where people tactfully avoid touching on the whys and wherefores of our various professions (and just as well since everyone knows I am a mediocre painter, not even a painter, since my paintings are not to be seen anywhere) even in this group, as I was saying, misunderstandings and disagreements often arise when one of us suddenly finds he is being judged by all the others and an outburst of reciprocal sado-masochism erupts, almost invariably ending in tears and insults. And this is provoked by someone introducing into the conversation, either deliberately or simply because tired of pretending, some wounding remark about the profession of the victim of the day. And here, because of the professions we pursue, all of us define ourselves as exploiters and social parasites. The architect because it is true, the editor because that is culture, the advertising agents because it is obvious, the doctor because we all know what doctors are, as for the interior decorator, well! Adelina, well, well, well! and I, the portrait painter, well! As for me, I am usually spared any embarrassment, I repeat, because they are all competent at the jobs they have chosen to do, while my technical competence only serves to accentuate the poor quality of the paintings I produce.

Was Antonio, the architect, drunk? I would say not. Our kind of drinking rarely ends in drunkenness. But if it is true that *in vino est veritas*, then in this type of reunion the threshold of truth is crossed by those closest to it. This must be the explanation. Despite the open windows, the heat inside the studio was almost unbearable. We had talked about a thousand different things, unconnected and absurd, and as the night wore on, the lively discussions began to wane. Sitting on the floor, Adelina rested her head against my thighs (people usually says knees probably because it sounds better but what they mean are thighs because knees are invariably hard, as you can see from mine). Out of affection and for the sheer tactile pleasure, I slowly ran my fingers through her hair as I drank my Gin and Tony, an expression I often use when I get tipsy. The interior decorator, whom I shall refer to as Sandra although that is not her name, has started flirting again with the doctor, quite harmlessly, but enough to make Carmo, the publisher (older than me, I hasten to repeat), suffer greater pangs of jealousy than Shakespeare's Othello. It is also enough to make the doctor's wife allow herself to be courted (such a nice old-fashioned expression) by Chico, the advertising agent, who fancies himself as a lady-killer and cannot resist a little innocent flirtation without getting involved. Deep down everyone knows this is all meaningless. Anything more serious or risky would break up the group, and that is the last thing any of us would want. Ana and Francisco (who complete the group) also work in advertising. Still in their early thirties, they are head over heels in love and truly alarmed at the strength of their own passion. Sitting there on the sofa, they are waiting for us

JOSÉ SARAMAGO

to attribute their obvious excitement to the influence of alcohol. I know Carmo disapproves of such behaviour in public and I myself do not encourage it, but I can understand the terror which has taken possession of those poor hearts, minds, veins and sexual organs, that metronomic oscillation between life and death, that frenzied need to proclaim as eternal one's own definition of the precarious. Carmo does not accept these things, but what would he do should Sandra accept him one day and share her bed with him, even if only for an hour?

And what about Antonio, the architect in our group, who says he will design houses for all of us one day? Where can Antonio be? Antonio, who had gone to the bathroom, now appeared in the doorway of the studio with a fixed, determined smile on his face, which could have been mistaken for malice, unlikely in the case of Antonio, always so quiet and unobtrusive. On one forefinger he was holding up the second portrait of S., invisible beneath the black paint, and I thought he must have discovered it by chance for the light was on in the storeroom and naturally he had peeped in, after all it was after midnight and we were becoming bored (except for Ana and Francisco) or starting to get into silly arguments about culture (how the bourgeoisie love going on about culture), and also being my friend, avowed and proven, everything concerning me concerned him. For this and other reasons which could not be defined or confided there and then, Antonio asked me: 'Have you moved on to abstract painting? So much so that you now use only one colour? And what about those little portraits of yours?' What I thought of Antonio between the moment I saw him in the doorway with the portrait in his hand and the moment when I heard him speak, I shall only mention here because I do not want to rush things. It is important not to rush things but give things time to become clearer and if they do not become clearer then it should not be for lack of time because time is the one thing I have right now, unless death decrees otherwise. And having got that off my chest, I can finally say that I leapt to my feet in a rage (sending Adelina onto the floor) and before reaching Antonio I was able to control myself sufficiently to simply snatch (yes, with violence) the picture he was now holding in both hands. I restrained myself from punching him because of that black picture which I would never be able to explain (Adelina herself knew nothing of its existence, her lack of curiosity assisted by the precautions I usually took to conceal it in a corner behind other recent paintings, so that the wet paint would come to no harm) and also because Antonio had deliberately infringed the rules of the group by classifying as 'little portraits' paintings which I alone had any right to belittle behind locked doors and with my head under the sheets. As I carried the picture back into the store-room, I could hear quite distinctly, as if he were speaking into my ear, Antonio's voice repeating over and over again: 'When is he going to start painting in earnest?' and the voices of the others begging him to be quiet in pleading tones as if rebuking someone who had thoughtlessly blurted out the word cancer at the bedside of someone dying of the disease. Antonio had forgotten (or chosen to forget) that one never mentions the gallows in the house of a condemned man, nor speaks of 'little portraits' to someone who paints nothing else. When I returned, Antonio had settled down, his expression obstinate but tranquil amidst the anxiety and consternation of all the others, deeply absorbed in their own affairs (yet taking care not to hurt my feelings any further). Sandra, for example, was simply chatting to Ricardo, the doctor; Chico was simply conversing with Concha, the doctor's wife; Francisco only had words for Ana, while Carmo was trying to engage Adelina in conversation, but nothing doing, she only had eyes for me, her face expressionless rather than glum, as if she were waiting for something to happen. No more was said on the subject and the night ended there. Ana and Francisco, poor things, rather than ask me to loan them my bed for a quarter of an hour, made some excuse or other and were the first to leave. Shortly afterwards Ricardo and his wife, Concha, left because he was on duty next day. And Antonio quickly disappeared, mumbling words of apology: 'Forgive me, I meant no harm.' Once people started leaving, Sandra made her departure, covering Adelina with kisses and taking Carmo and Chico with her as escorts, resigned to leaving me behind. I could imagine Carmo's excitement, hoping that Sandra would offer him a lift (Carmo has no car, has never possessed one) and that rogue Chico insisting 'Come on, Carmo, I'll drive you home', and so it would turn out unless Sandra decided to amuse herself by taking Carmo with her, watching him tremble and babble on about the weather before asking her if she would be interested in designing the jacket of a book. Chico could not care less, he is not one for beating about the bush. Anyhow, he suspects that Sandra is lesbian or on the way to becoming one (he has always told me so) and he wants nothing to do with lesbians. And he is almost certain to be magnanimous and allow Sandra to give Carmo a lift in her car, which smells of cigarette smoke and Chanel, so that Carmo may stretch out blissfully on his lonely widower's bed.

Adelina and I suddenly found ourselves alone in that great silence which reigns at two o'clock in the morning. She came to me and kissed me on the cheek, on the very spot where the flesh caves in a little. Then she began gathering up the dirty glasses and side plates, the ashtrays filled to the brim with cigarette butts. I helped her to clear up, more out of kindness than necessity. We both knew it and were kind to each other. And although she could not stay the night, she lingered a while, my arm round her shoulder, as seemed appropriate under the circumstances. We spoke of vague and forgotten things, and all of a sudden, as if suddenly remembering, I interrupted our aimless conversation and explained: 'I'm experimenting with a paint spray. That Antonio. But he's right.' Adelina said nothing, not even as much as 'Really?' She became rather more restless when she felt it was time to go and asked me with some formality: 'Could I ask you to drive me home?' Her car was being repaired and it had already been agreed that I would take her home after our little reunion (or party). I replied 'Of course', which was the answer she expected.

I left her on the corner of the road where she lives (her mother does not approve of me dropping her off right outside the door) and I sat there watching her as she walked along the pavement, one minute visible beneath the light of the streetlamps, the next minute hidden in the shadows between one lamp and another, until I could see her struggling with the lock before disappearing inside the building. I started the engine up gently, moving off slowly and heading across the city. This is something I enjoy doing from time to time: driving at my leisure through the deserted streets as if I were kerb-crawling, and women look at me puzzled and intrigued when I drive on without so much as looking at them. Sometimes, on the other hand, I do stare at them, knowing what they are hoping for but not likely to get from me, before driving on, not to the end of the night, but through a night I did not know how to end. Not entirely true on this occasion: there were the usual streets and women, and men, too, passing in the shadows, and cats knocking over sacks of rubbish and the terrible glare of asphalt, and the lamps, and water dribbling here and there, but inside the car I was being carried rather than driving, empty, without a thought in my head, brutalized. Because I was driving so slowly (and not for the first time), a policeman stopped me and wanted to know what I thought I was playing at. I explained (an excuse which had become second nature) that the engine was giving me trouble, that I was driving slowly to see if I could manage to get home. Through my rear mirror I could see the policeman was taking down my number as a precaution, craning his neck to catch the light from the street-lamp. This worthy upholder of law and order was simply doing his job. Were I to be found lying injured or dead in the night, he would have important evidence to bring to any inquiry by stating his suspicions and the laudable precautions he took with civic foresight. And if any bombs were to go off in the night, the work of the Armed Resistance Movement or the Revolutionary Brigades, I would certainly be in trouble. However, I suffered no such mishap.

It was three-thirty when I parked my car in the Rua Camões. I was far from home but I felt like having a stroll. I began walking uphill in the direction of the Rua Santa Catarina, and, on reaching the Mirador, I went down to the railings and stood there gazing at the river, thinking of nothing, not a thought in my head, clearing my

JOSÉ SARAMAGO

mind completely so that not even the lights of the ships should have any significance other than shining for no good reason. That was as much as I was prepared to concede. Finally I perched on one of the benches and, taken completely unawares, discovered I was weeping. If that could be called weeping. Perhaps our physiology has reasons unknown to our anxieties and emotions, hence the ability of women to weep in that fluent, continuous, uninterrupted fashion which can be so very moving, whereas men are said not to weep, or it is considered shameful if they do, because they have never been capable of tears and so some plausible excuse had to be invented. It is true that I have not enjoyed the privilege of watching a man weep and it would be wrong to judge others by myself, but I am honestly incapable of anything more than these two drops slowly being squeezed from my burning tear-glands, drops so meagre and oppressively concentrated that they do not roll down, but remain there between the eyelids, slowly burning up, so slowly that I suddenly discover my eyes are dry. I would swear there had been no tears, had there not been for a time, now beyond recovery, memory or recollection, a tremulous and glistening curtain between me and the outside world, as if I were inside a cave with a cascade at the entrance sending down great shining rivulets of water, but silent, apart from this buzzing inside my eyes, the burning sensation of that tear-drop. I most certainly wept. For a moment or an hour, the white and amber lights coming from the ships and the other bank of the river were like sunlight in my eyes. Like all short-sighted people, I had the advantage of not seeing the light but its multiplication. Still sitting there, I later discovered that at some time, immeasurable because gone forever (and I became even more aware of it as the sounds of the city started up again and began penetrating my consciousness), I knew (or find it gives a nice *prosic* touch [Does the adjective exist?] now to say that I knew) that during the immeasurable time that had elapsed, I was alone in the world, the first man, the first tear, the first light and the final moments of unconsciousness. I then began to examine my life, to take a careful look, to rake over it like someone lifting stones in search of diamonds, wood-lice or dense larvae of the white and plump variety which have never seen the sun and suddenly feel it on their soft skin, like a ghost incapable of revealing itself in any other way. I remained sitting there for the rest of the night, sometimes looking at the river, sometimes at the black sky and the stars (what more should a writer say about the stars other than to say he has looked at them? Lucky me who only writes like this and, therefore, feels no obligation to do any more) until just before daybreak there was some unexpected rain and the sky cleared to my left and the waters turned as grey as the sky. Bidding farewell to the shadows which continued to hover in the west, the lights gradually went out in various parts of the city. I felt somewhat humiliated that after such a night I should end up with a chill in my bones and receive a look of indifference from the first passerby I met on the road.

I am writing this at home, as you can see, after having slept for no more than four hours and, convinced that it is essential and useful, or at least harmless even for me, I have decided to carry on writing, perhaps about my life past and present, or perhaps just about life, because it suddenly occurs to me that it might be easier to talk about life in general rather than about my own life. But how can I ever hope to recover all those years behind me, and not just mine for they are inextricably mixed up with those of other people, and to rummage through mine is to disturb the years of others which do not belong to me now or then, however gently or brutally I might invade them each moment we share or think we share? Perhaps no life can be narrated, because life is the superimposed pages of a book or layers of paint which, opened or stripped away for reading and looking at, immediately turn to dust and perish. The invisible force which linked them is missing, their own weight, agglutination and continuity. Life also consists of minutes which cannot be separated from each other, and time becomes a thick, dense and obscure mass in which we swim with difficulty, while overhead an unfathomable light begins to fade, a dawn withdrawing into the night from which it has just emerged. If I once read these things I am now writing then I am copying them, but not deliberately. If I have never read them, then I am inventing them. If, on the other hand, I have read them, then I must have assimilated them and now have the right to use them as if they were my own and had just been invented.

I was born in the year 1632, in the city of York, of a good family, though not of that country, my father being a foreigner of Bremen, who settled first at Hull. He got a good estate by merchandise, and leaving off his trade, lived afterward at York, from whence he had married my mother, whose relations were named Robinson, a very good family in that country, and from whom I was called Robinson Kreutznaer; but by the usual corruption of words in England we are now called, nay call ourselves, and write our name, Crusoe, and so my companions always called me. I had two elder brothers, one of which was a lieutenant-colonel in an English regiment of foot in Flanders, formerly commanded by the famous Colonel Lockhart, and was killed at the battle near Dunkirk against the Spaniards; what became of my second brother I never knew, any more than my father and mother did know what was become of me.

Since starting to write, I have copied texts on a number of occasions for one reason or another: to reinforce or contradict some statement of mine, or because I could not have expressed it better myself. Here I have done it to keep my hand in training, as if I were copying a picture. By transcribing and copying, I learn to narrate a life, moreover in the first person, and in this way I try to understand the art of penetrating this veil of words and ordering the insights words provide. But once having copied out a text, I am prepared to affirm that everything which has been written is a lie. Deceitful on the part of the copyist who was not born in 1632 in the city of York. Deceitful on the part of the author whom he copied, Daniel Defoe, who was born in 1661 in the city of London. The truth, if it exists, could only be that of Robinson Crusoe or Kreutznaer, and in order to recognize it would have meant proving its existence from the outset, that his father came from Bremen and passed through Hull, that

JOSÉ SARAMAGO

his mother was, in fact, English, and that first name was his family name, that two more sons were born to the couple and that what we stated really happened to them. The same truth would require confirmation that Colonel Lockhart and his regiment actually existed and, obviously, confirmation of the battles he fought, especially the one of Dunkirk against the Spaniards. (About the existence of the latter there is not the slightest doubt.) I do not believe that anyone could unravel these tangled threads, untie them, distinguish the genuine from the false and (an even more delicate task) define and register the degree of falsehood in the truth or truth in the falsehood. Of all that Daniel Defoe-Robinson Crusoe (the youngest of the three brothers) wrote and left behind I need only quote a few sober words: 'Just as my parents were never to discover what happened to me.' Because I myself abandoned them? Or because they abandoned me? Wilful neglect during their lifetime or orphanhood brought about by their death? For none of these reasons. Simply because any one of us could say these things about our parents or our children about us. Because I, the painter of portraits and the author of this narrative, have no descendants, or do not know them if they exist, or will exist in some future which still has to be written. Robinson Crusoe (we are told on the penultimate page of the story Defoe narrates on his behalf) had three children, two boys and one girl: useless information for any understanding of the text, but which confirms my belief in the importance of the superfluous.

I was born in Geneva in 1712, the offspring of citizen Isaac Rousseau and citizeness Suzanne Bernard. A most modest patrimony divided amongst fifteen children had reduced my father's share to almost nothing so that all he had to live on was his craft as a watchmaker at which he truly excelled. My mother, the daughter of Pastor Bernard. was more affluent: she was bashful and comely. [...] I almost died at birth and was not expected to survive.

From the outset, these parents have the enormous advantage of being real and, therefore, promise greater veracity than all of Defoe's fiction. No less real is Jean-Jacques Rousseau, who was born in the city of Geneva in 1712. But on faithfully copying down these lines with the honest intention of learning, I cannot see any difference, other than in the writing, between reality and fiction. I am convinced that for my life as narrated here (how could I narrate it elsewhere?) I can only rely on what someone later told Rousseau (for he himself was not conscious, or sufficiently conscious, to have known it then): 'I almost died at birth.' Nor could I have known it when I was born, but unlike Jean-Jacques, I did not need anyone to come and tell me. Having been born, I was born at the beginning of my death, therefore, almost dead. The midwife who helped to deliver me from my mother's womb probably remarked: 'The child is full of life.' But she was mistaken.

Officially a Roman emperor is said to be born in Rome, but it was in Italica that I was born; it was upon that dry but fertile country that I later superposed so many regions of the world. The official fiction has some merit: it proves that decisions of the mind and of the will do prevail over circumstance. The true birthplace is that wherein for the first time one looks intelligently upon oneself [...].

Someone narrates the life of a person who never existed or did not exist in this way: Defoe invents. Someone narrates a life as if it were his own and trusts in our credulity: Rousseau opens his heart. Someone narrates the life of an historical character: Marguerite Yourcenar writes Hadrian's memoirs and becomes Hadrian in the memoirs she invents for him. Confronted by these examples, I, H., remain incognito with this initial as I studiously copy out and try to understand, inclined to affirm that all truth is fiction, basing myself on evidence of suspect veracity and convenient falsehood from six witnesses who go by the names of Robinson and Defoe, Hadrian and Yourcenar and Rousseau twice. I am particularly intrigued by the geographical game which jumps from Italica (Spain, near Seville) to Rome, from Rome to London, from London to York, from York to Geneva and from Geneva to the place where Marguerite Yourcenar was born, a place I neither know nor am ever likely to know. Tossing words over centuries and distances inferior to centuries, she herself made Hadrian write: 'The true birthplace is that wherein for the first time one looks intelligently upon oneself'. So

JOSÉ SARAMAGO

where was Defoe born? Or Rousseau? Or Yourcenar? Where was I born, painter, calligrapher, still-born until it was decided where, when and if I had cast an intelligent look over myself? It remains to be seen whether once our place of birth has been discovered, we shall be able to recover and sustain that look of understanding or lose ourselves in new geographical locations. Most likely they are all fictitious: the real life of Hadrian is gradually crushed, pulverized, dissolved and reconstituted in another guise in Marguerite Yourcenar's fiction. We may confidently wager that something of Hadrian is still missing, perhaps simply because it never occurred to Defoe or to Rousseau to write their own biography of that Roman emperor who was born in Italica but who, according to the official fiction, was born in Rome. If the official fiction is capable of such things, then we can expect something even more extraordinary from individual fictions.

Close observations of these subtleties (do they really exist or only in my head?) make me aware that there is not much difference between words which are often colours and colours which cannot resist the temptation of becoming words. And so my time passes with the time of others and the time invented for others. I write and think: what is time today for Defoe, for Rousseau, for Hadrian? What is time for someone who is dying at this very moment, without ever having discovered where he was born through the knowledge that comes with understanding.

First exercise in biography in the form of a traveller's tale. Title: Impossible Chronicles.

The very title puts the reader on his guard, a warning not to expect wonders from a narrative which begins so cautiously. It would be quite pretentious to think that a rapid journey through the regions of Italy gave anyone the right to speak of them to anyone other than interested friends, who are sometimes sceptical, never having been there themselves. I am convinced that there are still things to be said about Italy, although little remains for the ordinary traveller armed only with his sensibility and who, because of some avowed partiality, is almost certain to close his eyes before inevitable shadows. For my part, I can say that I shall always visit Italy in a state of total submission, on my knees, as it were, something which escapes most people because it is entirely psychological.

Once having marked out my own little space and prominently displayed the flags indicating the points of departure and arrival, no one can argue that Paul should not write where Peter has written, or that where better eyes have seen, all other eyes must remain closed. Italy must have been (forgive the exaggeration if no-one agrees with me) our reward for coming into this world. Some deity or other, solemnly entrusted with distributing justice and not sorrows, and with a profound knowledge of the arts, should whisper into everyone's ear at least once in his lifetime: 'You're born? Well, go to Italy.' Just as people head for Mecca or less contentious places to ensure the salvation of their souls.

But let us leave these thresholds and enter Milan. For one reason or another Milan had been excluded from my map of Italy, as if two million inhabitants and an area of almost two hundred square kilometres were unimportant. However, it is also true that large cities do

JOSÉ SARAMAGO

not appeal to me very much: there is never enough time to get to know them properly, so that we remember them as if they were tiny boroughs consisting of no more than a square, a cathedral, a museum and a few narrow streets which time has scarcely changed, or we think has scarcely changed, for they are old and silent and we do not live there. Unless the traveller expects from a city what he has found in others he has visited (shops, restaurants, night-clubs), whereby everything becomes even more restricted since he is simply travelling inside a protective sphere and safe from any adventures.

The same is true of me but for different reasons. I limited myself to taking fleeting possession of a tiny section of Milan, a polygon of which the closest apex was the Piazza del Duomo, a cathedral in a flamboyant Gothic style which for all its splendour (or perhaps because of it) leaves me cold. The other apexes of this geometrical figure into which I crammed the whole of Milan were the Brera Gallery, the Castello Sforzesco, the church of Santa Maria delle Grazie and the Pinacoteca Ambrosiana. I doubt whether anyone is expecting me to provide them with a catalogue or guide-book of the city's art treasures, let alone attempt to confirm or contradict opinions already expressed, directly or indirectly by others. But a man advances through spaces dictated by the architecture, through rooms crowded with faces and forms, and he certainly does not come out as he went in, otherwise he might as well have kept away. This is what prompts me to run the risk of expressing in plain language what the privileged may have explained in the style of an historical pageant or, more profitably, in the discreet whisperings of a catalogue.

Here in Portugal we visit our castles as if they were national shrines. But our castles are usually empty shells from which every trace of life has been scrupulously removed lest there should be any trace or odour of a human presence. Inside, the Castello Sforzesco is more palace than fortress, but few buildings give such an impression of might and power; few castles are so manifestly warlike. The solid brick walls seem more unassailable than if they had been hewn out of stone. In the vast inner courtyard cavalcades and military parades can be staged and the whole edifice, surrounded by a great tumultuous city, suddenly emerges amidst the silence of its other tiny courtyards or apartments transformed into museums, like some paradoxical place of peace. But in one of these rooms, an exhibition of works by the French artist Folon is an insidious tentacle of the octopus outside: men-buildings, men-roads, men-tools advance over barren hills as the skies become covered with curved arrows, criss-crossed, and pointing simultaneously in various directions.

But there is also a luminous and strangely terrifying happiness hovering there in the Museum of Ancient Art installed in the castle's Sala delle Asse. One enters by a low and narrow arched doorway and, looking straight ahead, all you can see are what look like columns painted all the way round the walls. It is simply another room until you raise your eyes to the ceiling. We pity those visitors who do not feel a sudden shiver go down their spine: they must be blind to beauty. The entire vault is covered with intertwining foliage, forming an inextricable network of trunks, branches and leaves where no birds sing, where only a murmur descends, perhaps the phantom sound of Leonardo da Vinci breathing as he stood on a lofty scaffold to paint a tree-cum-forest. Not even Michelangelo's *Pietà Rondanini* several rooms further ahead (on which he was still working four days before his death, an unfinished statue which seeks yet shuns our hands) can efface the memory of the paradise created by Leonardo da Vinci.

And now I shall say something about the Brera Gallery, where Raphael's *Nuptials of the Virgin* is on display and the awesome, rigorously foreshortened *Dead Christ* by Mantegna. But the painter whose work intrigues me most of all in this museum is Ambrogio Lorenzetti, especially his tender *Virgin and Child*, her mantle unexpectedly adorned with stylized flowers. Two remarkable landscapes by the same Ambrogio Lorenzetti can be seen in Siena, 'the most exquisite pictures in the world'. I shall return to them when the time comes for Siena to open 'the doors of her heart' to me, as she promises all travellers without ever disappointing them.

JOSÉ SARAMAGO

Then there is the church of Santa Maria delle Grazie. Alongside, at the spot where the refectory of the Dominican Convent stood, is Leonardo's painting of *The Last Supper,* already doomed to perish as the painter applied the final brushstroke, for the dampness of the site had already begun its work of corrosion. Today, dampness has transformed the figures of Christ and the apostles into wan shadows, has covered them in mist, pitting the picture all over where the paint has peeled, a constellation of dead stars within a luminous space. It is a question of time. Despite all the careful precautions being taken, *The Last Supper* is perishing, and besides the qualities of Leonardo's incomparable artistry, perhaps it is its encroaching demise which makes this magnificent painting even more precious. As we come away, we feel twice as apprehensive that we may never see it again. Even if there should never be another bombing to demolish the building, reducing it to rubble, protruding beams, debris and bricks pulverised to dust, *The Last Supper* seems inevitably destined for some other fate.

And now before departing, time to visit the Pinacoteca Ambrosiana. By no means large, the museum is half-hidden away in the Piazza Pio IX which, in its turn, could only conjure up a piazza in the Mediterranean mind, but it is here one finds the somewhat rustic profile of Beatrice d'Este (or is she Bianca Maria Sforza?), her hair tucked into a net covered in pearls which any modern hippy might envy. The portrait was painted by Giovanni Ambrogio de Predis, a Milanese artist who lived in the sixteenth or seventeenth century. But the main attraction in the Pinacoteca Ambrosiana is the enormous cartoon of the School of Athens, which is exhibited in a special room. Lit to perfection, Raphael's drawing with its spontaneity and almost imponderable lightness of touch, more chiaroscuro than line, foreshadows the wisdom and dignity of the figures in the room of the Vatican, momentarily glimpsed by tourists passing through.

This was what Milan meant for me. And then at night, groups of people in the Galleria Vittorio Emmanuele, youths engaged in heated arguments with their elders, *carabinieri* keeping a watchful eye, tension in the air. And the walls of the buildings all along the Via Brera, covered with graffiti: 'The Struggle Goes On', 'Power to the Workers'. Several days later, when I was already travelling around Tuscany, the police invaded the university. There were scenes of violence, demonstrators were wounded, imprisoned, dispersed with tear-gas. And the right-wing press, conservative, fascist, or with fascist sympathies, triumphed.

I called what I have just written my (first) exercise in autobiography and I do not believe I was deceiving myself or deceiving others (strictly speaking, to deceive oneself or deceive others must surely come to the same thing?). After all, Rousseau's confessions and the fictitious reminiscences or memoirs of Robinson Crusoe or Hadrian respectfully observe the rules of the genre: they all start from a common point which goes by the name 'birth' and, if we examine them closely, they are transposed biographies which could just as easily have started off in an even more traditional manner with the words: 'Once upon a time'. Rejecting the classical method of autobiography, which I personally find dull, I chose to cover my own glass-like transparency with a thousand fragments of circumstance, those particles of dust moving through the atmosphere, the shower of words which, like rainfall, can be enough to inundate everything, quietly seeking out faint stirrings, the first restless movements of my fingers, my response to the sun and the frustration of not being able to throw down firm roots and cling to space. In a word: to conceal in order to discover.

I have (or have had since adolescence) an obsession with death, well not so much with death as with dying. I am not sure if I should put it so bluntly, considering no one likes confessing to cowardice and this is the greatest cowardice of all, precisely because it assails us when we are alone, in silence and settling down for the night in the safety of our own home: just as we are about to fall asleep and our bedroom loses its dimensions, when not even the furniture offers any threat, and there is no enemy pointing a gun at our head or drawing a knife. Probably I would not. But this first exercise in dissembled biography betrays me at once: death and dying are mentioned five times, one dies but once. This reveals my nature, sets me apart from my fellow-creatures, and not only me, since this black mesh is common to many others. And so, through successive appearances, I should come (shall come?) to find myself individualized, a unique human being defined once and for all, and fully justified in cautiously and methodically putting one last full stop to this calligraphy. Even though motivated by sheer scruple, I should have to begin all over again to explain the movement of the full stop itself, once having squared and focused that tiny point where the eye and the message transmitted from the brain to the muscles of the hand converge so that the pressure put on the paper produces only a dot rather than a blot or splash of ink. From an imaginary brain which has nothing more to say about itself, from a brain as white as a sheet of paper which is not really white. Because white does not exist, as I who am a painter always knew. Only what exists can exist.

However there is no God. There are many ways of knowing and mine is enough for me. When the anthropomorphic image of the deity was lost, everything was lost. None of the subsequent attempts to justify immateriality were able to renourish or revive beliefs. The Greeks had excellent gods who thought nothing of fornicating with perspiring mortals in their sordid beds. The admirable Moloch proved his existence by feeding on human flesh in public. And no less praiseworthy was Jesus, the son of Joseph, who travelled on a donkey and was afraid of dying, but once these stories ended, stories about ancient gods and those who worshipped them, there was no longer any place or time for God and he could achieve no more than Defoe, writing and rewriting the life of Robinson. A God who is not solemnly enthroned in the heavens, a God whom we have no hope of knowing in person, one and triune, is an imaginary Robinson, the second creator of a religion of fear which needed a Man Friday in order to become a church.

I am saying things others have said before me, but this well-trodden fabric, known as culture, ideology, and even civilization, consists of a thousand and one strands, namely legacies, voices, superstitions, which have become hardened convictions. In this

JOSÉ SARAMAGO

first exercise in autobiography, the heads of the apostles Peter and Paul stick out of this fabric made from wool in different colours, and both apostles smile as if they were the last to do so. And not just them. I enter Italy on my knees. There I speak of a deity who metes out justice, there on the periphery rises Mecca where pilgrims flock, with whose culture I have nothing in common, whereas I can now see (or saw before) that I share the culture of the pilgrims who crawl (on their knees) to Fatima, along the roads and within the sanctuary, making votive offerings, confessing their sins aloud, and nourishing Moloch in their own way. First there is the smile, then laughter followed by loud guffaws. Religion comes fourth on the scale. 'He that has ears to hear, let him hear,' as the carpenter's son said when he spoke in riddles to his friends. But none of this prevents a man who started out writing as naturally as possible (without trying to be controversial or defensive, and with no other aim than to narrate a journey which he will subsequently call an exercise in biography) from discovering between the words religions he does not possess but which demand to be heard and frequently contradict what has already been said. This leads me to question whether we possess what is knowable about this world or are we simply the interpreters of the knowable or known, which hovers over the earth like one more atmospheric layer capable of surviving the death of civilizations and the gods they worship. In this age of formidable women, the Venus of Willendorf is probably still an obsession.

A man advances through spaces, through rooms crowded with faces and forms, and clearly does not emerge as he went in, otherwise he might as well have kept away. I said this in praise of museums. I say this every time I enter a museum so that no one may wonder at each new quest for the secret or message I know remains intact inside, even when brought to light. I say this to anyone who claims that museums are outdated institutions, tombs, musty-smelling warehouses and that art should come onto the streets and into the squares. Those who make such claims may be right. And I am such a mediocre artist that I feel I have no authority to contradict them. However, it strikes me that one sees two quite different expressions on the face of the same man when he stands still before a work of art in the silence and intimacy of a museum or attentively treads the paving stones around the statue of Donatello's *Gattamelata*. This question of what is good or bad about museums is nothing other than a pastime for scholars and critics. It is simply a matter, as far as I can see, of knowing where the works of art are kept, how one can get to see them and, above all, the reasons why any of this (being, seeing, looking) should be necessary. I believe (convinced as I am that no painting of mine is ever likely to arouse any interest) that no one visits any of these museums without some good reason for going there.

It has not been easy to express these thoughts. I keep having to remind myself that I am not in the habit of writing, that I have not acquired certain techniques (glimpsed in the act of writing, but not within one's grasp and difficult to master), yet I can see that by this route I am reaching certain conclusions which have so far escaped me, and one of them, however straightforward it may seem, comes to me at this point in my writing, namely the satisfaction of knowing that I can discuss painting, even though convinced I am a bad painter, without allowing it to worry me, that I can talk about works of art in the knowledge that my own paintings will not affect the discussions and opinions of the experts. It is as if I were to say to myself: 'Their views have no effect on me.' The man without talent is as immune as the genius, perhaps even more so, but it has not been proven that his life is any less useful. An odd conclusion. And not just mine, not just some facile self-justification, for it is, and always has been, a universal fact that the rich and endowed have resorted to deceit in order to conceal their various methods of control; everything in our museums deserves to be salvaged, the paint on the canvas and the canvas beneath the paint, the roof covering everything and the guide who repeats what he has been taught, the wooden floor I am treading and the soles of my feet doing the treading, the inscription identifying the painting and the absent hand that wrote it.

So many words written from the beginning, so many lines, markings, paintings, such a need to explain and understand and, at the same time, so much effort, for we have still not finished explaining or reached any real understanding. In Milan, some of the walls spoke, used words which surprised me since they are prohibited in my own country plagued with disquiet and fear: 'The struggle goes on', 'Power to the workers'. In Milan the police invaded the university, attacked and wounded demonstrators and carried out arrests, while the reactionary press gloated and praised the authorities. I declare that men are not brothers. Or rather: not all men can be brothers. Capitalists like Rockefeller, Melo, Krupp, Schneider, Champalimaud, Brito, Vinhas, Agnelli, Dupont de Nemours are not my brothers, just as the police in their service are not my brothers. The police and financiers behave like brothers even though not born of the same father and mother. In Milan the brothers of this fraternity, poor bastards and rich bastards, were congratulated by the bastardised press. The world is old and sorrowful.

Could I have been born then? I doubt it. I should have known before now and would not be here after all these years, interrogating myself like Hadrian about the date and place of my birth. But it could have been during the time of the Spanish Civil War (1936–1939) when a policeman in Lisbon caught me with some leaflets in my hand, rectangular sheets of paper, crudely printed and with the ink not yet dry, leaflets protesting about the supplies of wheat being sent to feed Franco's troops, and attacking fascism both at home and abroad. These leaflets carried the signature of the Portuguese Popular Front (undoubtedly influenced by the French Movement) and I had no idea what it meant. There was some feast-day or other being celebrated in Amoreiras and I had gone there, who knows why, since I never much cared for such festivities, especially when on my own, for even at that age I was prone to this melancholy which has never left me. The leaflets were piled up on top of a low wall and even now I can sense how nervous the person must have felt who put them there, lying in a pile for any passers-by who might be curious to learn of the crimes that were being committed. I was much too young. Grabbing the pile of leaflets, I stood under a streetlamp to get a better look. There was music, some popular melody coming from a band, people dancing in the streets, fairy-lights, shooting-galleries and something else I can no longer remember. But I do remember ('One never tires of nursing old grievances', as Luis Augusto Rebelo da Silva once wrote) the hand which suddenly gripped me by the arm (with such force that all the leaflets scattered to the ground) and the policeman's voice. The only thing I cannot remember is his face. I know he was no longer young, and must be dead by now, but I continue to ask myself if he ever thought about what he had done, whether his suffering was that little bit greater at the hour of death (if there is any justice and he had no more serious crimes on his conscience). He bent down to pick up a leaflet, read it and ordered me to pick up the rest and hand them over to him, gripping my arm all the while with unnecessary force because there was little chance of my being able to escape. I experienced a fear I had never known before: the fear of the chosen victim, of those condemned without trial, the fear of the guilty, doomed from birth. I am now trying to define this fear and am in danger of exaggerating as I struggle to find the right words: 'You're coming with me to the police station,' he told me. I protested my innocence, pleaded with him to let me go, explained how I had found the leaflets and only started reading them to see what was written there and nothing else. The policeman asked if someone had given me the leaflets to hand out ('Own up, you little rogue, you were going to hand them out'). Sobbing, I repeated my story, which was true but difficult to prove. For the policeman my truth could only be false. The people who had gathered round at first now moved away when it dawned on them that this had something to do with politics. They were careful not to look back, showed no further interest, nervous and relieved, as I now realize, that they had escaped any danger of becoming involved. And I began to ask myself if the person who left the leaflets on top of the wall could still have been there, gazing at me from afar with compassion and hoping they would do me no harm. I was taken to the police station some blocks away, after

86   JOSÉ SARAMAGO

being roughed up and threatened as I was led through the silent streets. And all because of something so trivial and innocent. Just to remember that episode fills me with uncontrollable rage.

I was interrogated by the chief of police. I was kept standing while he remained seated. Then they locked me up in a cell for two hours. I was no longer weeping. Slumped in a chair, I was dumbfounded, sitting there in almost total darkness. The guards outside were chatting amongst themselves while their chief telephoned headquarters two or three times, repeating the same question over and over again: 'Should the prisoner be taken below or what?' They finally released me and said I should consider myself fortunate. Those 'below' had decided I was not worth bothering about. However they took my name and address. It was unusual for me to arrive home at such a late hour and I was severely rebuked. I was asked where I had been but said nothing. My parents must have thought I had decided to lose my virginity that night. It was true, but not as they imagined, the only thing they could imagine.

Writing in the first person is an advantage but it is also akin to amputation. We are told what is happening in the presence of the narrator, what he is thinking (should he wish to divulge his thoughts), what he is saying and doing and what those who are with him are saying and doing, but not what they are thinking, except when what is said coincides with what is thought and this is something about which no one can be certain. If my friends were characters out of a novel not written by me or one of them, but by a third party other than ourselves (the author), each one of us would only have to read this novel in order to become as omniscient as the author himself presumes to be. And so, since they are as real as I am and just as reserved or not so open that others might truly say 'I know', and because I can only convey some of my thoughts in this narrative which is not a novel, I resign myself to ignorance, to the impenetrable nature of faces and the words those faces utter (it is the faces that speak, the faces that understand) and I shall go on speaking about my friends without knowing what they are think-ing, but only what they are saying and doing. And even then, on condition that they say and do it in my presence, otherwise I shall never know whether they are telling the truth about what they did and said when I was not there. And if they were to tell me any of this I should have no way of knowing whether they had agreed amongst themselves what they would tell me if they should testify on behalf of each other. If this narrative were not in the first person, I should have found it an even better way of deceiving myself. In this way I should be able to imagine every thought as well as every action and word, and in putting them all together I would believe in the truth of everything, even in any inherent falsehood, because that falsehood, too, would be true. The real falsehood is what is unknown and not

JOSÉ SARAMAGO

what was merely formulated in accordance with that hundredth of the hundred ways of formulating what one normally calls a lie.

I showed Adelina my traveller's tale, detached, of course, from the other pages coming before and after. I felt rather wicked as I smugly watched her reading it in front of me, calmly sitting there with her legs crossed, so self-assured, while I knew (the only person on earth to know) that on previous pages she was more than the figure visible to me and aware of herself, because she was something I alone manipulated, pulled towards me or pushed away, without her knowing it, without her so much as suspecting anything. I discovered that my feeling (or should I say impression?) was not merely mischievous but one of genuine malice, malevolence, ill-will, something the slave-master, a despot or the powerful owner of a plantation might have felt. I had good reason to feel embarrassed and fortunately felt ashamed of myself. I can lay Adelina naked on my bed, yet cannot bring myself to force my hand up her skirt.

'I had no idea you had a talent for writing.' Those were the words she used as she rested the papers on her lap. There was an expression of surprise in her eyes (do eyes have an expression, or is it because of what surrounds them, eyelashes, eyelids, eyebrows, wrinkles?) and an impending question mark, which I might have placed at the end of her sentence had I felt more certain. 'I have decided to write an account of my travels until another commission turns up.' 'It's nicely written. Not that I understand much about writing, but in my opinion it's good.' She paused and then, averting her eyes from mine, she added: 'I don't understand why you've called this article (it is an article, isn't it?) "a first exercise in biography". How can a travel book be considered biography?' 'I'm not sure that it can, I really don't know, but I couldn't find anything more interesting to write about.' 'Either it's a travel book or a genuine autobiography. In any case, why should you want to write your biography?'

Logic personified. I know my own feelings and susceptibilities play some part in this, but Adelina, though not normally aggressive, might just as well have asked me: 'What could there possibly be in your life that is worth narrating?' I had no answer to give to either question, even less so had she remembered to add: 'And to whom?' Therefore I seized the alternative which Adelina had earlier proposed: 'Either it's a travel book or an autobiography.' 'I believe we reveal something of ourselves in everything we do and say, in our every gesture, in the way we sit, walk and observe, in the way we turn our head or pick up an object from the ground. This is what painting tries to do. Obviously I'm not talking about my own painting.' I saw Adelina blush: 'Why not?' I took pity on her and broke off at once: 'Well, in that case a travel book is just as good as a genuine autobiography. The problem is knowing how to read it.' 'But anyone who reads a travel book knows what he is reading and it never occurs to him to look for anything else.' 'Perhaps people ought to be warned. If they don't need to be told that a picture has two dimensions rather than three, then they should not have to be warned that everything is biography, or to be more precise, autobiography.' Adelina carefully assembled the sheets of paper and handed them to me: 'You haven't numbered the pages.' Of course I had not numbered them. I only copied them out to show her. I had no intention of coming clean. 'What you're saying is interesting, but I'm in no position to argue with you. It never dawned on me you had these ideas.' 'What ideas?' 'This business about writing and thinking about what you are writing. I only saw you as a painter.' 'A bad one.' 'I never said that.' 'But it's what you are thinking. It's what everyone thinks.'

I suddenly found myself saying the wrong thing, something I had no intention of saying. Adelina had risen to her feet, was looking flushed again as if I had offended her. And this impression was so strong that I felt I must apologize. She came up to me and said what she should have left unsaid: 'Idiot', and did what she should not have done: she patted me on the wrist (I have two wrists, so perhaps I should have specified which wrist Adelina patted, but apparently one does not explain these things in a narrative unless it is absolutely essential, for example, if my wrist were bruised and painful and I complained, because then it might be crucial for the rest of the plot, if I happened to be writing a narrative). I simply asked her: 'Shall we go?' 'Let's go.' We had arranged to have dinner together and

Carmo was to meet us at the restaurant, perhaps with Sandra who, as Adelina, smiling without malice, informed me 'is sure to flirt with you'. 'To amuse herself,' I suggested, paying no attention. Whereupon Adelina, as if thinking about something else, remarked: 'People feel this need.' Uttered in all innocence, certain phrases coming from Adelina leave me intrigued. I would even go so far as to say that there is something irritating, barbed, sharp and abrasive about them, yet if written down none of this would show. When I hear them, I feel somewhat betrayed. It sounds as if she is threatening to leave me while I had always assumed that when the time came to split up she would be the one to suffer and not me, because I would be the one to take the initiative. As we walked downstairs, she went first and I followed behind. Listening to the tapping of her heels on the stairs, I went on repeating and pondering her words: 'People feel this need'. What do people need when they come together? What are they, or what were they unwittingly looking for when they decided to separate? I realized that our little stroll together was almost over, not because I wanted it to end (always lost in thought and somewhat remote) but because she had become tired for some reason, one more reason why we should separate without delay, before enough time elapsed to warrant further explanations, increasingly futile and compelling, when all it needed was a simple and somewhat discreet gesture to put a full stop once there was nothing more to be said.

Already in the car, Adelina asked me: 'When did you make that journey?' 'About two years ago.' 'Are you thinking of doing some more writing?' 'It's possible. I didn't give it much thought when I began writing. But perhaps I'll carry on.' We kept silent for a few moments. She returned to the subject: 'You should try publishing your story in a newspaper. Or in some magazine.' Then she paused before adding: 'But I suggest you get rid of that title about an exercise in biography. People won't know what you mean.' That word 'people' again. Such an odd expression. I decided to cut the conversation short. 'One can never tell what people need or understand.' Out of the corner of my eye I saw Adelina turn her head in my direction. I heard or thought I heard her take a deep breath as if determined to ask a serious question, but then I could feel or hear her relaxing and her expression became less bright as she turned her head away again. We said nothing more until we reached the restaurant.

Carmo and Sandra were already seated, poetically nibbling at fresh cheese and sipping wine. These friends of mine appreciate this kind of restaurant, popular *ma non troppo*, with floral-patterned table-cloths and tiled walls, a real family atmosphere with homely types doing the serving and cooking. Yet for some strange reason the clientele always has that civilized look which smacks of intellectualism and pretentious simplicity, a new way of giving the impression that one is cosmopolitan in an age when everyone either is or is on the way to becoming so. Carmo's eyes were shining, his lips moist. Sandra was laughing as if greatly amused, but knowing her as well as I do, I could tell she was also furious at our late arrival while she sat there being seen with an old man. As we took our seats, I looked coldly at Carmo. I bear him no grudge, I even like him, but it is myself I detest as I look at him, and see what I shall look like in a few years, as old as him and with whom at my side? Whom will I amuse? What younger man, no matter how little the difference in our ages, will sit and stare at me like this? Sandra took over the conversation, interrupted Carmo in the middle of a sentence. The waiter arrived with the menu, we made our choice, settled down to enjoy our meal, the wine was from Alentejo and excellent, Peace be with us.

During dinner, Sandra, fickle as ever, started being sweet to Carmo. It is true that she kept giving me signs with her foot, but I am sure with no intention other than to make me watch her amusing herself as she flirted with Carmo. And my oldest friend (and certainly older than me), as the saying went in my childhood days, was in his seventh heaven. The rules of our frivolous little game demand that we should ask no questions when we are with friends spellbound by love: they will confide in us whenever they find it necessary, if they should find it necessary, because more often than not the hard facts fit into our daily routine without the need for any questions or explanations. In this case, the flirtation was simply a

JOSÉ SARAMAGO

more serious replay of previous episodes. But Carmo probably had his own good reasons. In appearance he looked twenty years younger and seemed to be intoxicated by something other than wine. Lucky Carmo. If he can hold on to Sandra for at least a week, he will either die or pass into immortality.

Adelina asked: 'Did you know that H. (which is my name here) is going to write about a journey he made in Italy two years ago?' Sandra politely said: 'Really?' Surprised, but smiling, and resolutely happy, Carmo asked me: 'Are you serious, old boy?' I looked at Adelina slowly, fixing her eyes with mine: 'It didn't seem worth mentioning.' 'You do keep things very much to yourself. Among friends there is no need to be quite so secretive.' I raised my glass of wine, swayed a little: 'I don't like divulging my affairs. I'm among friends and wasn't trying to be secretive. Or perhaps I was. It was something I had to resolve but you've resolved it for me.' My words were unnecessarily brutal. I finally added: 'But who cares.' Sandra jangled her bracelets to banish the shadow which had been cast over our table and asked Adelina: 'Have you read it? Did you like it?' 'Yes, very much.' Expressed with such simplicity, this judgement pleased me. My remorseful eyes caressed those of Adelina, but I suddenly flinched because something resembling a smile passed over her face and, whatever it was, it meant that she had stopped being on the defensive. It was then that Carmo, who was leaning towards me from the other side of the table (which allowed him to take advantage and rest on Sandra's arm and left breast) blurted out: 'Write your book and I'll publish it.' I felt a kind of knot in my stomach, lodged near my solar plexus, and turned down Carmo's offer: 'Either you're mad or downright stupid.' To which he replied: 'I'm serious. Write your book and I'll see that it gets published. I'll even pay you royalties.' Of course Carmo was not going to lose the opportunity of publishing the work of the Hemingway sitting opposite him, he was not going to lose Sandra, he was not going to relinquish that arm and breast. I pursued the conversation. 'You're both mad. And if this is your idea of publishing you'll soon go bust. How do you know whether my book is any good? The fact that Adelina likes it means nothing. She is not one of your readers and, as far as I know, you have no trust whatsoever in your readers.' Carmo wisely accepted this reservation: 'All right then, I haven't read it and I can't really be sure if it's any good. But once you've finished writing it, let me read the book and if I'm sufficiently impressed I'll keep my promise and publish it.' As if she were taking part in my little game, Sandra suddenly turned to Carmo and kissed his flushed cheek. The kisses we exchange are never taken very seriously, yet I am convinced that same night Carmo slept with Sandra for the very first time.

Second exercise in autobiography in the form of a chapter of a book. Title: The Venice Biennale.

Watching the film *Death in Venice*, I found myself mentally asking the director when he would decide to show, however fleetingly, at least one of the city's 'famous landmarks': St Mark's Square, the Moors on the Clock Tower, the Campanile, Sansovino's Loggetta, the Doge's Palace, the façade and domes of the Basilica. But the film ran on and we reached the last reel without lapsing even once into the facile picturesque. Why? I left the question in mid-air, expecting to find an answer one day. Never expecting it to come so soon.

On my first visit to Venice I used my time to explore the city's epidermis, scrupulously fixing my feet and eyes where millions of other people had already fixed theirs. For this ingenuous lack of originality let the man who has committed no greater crime punish me by casting the first stone. But on this occasion, once I had revisited all the familiar places and confirmed the incomparable attractions of Venice for tourists, I decided to turn my back on the coastal splendours of the Grand Canal and probe the interior of the city. I deliberately shunned the open spaces and allowed myself to wander without map or itinerary through the most tortuous and deserted streets (or *calli*) until I found myself in the obscure heart of a city prepared to reveal itself at last. And this was when I presumed (and still presume) to have understood Visconti's conception: if by some magical spell all the salient features of Venice were suddenly to be removed, the city would lose nothing of its unique fascination. The film *Death in Venice* is set in the only authentic Venice: a city of silence and shadows, with that black fringe imprinted on façades by the water in the canals and that all-pervading stench of dampness which no amount of sunshine can remove. Of all the cities I know,

Venice is the only one that is manifestly dying, she knows it and, being a fatalist, is not unduly concerned.

On my last day it rained. The Grand Canal was a great pulsating river and the low tide, forced by the wind, gurgled on the ground of St Mark's Square and against the great doors of the Basilica. Venice swayed like an immense raft, she appeared to be sinking, now she was afloat, miraculously sustained at the last minute by some tiny bridge or other there on the city boundaries. In compensation for the inevitable, I found myself thinking of Fabrizio Clerici's painting which shows Venice without any water, the city's buildings raised on tall stakes while the bottom of the Adriatic is covered in the same mist which earlier had enveloped the city, now open and with clear, sunny skies overhead.

I have no intention of entering into any arguments about the Biennale. Amidst the frenzied protests and impassioned eulogies I wander around with my tiny instruments of understanding, accepting and rejecting (frequently accepting and rejecting in rapid succession or vice versa), and I cherish the memory of a turbulent chaos which, in retrospect, strikes me as being singularly harmonious.

I shall never be able to forget Trubbiani's birds made of zinc, aluminium and copper, birds with huge wings, tied onto racks used for torture, and paralysed in that instant preceding death, before that shriek-cum-croak we are asked to conjure up in our minds. And I fear that my nights will be disturbed by nightmares inside that *Nursery* painted by the Austrian artist Oberhuber: a suffocating, empty room, the walls lined in canvas, with monstrously large children painted in vague tones, almost indistinguishable yet quietly intimidating.

What else should I mention here? *Cattle raising* by the Brazilian artist Espíndola, a genre painting with a feeling for ambience which engaged one's vision, touch and smell; the glass fibres of the Canadian, Redinger, crumpled cylinders scattered over the floor and reminiscent of huge, blind worms; the painted panels of *The Five Seasons* by Otasevic from Yugoslavia; *People* by the Polish artist

Karol Broniatowski, dozens of human figures made of papier-mâché, life-size and naked, but covered in newspaper and arranged in every conceivable position, on the ground, seated, lying down, dangling in clusters from the ceiling, invading the space where visitors move around as if trying to attack them, to embrace and possess them; bronze figures by the Hungarian Andras Kiss Nagy, which resemble prismatic formations of basalt; etchings by the Uruguayan artist Luis Solari, most of them quite small, Goyaesque, human figures replaced or accompanied by animal doubles; hideous photographs by the American Diane Arbus, or the hideous captured on film.

These references will suffice to show how I responded to works which, in one sense or another, are rooted in an exalted and controversial expressionism. This is probably due to my personal inclinations rather than any attempt on my part to make value judgements which are beyond my competence.

On leaving the castle gardens, where the Biennale wearily scatters its pavilions, I prepare for my departure. The *vaporetto* advances slowly through the restless, murky waters, along the Riva dei Sette Martiri and the Riva degli Schiavoni from where I have just emerged. A chilly melancholy hangs over the entire city. The façade of the Ducal Palace, which in sunlight becomes pale orange, turns to dusty pink and becomes quite delicate as the rain starts falling. Under the arcade, looking onto the Piazzetta, five American youths are seated on a long stone bench, genuine hippies who doze off leaning against each other in a fraternity which is altogether touching.

I take my leave of the Tetrarchs, the warriors of porphyry, Egyptians or Syrians embedded in the corner of the Basilica, right at the entrance of the Porta della Carta. Embracing each other fraternally, these comrades-in-arms, like the hippies, have come from afar but here they will remain, watching the multitudes, clutching their swords in one hand, the other resting on their companion's shoulder. I love these Tetrarchs, I run my fingers over the red stone as a farewell gesture, then walk on. When shall I return?

On the 11th of March 1944 (almost thirty years ago) bombs fell on Padua. The church of the Eremitani was virtually destroyed and

Mantegna's frescoes depicting the life of St James either disappeared or were severely damaged (the painter was seventeen when he first stood with his paints and brushes before the bare surface of a wall). I look at what remains of Mantegna's pictorial world: monumental architecture, human forms as ample and robust as rocky landscapes. I am alone in the church. I can hear the sounds of a city which has forgotten the war, the drone of aeroplanes and explosion of bombs. Just as I am about to leave, an elderly English couple arrive, tall, dried up, wrinkled, so alike. As if in familiar surroundings, they head straight for the Ovetari Chapel painted by Mantegna and there they stand, lost in contemplation.

But Padua (the city of St Antony and of Gattamelata, Donatello's equestrian statue which no one making equestrian statues in Portugal today appears ever to have seen) is, above all, the Chapel of the Scrovegni where Giotto painted the frescoes of *The Life of the Virgin, The Life of Jesus, Christ's Passion, The Ascension and Pentecost,* and *The Last Judgement.*

These paintings may lack the narrative appeal of the cycle of *The Life of St Francis* which Giotto painted in Assisi, but I can think of no style more suited to this warm cocoon, to these perfect proportions in the Scrovegni Chapel. The figures appear aloof and at times almost priestly. For Giotto they belong to an ideal world of premonition. In a world thus described the divine extends serenely over the concerns and vicissitudes of this world, like some predestination or fatality. No one there knows how to smile with their lips, perhaps because of some flaw in the painter's powers of expression. But the open eyes, with long, heavy eyelids, often light up and exude a tranquil and benign wisdom which causes the figures to hover above and beyond the dramas narrated in the frescoes.

As I strolled through the chapel, once, twice and for a third time, examining the three cycles in chronological order, a thought suddenly occurred to me which I have still not been able to unravel. It was a wish rather than a thought: to be able to spend a night there in the middle of the chapel and wake up before dawn in time to see those groups slowly emerging in procession from the shadows, like ghosts, their gestures and faces, that translucent blue, which must be one of Giotto's secrets, for it is not to be found in any other painter. At least not in my experience.

Let no one imagine I am betraying some deep religious feeling. I am simply trying to find out in the most mundane terms how an artist can create such a world.

If I am capable of being at the same time, or successively, the author and judge of my actions, then I believe Carmo's offer had some influence over this second exercise. This time (at least this is my impression) the narrative is much more vigorous, the style more polished and controlled, as if aware of being observed. Both exercises are linked, as much in the period they describe as in the period when I wrote them, but the first exercise is unprepared, exempt, innocent, whereas this one has become literary, who knows whether for better or for worse. I would say probably for worse when one tries to ennoble gestures and phrases, the expressions becoming laboured and no longer natural or fluent, and the same care could have been taken to say something more meaningful, more considered, more immediate and, therefore, probably more personal. If this is the case, then spontaneity should be greatly mistrusted and artifice warrant the highest praise, this so-called art, artefact or *artemages* as one says in the Alentejo (or used to say at a time when the word was still common) and which is clearly a popular expression for the magic arts. Or do I mean the art of images? Not having entirely forgotten that I am a painter, this last hypothesis whereby painting is called *artemages* appeals to me. How much nicer to be known as an *artemagista* than a painter, and how much more suitable a name for someone who can do so many different things remote from painting.

No doubt I am being extremely ingenuous. These writings of mine are worthless and Carmo was not serious when he spoke of publishing a manuscript he has never read and will do everything possible to avoid reading once he has sobered up. Sitting beside Sandra, feeling her heavy breasts and perhaps rubbing his leg against hers, Carmo would have volunteered to go into space, the first man ever to do so should Gagarin have fallen ill at the last moment and the Soviet Union no other astronaut in reserve. There are many ways of making heroes and saints: the difficulty is finding them in that brief moment when three or four vectors previously disconnected meet each other in optimum space. That moment is brief and it is common knowledge that the point of encounter is also the point of crossing, and the factors which fail to meet immediately disperse forevermore, unless, as I was taught at school, space is infinite and circular or spherical, and, therefore, the encounter can be repeated. It is a simple fact that none of us can yet have touched this precarious point: time is incapable of waiting so long. Anyhow, there is still some hope: so long as Sandra, out of whatever caprice or deep despair, should be or appear to be interested in Carmo, the promise, guarantee, or what was virtually an oath, cannot be forgotten. Carmo will not want to descend from the heights he scaled that evening. There is only one way of playing Don Quixote: to enlarge one's ideals. There is only one way of slowing down the passage of time: to live someone else's time. The astute take advantage of the one and the other, unlike me, for I shall say no more to Carmo about my travel notes on Italy.

I would probably exchange all my talent as a painter (which does not amount to much but is all I have) in order to discover the deeper motivations which lead people to write. The same could be said of painting, but I repeat, writing strikes me as being the more subtle art and probably reveals more about the writer. I can swear that in Venice (let anyone who doubts me check the catalogues) those birds I mentioned were really there, those birds by Trubbiani made of zinc, aluminium and copper, held down by their half-severed wings on a torturing-rack, the mechanical device which aims and releases the blade of the guillotine, fires a revolver or simply prolongs a painful death. But why should this have made such a deep impression, why should this have so caught my imagination that it was the first thing I mentioned, thus betraying myself? I was not conscious of this when I wrote it, but I am aware of it now as I write it again (an important lesson: nothing should be written only once). Frankly, I betrayed myself, but who was to know, because the first time one always uses the secret language which divulges everything yet allows no understanding whatsoever. Only the second language explains, yet everything would go back to being obscure if the code of the first language were to be forgotten or lost at this precise moment. The second language, without the first, is useful for telling stories and together the two of them constitute the truth. So what did I betray? I betrayed a torture practised for many years, long before the episode with the police and the leaflets of the Portuguese Popular Front. How time passes. There are those who say there is a cruelty one can associate specifically with childhood and there are those who deny it. But if pressed, I should say that this cruelty certainly exists, when the person concerned can testify to this experience at a later date and in different circumstances. At a later date and in different circumstances, but in the right place in my judgement.

High up on a tree (an olive-tree to be exact) sits a bird. A sparrow. Creeping about below is a young lad with a catapult in his hands. The picture is familiar, the objective simple. Nothing cruel about it: sparrows were born to be stoned, boys to stone sparrows. This has been so since the world began and, just as sparrows refused to emigrate to Mars, boys have not taken refuge in monasteries overcome with remorse. (Although that is what the pilot did who dropped the atom bomb over Hiroshima [or was it Nagasaki?] but this time the exception does not prove the rule.) So once the elastic has been stretched and aim taken, there goes the stone. However, the sparrow did not come down. It neither came down nor flew away. It remained in the same spot on the same branch, chirping in a manner difficult to define but which, as later became apparent, was one of resignation. The stone had missed its aim, breaking off several leaves from the olive-tree, which came floating down, swaying like the pendulums from a wire extending all the way down to the ground. The boy felt successively annoyed, bewildered and pleased. Annoyed because he had missed, bewildered because the sparrow had not flown away, and pleased for the same reason. Another stone in the sling (also known as a catapult), another and more cautious aim and the sudden noise of friction in the air, the sound of humming. Discharged upwards, the stone soared above the tree, a black dot getting smaller against the blue background of the sky, almost touching the white border of a tiny round cloud and, once on high, it paused for a second as if taking the opportunity to examine the landscape. Then, as if going into a swoon, it dropped, having already chosen the spot where it would settle on the ground once more. The sparrow remained on the branch. It had neither stirred nor noticed anything, the poor bird did nothing except chirp and shake its feathers. From being annoyed-bewildered-pleased, I began to feel simply ashamed. Two stones, one bird quiescent and alive. I looked around me hoping to find someone to help me improve my wretched aim. The olive-grove was deserted. There was nothing to be heard other than snatches of song from the other birds, and perhaps a few metres away a green lizard at the entrance to its lair in the hole of a tree might be looking at me with fixed, stony eyes, trying to grasp what it was seeing. A third stone whizzed through the air, and then another, and another. Seven or eight stones were fired, increasingly less steady, my hand becoming more and more shaky, until the sparrow, without so much as moving or interrupting its chirping, was accidentally and almost without force struck on the breast by one of them. The bird flitted from branch to branch, beating its wings with that restless flutter of something taking its leave of the atmosphere's elastic stability before dropping at my feet, its claws quivering spasmodically and opening its malformed remiges like fingers (remiges, artemages, both words clearly gallicisms). It was a young sparrow which must have left its nest for the first time that day, so young that its beak still had yellow corners. It had managed to fly onto that branch and there it perched until it could regain some strength in its wings and tiny soul. How beautiful the crested peaks of the olive-trees look when seen from the air and there in the distance, if the sparrow's vision does not deceive it, those other trees, ash-trees and poplars planted in rows and covered with leaves resembling tiny waving hands or fans stirring up a breeze. I lifted the sparrow from the ground. I watched it die in my cupped hands, first the black pupils dimmed, the eyelids, almost translucent, went up and stayed there, leaving the tiniest of gaps for sight to pass through during those last few moments. It died in my hand. Alive to begin with, then it died. It died for a second time in Venice, tied down onto a torture-rack. Twisted slightly to one side, the head turned an eye swollen with horror in my direction. Which death is the real one? Travelling backwards in time and therefore displacing itself in space over Italy, France and Spain, or hovering dead over the rejuvenated waters of the Mediterranean, Trubbiani's bird in copper and aluminium came to rest in the palm of my hand to take the place of the bird I had killed, its corpse still lukewarm but beginning to turn cold. In the hot and silent olive-grove, the boy begins to perceive that crimes have their own dimensions. He takes the dead sparrow home and buries it in the yard, right up against the fence where the hoe cannot reach: a tomb for eternity.

What has yet to be, what has come and gone, what no longer is. The place nothing but space, and not a place, the place occupied and therefore designated, the place once more space and the sediment of what remains. This is the most straightforward biography of a man, of a world, and perhaps even of a picture. Or of a book. I insist that everything is biography. Everything is life, lived, painted and written: to be living, to be painting, to be writing: to have lived, to have written, to have painted. And the prelude to all this, the world still uninhabited, waiting or preparing for the arrival of man and the other animals, all the animals, the birds of tender flesh, of feathers and songs. A great silence over the mountains and plains. And then, very much later, the same silence over different mountains and plains and over deserted cities, loose sheets of paper still being blown through the streets by a questioning wind which moves off into the countryside without any response. Between the two imaginings, the one the before demands and the other which the afterwards threatens, there is biography, man, the book, the picture.

The water drained from the Mediterranean, Venice balanced on tall stakes as if they were her bones, so tall that only the birds visit the city. Broniatowski's figures of men and women might be strolling the streets and squares, naked figures covered or dressed in newspaper, headlines covering their skin, mouth, limbs, sex and eyes. This is a possible afterwards. I inhabit my obsession with these images but wish that it were otherwise. One has to imagine the desert, contemplate the desert like Lawrence of Arabia in the film, to strip away everything, to create perfect silence, that which only the sounds of our body inhabit, to listen to blood coursing through the undulating softness of our veins, the throbbing of blood, the artery of our throat pounding, our heart beating, ribs vibrating, intestines gurgling, air whistling between the hairs of our nostrils. And now is the moment. Now day may dawn, slowly, slower still, without haste. Lying on the ground, on one's back, looking up where the sky will start to clear, then turning one's head from side to side, because there is no certainty in this world that the sun will rise in the east, one has to catch the first glimmer of light, the first fringe, perhaps another bird, that spot on the mountain where the sky settles, a glance, a smile, two hands ready to build. In the end, it might just as well be the Scrovegni Chapel as the brotherhood of Tetrarchs, shoulder to shoulder, the common gesture of laying their hand on their sword-hilts as they pursue a common goal. Daylight at last. Seated on the scaffold, Giotto paints Lazarus restored to life. And far, far away, in Egypt (or perhaps in Syria) one can still see today the enormous slab of porphyry showing the scar left by the block from which the Tetrarchs were carved.

Between life and death, between the spelling of death and the spelling of life, I go on writing these things, balanced on the narrowest of bridges, my open arms clutching the air, wishing it were more dense so that the fall might or may not be so hasty. Might not, may not. In a painting these would be two very similar shades of the same colour, the colour 'to be' to be precise. A verb is a colour, a noun a symbol. In the desert, only nothingness is everything. Here we separate, distinguish, arrange things in drawers, storerooms and warehouses. We commit everything to biography. Sometimes we give an accurate account, but our judgement is much more reliable when we invent. Invention cannot be compared with reality, therefore it is more likely to be faithful. Reality is untranslatable because it is plastic and dynamic. It is also dialectic. I know something about this because I studied it at one time, because I have painted, because I am writing. Even as I write, the world outside is changing. No image can capture it, the instant does not exist. The wave that came rolling has already broken, the leaf has ceased to be a wing and will soon snap, withered under our feet. And there is the swollen belly which rapidly goes down, the stretched skin which contracts again, while a child struggles for breath and calls out. This is not the time for the desert. It is no longer time. It is not yet time.

I have been offered another commission but I have no intention of starting to paint just yet. In this profession of mine it is sometimes useful, without overdoing it, to show that one is not readily available. If someone expects to have his portrait painted and the painter says without a moment's hesitation: 'At your service', the client is almost certain to feel disappointed. We portrait painters must try to be more astute. The basic rule is to treat the person who wants his portrait painted like a patient. What does the patient do? The patient rings the doctor's surgery, speaks to his receptionist and makes an appointment three weeks in advance. Could anyone wish for better attention? During the weeks of waiting, the patient considers himself as important as the doctor who keeps him waiting. He takes pride in having a doctor who is in such great demand, preoccupies himself with the affairs of a man who will be unavailable for three weeks, before finally being able to see him, listen to him, examine him and then arrange for tests and further analyses. And, if possible, cure him. But the waiting in such cases is almost as good as the remedy. As everyone knows, only the poor die from a lack of medical attention.

The same is true of portrait painting, although here there is the additional advantage that the person about to be portrayed still has a few more days to prepare himself. He will take care over his appearance, make every effort not to give the impression of being diminished psychologically, because this portrait is going to be an examination when the time for examinations has already passed. And when the time comes for the first sitting, the person about to be painted will look at the painter as I imagine the penitent must feel tempted to look at his confessor or the patient at his doctor: what secrets or mysteries are his secrets and mysteries about to encounter? What words will attach themselves to mine? What face existed before mine? Who inhabited this place before me? All of them good reasons for keeping the client waiting. And meanwhile, I need the money. Even this quiet life I lead, the rare outings, my painting (writing in recent months), simply breathing, eating, the clothes I wear, painting and writing materials, the car I hardly ever use, all of these things constantly require money. They are not luxuries but the cost of living is steadily rising. Everyone complains. It is true that my needs are few. If necessary, I would be quite happy to settle for some writing paper, a bed, a table and a chair. Or perhaps two chairs rather than keep a visitor standing. And my easel because I need it. Let me say here and now that my childhood and adolescence were not easy. I know something about privations. In my parents' house (both of them are dead) there was little money and barely enough food to go round. And for some years (far too many in a child's eyes) home consisted of a single rented room, in addition to what one referred to in those days as 'use of the kitchen at mealtimes' and that was precisely what it meant. It was only later that bathrooms were to become a common feature in the construction of houses. Here in Lisbon, at a time when there were few slums of any size and poor living conditions were confined to dilapidated tenement buildings and old farmhouses in the suburbs, there were many homes where the kitchen sink was used for disposing of all garbage and excrement. Each room had its own chamberpot and the servant who cleaned out the rooms would empty the chamberpot in the kitchen after giving fair warning so that the other women and children had time to get out of the way. The chamberpot was covered with a cloth as it was carried to the kitchen, not because of the stench which no cloth could ever suppress (everyone knew everyone else by their smell), but simply out of modesty and discretion, and even after all these years, just to think of it makes me shake my head and quietly smile.

I must be getting old. Because life is becoming costly I find myself remembering things from a difficult past. Perhaps I am giving the impression of being the sort of man who thinks the world owes

JOSÉ SARAMAGO

him a living, but I do not believe this is helpful for one's psychological stability. No one should feel sorry for himself. This is the first commandment of human respect (contradiction: No man can take pity on others unless he has taken pity on himself). But this facility for recalling episodes of no significance and long since forgotten is clearly a sign of old age (if what we read in books is true). I can still see, even after all these years, that drunk old woman who lived in the tenement, sprawled out amidst the skirts of the other women who were both scandalized and amused as they watched her lying there, plastered, singing to herself and masturbating on the highly polished floor (such incongruity: plastered, polished). At that age I only knew about singing. And I only caught the briefest glimpse. The women closed ranks and screened the entrance to her room and one of them (not my mother) led me out onto the veranda where I can remember feeling much more indifferent than I am today. I was expelled onto the veranda of another house after being given two hard smacks (or was it three? or four?) when I was discovered in bed with a little girl who was not much older than myself (by now she must be ancient). What were the two of us up to? Obviously nothing. We were simply experimenting, trying to imitate what we had both seen our parents do in bed when they thought we were asleep and our hearts beat furiously as we were confronted by this mystery from which we were excluded. Seated on the long veranda at the back of the house, which looked onto a vast expanse of yards, one for each tenement (how often I flew over those yards in my dreams), she and I wept, not because of our interrupted lesson but because of the sting of those smacks and the shame those shrieking women tried to inflict on our souls. Those same women who, in the privacy of their bedrooms, sighed and moaned once they and their husbands (our fathers) had made up their minds that we were fast asleep and there was no danger of our waking up. Childhood is full of so many little episodes.

I have not been out much. Adelina went back home, as one would say, to spend her holidays with her mother. She cultivates this tranquil, bourgeois habit of going home for a fortnight (the third week she reserves for us, as we agreed, not the entire week but the odd day here and there) to a village where she was either born or brought up. She gets back to her roots, as that man would say who, after being set down on the Moon or Mars to live and work, returns to earth for a holiday or simply to re-adapt (if worth his while) to customs here and bring himself up to date with the ways and passing convictions of the inhabitants of this third planet of the solar system, counting from the one closest to the Sun to the one farthest away. In short, back to Earth. Summer is over and I am alone. It is still easy to find parking-space, the gutters can be seen again, the streets seem to have regained their appearance of old, the traffic moves without difficulty. But I am alone. Nearly all of my friends are away. Some said goodbye. Others not even that. And why should they? Carmo and Sandra are probably in the Algarve or were they heading for Spain? I've forgotten. Chico is still infatuated with an English dancer appearing at the Casino in Estoril and no one sees him these days. He calls me now and then to brag. As for Ana and Francisco (it is easier for me to refer to the other Francisco as Chico), I get the impression their affair is cooling off. Probably no bad thing. They gave everything they had, perhaps convinced that in this way they would satisfy those forever vague precepts about love, and prove to friends and acquaintances that they took their affair seriously. And it was serious. It continues to be serious but different. They still go around holding hands but this is a role they learned to play which an appreciative audience once acclaimed, but now all they can expect is the occasional handclap. I can sense their disquiet, how anxious they are to keep up the pretence, to smile as they put a brave face on things, and my heart goes out to them. I think of them with affection and put it in writing. As for Antonio, he has not been seen ever since that disastrous scene (or episode) of the canvas covered in black paint, which I alone knew was hiding a portrait I had been unable to finish. I should like to see him, to talk to him. There is probably a masochistic streak in my nature. At this moment (just at this moment, for I am sure to change my mind almost immediately) I should like to hand him these written pages. Perhaps to take my revenge, perhaps to throw down the gauntlet once more. A challenge I might lose, but the gesture itself would ensure me some kind of irrefutable victory. Of this I am convinced.

It is already night. Not too far advanced, eleven o'clock, perhaps a little later. I always remove my watch when I am painting, I also take it off to write and usually hang it from one of St Antony's fingers or respectfully put it round his wrist so that he will stand out even more from the other saints and at least know how the time is going while I go in search of myself by writing or painting. This St Antony is made of wood which could be described as worm-eaten. A trunk for the rigid body, a block for the head, two branches (from a tree) for the arms, a lot of gouging, painted in the conventional manner, a hole in the nape of the neck to secure his halo, everything that is required to make Antony a saint. I took care to place him against a white wall reminiscent of his monastic cell, when miracles were no longer spreading faith in the outside world. With this wood (all from the same tree? or from trees which grew side by side? or from others which could only be found here?) other saints could have been carved, the entire Golden Legend, one of the Eleven Thousand Virgins, Eve, Magdalen, Mother Eternal and Earthly Father, the angel of annunciations, the first proclaiming life, the second death, none proclaiming resurrection. I look at the saint and start writing and it is as if I were painting. I fidget in my chair, can hear it creak, and everything about this world strikes me as being as simple as the fact that this chair in which I am sitting and this saint I am looking at are both made of wood. The greatest irreverence and the most sublime veneration.

I am back at my writing, but had broken off to place the chair on which I was sitting beside the saint. Now I am on the floor with my legs crossed like the Egyptian scribe in the Louvre. I raise my eyes and look at the saint, I lower them, look at the chair, two man-made objects, two reasons for living, and I ask myself which is the more perfect, the more apt for its purpose, the more useful. And after much debate I withhold the prize from both the saint and the chair. An honourable draw, as sports commentators might say, the most conciliatory and unctuous writers of all, the high priests of the most reassuring religion ever invented. I should add that I nearly chose the chair, disloyally influenced by that other chair painted by Van Gogh. It would have been a case of blatant partiality, which I resisted. And in order to balance the world and its influences, I decided to paint the saint. Careful! What have I just written? Paint the saint. I know exactly what I am about to do, but could anyone reading these three words know it? To paint the saint, means what? And what does it mean to paint the saint? Whatever I do will be right, I shall have kept my word, the three words I wrote, but no one will ever know if I have done what I said I would do: paint the saint.

I went to the window and gazed at the river and the lights. The air is heavy and the faintest mist lightens the sky. Tomorrow I shall telephone my client at long last. I shall paint quickly, I feel confident that I shall paint quickly. It is a double portrait: husband and wife. Their daughter is getting married, as the man explained, and they want the newly-weds to have this oil painting of her loving parents for their new home. An excellent idea. But what does it mean to paint the saint?

Third exercise in autobiography in the form of the chapter of a book. Title:
Buying Postcards.

They are timid, nervous people, already overwhelmed by the naves of cathedrals evoking skies laden with shadows, or by vast rooms where mysterious objects are on display. They have just arrived and are about to be subjected to the solemn test, the interrogation of the sphinx, to the challenge of the labyrinth, and because they come from an ordered world with traffic signs forbidding access or indicating speed-limits everywhere, they feel lost in this new kingdom where there is a freedom to be won: that freedom commonly described as a work of art.

And then they make a beeline for the stands where there are dozens of postcards on display, keeping the tourists occupied before they invade the galleries. The picture postcard, in the hands of the bewildered traveller, is a surface he can cover easily, something he can take in at a glance, which reduces everything to the tiny dimensions of an inert hand. Because the real work of art awaiting him inside, even when not much bigger, is protected from untrained eyes by an invisible net which the living hands of the painter or sculptor outlined as they laboriously invented the gestures which brought it into being.

Fearful of appearing cowardly, the traveller has no choice but to venture forth into the petrified forest of statues and wooden panels, amidst noisy multitudes if the gallery is famous and a mecca for tourists, or in a silence which allows one to hear the muffled creaking of old floorboards (another use to which wood is put) if he happens to be in some small provincial museum where the security guards eye visitors with surprise and gratitude. Very much later, when the traveller is back home, the picture postcard will be of value as a means of confirmation. He really did make that journey. He was not simply dreaming.

Yet I fail to recognize this view of the Castello Estense in Ferrara which I am holding in my hand. I circled its great walls like some tiny insect while the postcard has been photographed from the air, from the wings of a bird in flight. This image was missing from my dream, but I rapidly weave it into an aerial view of Venice, minute in the centre of the Lagoon, surrounded by waterlilies almost floating on the surface of the water, and with slow currents which, seen from on high, become laurel leaves in a state of perpetual transformation.

(I HAVE RECEIVED A LETTER FROM ADELINA. SHE HAS DECIDED TO END OUR AFFAIR.)

Ferrara is a tranquil place with long streets which even in the city centre have a quiet, suburban air, with high walls overlooking gardens which at the slightest breeze send up invisible clouds perfumed with spikenard, an overpowering aroma which stops me in my tracks. In one of these streets, the Corso Ercole I d'Este, stands the Palazzo dei Diamanti, which is nothing other than that Casa dos Bicos the citizens of Lisbon would love to have in the Campo das Cebolas. There are eight thousand five hundred diamond-shaped stones on which sun and shadow play as within rock crystal. Situated in this same street is the Pinacoteca Nazionale, and no sooner do I pass through the modest entrance than I come face to face with a temporary exhibition of works by Man Ray, some two hundred of them, paintings, drawings, sculptures, photographs and all those other works by Man Ray which embrace all those genres without specifically being any of them.

The museum is as peaceful as a garden. It has two *tondi* by Cosimo Tura which represent episodes from the life of San Maurelio (whoever he is?) and a Jerome attributed to Ercole de' Roberti, which fully justify my visit. I sign the visitors' book. And I can still see the affectionate look in the security guard's eyes on learning I had come all this way (from Portugal) and chosen 'his' museum.

From there I make my way to the Palazzo Schifanoia to see the frescoes of Francesca del Cossa, Cosimo Tura, Ercole de'Roberti and various other painters. The Salone dei Mesi, with its seven divisions which are virtually intact, presents a riot of colour which can be quite overwhelming. I find myself absorbed in the wealth of detail and smile quietly to myself as I examine Ercole's painting of the Loves of Venus and Mars: their bodies discreetly covered with a sheet in folds which foreshadows abstract design. Mars and Venus lying side by side appear to be resting after making love. Of her there is only a fleeting profile, whereas Mars, in the background but half-turned towards the viewer, stares at us over the face of his beloved with one eye, his expression at once defiant and embarrassed. On the ground and strewn over a chest are the warrior's arms and his lady's attire.

A city with four attributes: *dotta* (wise), *turrita* (towered), *città dei portici* (city of arcades), *grassa* (fertile). Bologna is seductive, feminine, gentle. One accepts these platitudes which give a better description of the city than a thousand precious epithets. Bologna is also an ancient city which has achieved the miracle of preserving its antiquities, defending them from the scourge of tourism which makes everything uniform. Take the Casa Isolani, for example, a private residence situated in the Strada Maggiore, which dates from the twelfth century, where people actually live and tourists are fortunately not admitted. I also try to visualise the Bologna of Dante around the year 1287, with its hundred and eighty noble towers competing in height and supremacy.

The luminous Basilica di San Petronio is equally magnificent, its arches creating a perfect balance between religious ecstasy and a more human dimension, as if reluctant to abandon the ground from whence it sprang, even for heaven. Here on the outside, Bolognese life weaves its tempting spells of earthly pleasures. But in the nearby church of Santa Maria della Vita there is one of the most dramatic sculptured groups in terracotta I have ever seen. It is *The Lamentation of Christ* by Nicolò dell'Arca, modelled some time after 1485. These women, who throw themselves over the outstretched body, wail with a most human sorrow over a corpse which is not that of God: here no one awaits the resurrection of the flesh.

But on this particular visit the towered city meant, most of all, the discovery of a great painter who lived in the fourteenth century: Vitale da Bologna. His *St George Slaying the Dragon* has both the simplicity of the best of primitive painting and a convulsive photographic quality which envelops the figures in a constant vortex. Deprived of a stirrup, the horseman's right foot appears to rest unsteadily on the flank although firmly attached to the horse's flesh. And straining its head upwards in terror. the horse pulls on the reins as the saint tries to force it to confront the dragon. I am reminded of the horse Picasso painted in *Guernica*: there is the same horror, the same frantic neighing.

In another painting Christ crowns the Virgin as she kneels on a crimson cushion. Vitale da Bologna has depicted two adolescents who could be mistaken for brother and sister or even lovers. There is no hint of religion in the graceful way the Virgin crosses her arms or in the sinuous movement of Christ's left hand, where an almost imperceptible wound evokes chapters of blood and agony.

The Scenes from the *Life of St Antony Abbot* are as fantastic as a dream lived within another dream. Almost indecipherable for anyone who, like me, is not familiar with *The Golden Legend* or the *Vitae Patrum*, episodes which narrate as much as anything the history of painting, and in this context are constructed with a knowledge which is not simply precious because of those backgrounds covered in gold, but also in the arrangement of the various planes with multiple perspectives which place the viewer at every possible angle simultaneously. And such is the incongruity that one is confronted with a tiled floor receding into the picture, contrary to all the rules of Renaissance perspective, on which the artist has set a prison building in strict conformity with those very same laws to the point of absurdity. The effect (not because scientifically proven but in order to express myself more clearly in writing) is probably the same as that created by representing a fourth dimension wherein one can imagine an additional dimension.

I come across Francesco del Cossa again and also a certain Marco Zoppo, whose work is unknown to me, apart from this truculent St

Jerome kneeling in a rocky landscape, with a winding river in the background and even more remote hills fading into mist, an unconventional touch for the period. Several fine pictures by Carracci do not erase the memory of a polyptych by Giotto or *The Enthroned Virgin* by Perugino. At the far end of one of the rooms, as a sign that there all turmoil has ceased and every human gesture should be noble and considered, hangs Raphael's *St Cecilia in Ecstasy*. My reaction to Raphael is purely personal: I find myself won over and at the same time irritated, waiting for something to happen to disturb that cold perfection, waiting for some rapport between myself and the picture. And then I rush back to Vitale da Bologna's convulsive and dramatic *St George*.

As I take my leave of these cities, I keep saying to myself: 'This is where I should live.' And that is meant to be a tribute. But I am now approaching two cities where I should be happy to die: Florence and Siena. And that is a far greater tribute.

Letter from Adelina.

I know it is unfair of me to be telling you what I have to say in a letter. I had thought of speaking to you before coming here but did not have the courage. And for the last eight days I have been telling myself that I must talk to you when I return to Lisbon, but I know my courage will fail me. Not because I think you will be upset. Nor because I feel it will be any more painful for me than for anyone else. We are both old enough not to expect any great surprises in life, but it really is very difficult to confront someone whom one has loved and, for whatever reason, tell him: I no longer love you. This is all I have to say. I no longer love you. These words say everything. And now that I have written them I feel much relieved. I have not yet posted the letter but it is as if you had already received it. I have no intention of going back on my word and perhaps that is why I decided to settle this matter in writing. Were I in your presence, my courage would probably fail me. And so, although you do not know yet, I know: our affair is over. Will this decision surprise you? I doubt it. For some time now, perhaps from the very beginning, I found you evasive, reserved, wrapped up in yourself, as if you were in the middle of some desert and preferred to remain there. I am not complaining. You have never made me feel unwanted, but I am no fool and, like most women, I can sense when something is wrong. I can no longer bear to hold you in my arms and feel you are not there. We needn't be enemies even if we cease to be friends. Perhaps I still care for you, but it is useless. Perhaps you still care for me, but it is useless. Nothing could be worse than keeping up this pretence. People can be in love and suffer a great deal but it has to mean something. Then people should go on loving each other no matter the cost. But our situation is different. We had an affair which, like so many affairs, inevitably had to end. I have taken the decision, but I know you would have been just as happy to end it. Despite everything, I feel sorry. Things could have been so different were it not for the want of that difference, that difference which distinguishes one thing from another. I have said more than enough. Goodbye. Adelina. P.S. I think you should go on writing. Forgive me. I have no right to give you advice since your life is no longer any concern of mine. But then, did it ever concern me?

I feel numb. At the time, mild shock, a moment of resentment, the annoyance felt by any male who has been given his marching orders, and then enormous relief and a strange feeling I can only assume to be gratitude or something akin to gratitude. I realize there is something monstrous about this feeling: in fact, if I start to think, it is as if women should have been born only for such gestures, to be exemplary and spare men certain disagreeable actions, certain tiresome and dubious, not to say downright obscene tasks. Women are expected to sweep the floor, wipe their children's noses, wash clothes and dishes, scrape away with an affectionate thumb any shit stuck to the seat of their menfolk's underpants. This would appear to have been the situation ever since the world began. Therefore it is no less just (or essential, which is another form of justice) that women should look after the thermometers, barometers and altimeters which measure affections and passions and, once having checked and appraised them, should draw up reports about the combustible waste and energy produced for the male to approve and sign because no more is expected or asked of men. It is monstrous, I repeat, to have felt gratitude, because this gratitude is once again relief, conclusive proof of the constant selfishness of man, of his inherent cowardice, not to mention his insolence when he starts to boast, at least to himself, and lie to himself in so doing, that all his earlier actions and words had been intended, on reflection, to force the other person (the woman) to take the final decision. In this way, the man can go on being romantically melancholic or histrionically outraged (whichever he finds more convenient) and declare himself the victim of female incomprehension, or, getting back to the point, imply, like someone not fully in control of what they are saying, that Adelina did what I expected her to do, for this is where I had guided her without her being aware of the doors I was opening and closing for her, of being pressurised, of the gentle pressure I was exerting as I amiably pushed her towards an inevitable breach.

I must confess that I never noticed before just how well Adelina writes. She uses few words and short sentences of which I am incapable or only rarely capable of using as she does. Her letter is worth keeping. I wonder how she wrote it? At one stretch, on a sudden impulse, or did she have to write it out several times, play around with words until she hit the right note, not too dry or too maudlin, neither disdainful nor tearful? I should love to know. I ask myself how this letter would have sounded if written by me, and I can imagine how long-winded it would have been, with interminable phrases, trying to explain the inexplicable or, worse still, giving vent to recriminations and insults, knowing full well, even as I write, that a deep anguish (but futile and damaging) could be breathed over the written words, however cruel or even malicious they might be.

Earlier on I wrote that it is not yet time for the desert. I reread those words but cannot understand why I ever wrote them. Nor can I understand why I wrote that it is no longer time for the desert. Let us examine this more carefully. People speak of having premonitions. However to believe in premonitions is far too easy, especially since it makes us seem interesting. An external force, but not alien to some, must be hovering out there, probably not in the common space inhabited by everyone, but in another space (which we can only enter by displacing ourselves, that non-terrestrial measurement which I call a hundredth of a second, a simultaneous dislocation in time: a second, and in space: a centimetre), and from there, by impenetrable methods of transmission and reception, we are forewarned as to what we shall say, think and (or) do much later, or what others will say or do to us. The only thing we are not told is what they will think, just as we were not told in time, if we were ever told, about what they thought.

Could it now be time for the desert? And why the desert? Because Adelina, too, has walked out of my life, as that familiar and silly saying goes, which presumes someone can be inside another's life? And what is the desert, after all? The one Lawrence of Arabia contemplated all night long as in the film? As films go, the scene certainly makes an impact and is skilfully done, but on reflection, not very original. To re-enact the famous gospel scene at Gethsemane might be effective, I concede, but shows little imagination. It was written: 'And he came out and went, as he was wont, to the Mount of Olives; and his disciples also followed him. / And when he was at the place, he said unto them: Pray that you enter not into temptation. / And he was withdrawn from them about a stone's cast, and knelt down and prayed, / Saying: Father, if You be willing, remove this cup from me: nevertheless, not my will, but Thine be done./ And there appeared an angel unto him from heaven, strengthening him. And being in an agony he prayed more earnestly: and his sweat was, as it were, great drops of blood falling down to the ground. / And when he rose up from prayer and was come to his disciples, he found them sleeping for sorrow. / And said unto them: Why are you asleep? Rise and pray lest you enter into temptation.' (Luke 22, 39–46) Transposed and without the disciples (who were twelve in the episode quoted), this is the scene with Lawrence, eyes turned in anguish towards the desert all night long. By night, not by day, because the sun would not permit this dramatic moment, or would make it dramatic in a different way, with Lawrence dying of sunstroke, thus jeopardizing British policy in the Arab world and obliging the British to wait for some other Lawrence less given to contemplation. The same is true of Jesus. If Jesus had died on the Mount of Olives from that haemorrhage which turned out to be benign and not fatal, would there have been any Christianity? And without Christianity history would have been altogether different, the history of men and their deeds; so many people would not have been immured in cells, so many people would have met a different death, not in the holy wars nor at the stake with which the Inquisition tried to justify its own relapsed, heretical and schismatic nature. As for this attempt at autobiography in the form of a traveller's tale divided into chapters, I am convinced it, too, would be different. For example: what would Giotto have painted in the Chapel of Scrovegni? Arcadian orgies of a mythology which persisted into the Middle Ages if not to the present day? Or would he simply have been a house-painter who was not there to paint the chapel but simply to whitewash the walls in the Scrovegni household?

Desert – to desert. The dictionary defines the first of these as 'noun. desolate, uninhabited, uncultivated, solitary place. Abandoned, unfrequented. A place where no one wishes to go. jur. The wilful abandonment of a loyal or moral obligation. n. desolate or barren tract: a waste: a solitude.'And the dictionary says of the latter: 'v.t. to leave: to forsake. v.i. to run away: to quit a service, as the army, without permission.'

I ask myself how writers and poets have the nerve to write hundreds or thousands of pages, millions upon millions if you put them all together, when a simple dictionary definition or two would suffice, if carefully pondered, to fill these hundreds or thousands or millions upon millions of pages. Today I am of the opinion that writers have shown far too much haste: they micrometrically complicate sentiments without probing the various meanings of words beforehand. Take these two straightforward examples of mine, which resulted from a conjectural premonition which led me from desert to desert after having passed via T.E. Lawrence (Thomas Edward) (1883–1935), born in Tremadoc, a British Secret Service agent in Arabia and Asia Minor during the 1914–1918 War, *The Seven Pillars of Wisdom* (1928); and via Christ which means the Messiah or the Lord's anointed, a name given to Jesus who, according to the venerable manuscripts which are capable of revealing everything apart from their ignorance, was born in Belém (situated between Pedrouços and Junqueira) on the 25th of December in the year 4004 of the universe (4963 according to *The Art of Verifying Dates*), in the year 753 of Rome, in the thirty-first year of Augustus' reign. This authoritative source claims that the year of Jesus' birth was almost certainly established by Dionysius Exiguus. But according to other calculations no less worthy of trust and respect, the date of the aforesaid birth (without sin, pain, carnal copulation or tearing of the hymen) has to be referred back to the 25th of December of the year 745 of Rome, six years before the common era. Therefore Jesus would have lived for thirty-nine years instead of thirty-three. Fortunate man.

Here I am then, abandoned and in the desert. Seeing things as I do now, Adelina was merely that last shadowy form which, not so long ago, although already remote, could still be seen on the steep slope of a shifting dune, a blurred double shadow or the double blade of open scissors cutting into themselves, becoming ever smaller and then a mere sign on the crest of the sand where the wind blows minute chippings (loose substance, powdery and vitrescent, produced by the crumbling of siliceous, granitic or argillous rocks) and suddenly, in the time it takes to open and read a letter, she has disappeared onto the other side. Are we the desert or are we deserted? Abandoned, forsaken, lost, or are we responsible for this wilderness and solitude? As someone who has never been a soldier and, therefore, never had the opportunity of absenting himself without leave, I must confess that I have always been fascinated by ranks, that plural entity; I have always dreamt of having my own force and at the same time all the military force of the Tetrarchs multiplied, a thousand times four, four thousand times one, and my intelligence multiplied as well, and sensibility and sweat and labour, yes, labour, four thousand times one. However, if every regiment has its ranks, all those ranks do not make a regiment. And since the desert can have inhabitants and still be a desert, inhabitants are not enough for the desert to be no longer desert. With all my festive friends here in the flat, or out there while I think of them as my friends, no desert of mine (or I the desert) has been populated. I became conscious of this when I began writing. In the end I put all my effort into recovering the desert, (trying) to understand afterwards what might have remained, what did remain, what might come to remain. Solitude certainly, but perhaps not sterility. Uninhabited, I concede, but not uninhabitable. Dry but with water inside, the terrible water of

JOSÉ SARAMAGO

tears, perhaps that fresh feeling pouring over one's hands. H_2O. Primordial water and whatever is suspended therein.

The portrait of the couple who are about to marry off their daughter will not be painted here in the studio where so many people, from A. to S., have already been. Where I had Olga the secretary on the divan. And Adelina. Only a deep love of the picturesque (however mistaken) or sheer necessity would induce anyone to climb those four awkward flights of stairs. People with a daughter of marrying age need not be old but this couple is, either because the bride-to-be was a late child or because respectability has aged them prematurely. So off I went then, to that grand, solemn and silent house in Lapa and there I painted the portrait. I began by positioning the husband and wife in the actual space their bodies continue to occupy, and then in the unstable space of the canvas. During the second session I told the husband he could go while I painted his wife. The perfect lady. Polite but distant, icy behind the thin veneer of courtesy, or because of this very same veneer which, like the one I use in my profession, is glossy, smooth and cold. On the third day I was introduced to the daughter, on the fourth (day) to their future son-in-law. She crossed her legs ostentatiously, he came to examine the effect. It is obvious that neither of them (from my point of view since I neither marry nor unmarry them) attaches any real importance to the portrait, which is simply a foible of the middle-aged or a convention being played out in a house in Lapa, a district where there can be few people left who indulge similar whims. The mother remains quite still, unbending, scarcely says a word however much I try to get her to relax; she looks as if she were in a state of shock. The daughter approached the scent of my frontier while the clouds of smoke from her fiancé's cigarette and her father's cigar passed over it. 'I used to smoke Havanas, but now ... ', the head of the household broke off, offering me a Dutch cigar probably made with the finest tobacco from Cuba. Meanwhile I go on painting.

It is so easy. The hand captures from afar what is in the face while one's mind wanders, the painter takes another look, using his eyes in a different manner as they pass from the face to the canvas; he can see once more the currents of the Lagoon, sluggish and turgid in the underlying mire, divided into greens and blues, with lighter veins breaking up the large strips of colour, and several white boats resembling tiny lice in that realm which is more vegetal than aquatic. I run my brush over the canvas with the same slow movements as that of the Lagoon's currents; it is not the face I paint, but the Lagoon in my mind's eye. I wonder how this portrait will turn out.

At home, I paint the saint, I copy (from the postcard) the architecture of the prison and the tiled floor in Vitale da Bologna's painting, and I am going to put on that floor and in the shadows of that grating my statue of St Antony, without any child, halo or book. I discover that the Bolognese painter long before me used the measure I defined in passing as the hundredth second. Otherwise he could never have achieved this particular effect of unreal perspective and time which successively recedes into space or this advance of space on time. But since I shall not use any of the figures from the original picture, I shall have to find some other way of putting the saint into my picture with the same distortion of space and time, the same fluid dimension, which subsequently makes everything as solid as the texture of tiles and the molecular consistency of iron. These are the daydreams of the solitary painter, devious means of approximation and discovery, weightless gymnastics, movements in slow motion, capable of being decomposed and repeated, the providence of those anxious people for whom this is one last chance of duplicating life. To turn everything back in time, not in order to repeat everything, but to be able to choose and pause from time to time. To take St George's horse as painted by Vitale da Bologna and lead it away, heading for Lisbon or coming from Bologna, through Spain and France, through France and Spain, to Paris, to the Latin Quarter, to the rue des Grands-Augustins, and to say to Picasso: 'I say, old man, here's your model.' At that time in Lisbon, a child who knew nothing about Guernica and very little about Spain except for the Battle of Aljubarrota, was clutching some soggy leaflets in his hands, and unwittingly distributing the political manifesto of the Portuguese Popular Front which for a time lived up to its name in word and deed.

Death and destruction. At a much later date, counted in years, I shall learn about the battle cry of the pro-Franco General Millan Astray. And even later, I shall finally come to know almost by heart the words of Unamuno: 'There are circumstances in which to remain silent is to lie. I have just heard a languid cry devoid of any meaning: Long live death! This barbarous paradox revolts me. General Millan Astray is a cripple. I mean no discourtesy. Cervantes, too, was a cripple. Alas, in Spain today there are far too many cripples. But it appals me to think that General Millan Astray could lay down the basis for mass psychology. A cripple without the spiritual qualities of Cervantes tends to take comfort in the mutilations which may inflict suffering on others.' And much later in life I would blush with shame when I read the words of the Spanish National Anthem for the first time: 'I believe in Franco, all-powerful man, creator of a supreme Spain and of a well-organized army, crowned with the most glorious of laurels; the Liberator of a dying nation and the Architect of a Spain born under the protection of the strictest social justice. I believe in the Heritage and Glory of a Spain which will continue to uphold traditional values for all Spaniards to follow; I believe in pardon for the truly repentant, in the revival of the ancient Guilds for the organization of labour, and in lasting peace. Amen.'

I am now repeating this so that everything may be corroborated by the missing witness: me. Me, Portuguese, painter, alive in the year 1973, in this Summer which is almost at an end, in this encroaching Autumn. Me, alive, while men are dying in Africa, Portuguese men whom I sent to their deaths or consented should die, men so much younger than me, so much simpler, and with so much more to offer than me, a mere painter. The painter of this saint, this Lapa, this martyr, this crime and complicity. In 1485 Nicolò dell' Arca had already understood so much: from his *Lamentation of Christ* which only appears to mourn the death of a god, one can remove Christ and replace him with other corpses: the white corpse blown up by a land-mine with the entire lower part of the abdomen torn out (farewell, son never to be), the black corpse burned with napalm, the ears cut off and preserved somewhere in a jar of alcohol (farewell Angola, farewell Guinea, farewell Mozambique, farewell Africa). There is little point in removing the women: weeping is always the same.

On reflection, I have achieved very little.

Fourth exercise in autobiography in the form of the chapter of a book.
Title: The two hearts of the world.

Florence is a hundred kilometres away from Bologna. Leaving the flat fields on the eastern side of the province of Emilia, the autostrada goes up as far as the Pass of Monte Citerna and, after passing through tunnels lit up like Christmas trees and across viaducts resting on giant legs, it bridges valleys and deep gorges, then descends for what seems an eternity before finally reaching Florence. And when I write 'for what seems an eternity', this is no mere rhetorical flourish. Entering Florence, as that Frenchman I met in the *tavola calda* told me, is a traumatic experience: the poor road-signs, the apparent confusion of innumerable one-way streets, so that trying to find the city centre or the Piazza della Signoria, for example, is like searching for a needle in a haystack. Florence must have a great deal of confidence in herself to play such havoc with any traveller who ventures there without the assistance of a guide.

And now that I have arrived, I am living in the Via Osteria del Guanto, two paces away from the Via del Corno, where I am not certain that Vasco Pratolini was born, but where most of the action takes place in his *Cronica dei Poveri Amanti*, and also very close to the Uffizi and the Palazzo Vecchio, the Loggia dell'Orcagna and the Museo Bargello (the National Sculpture Museum) which has works by Michelangelo, Donatello, not to mention Della Robbia, that admirable Luca who 're-invented' the art of ceramics so that it might become at once sculpture and painting.

As I sleep, this silent gathering of statues and paintings, this surviving parallel humanity continues to keep vigil over the world which I renounce when asleep. So that I, older and more fragile, encounter it once more on walking down the street, for, after all, statues and paintings last longer than this frail flesh.

Florence for two days, two weeks, two months? Florence for the duration of a sigh? But this city is as vast as some inexhaustible continent or universe. There is a certain air of remoteness which does not simply stem from the reserved and condescending manner of the Florentines, perhaps weary of tourists or, even more likely, because they know they will never again have the city to themselves. The traveller leaving Florence goes away feeling frustrated, unless he is just an ordinary tourist. However much he may have seen and heard, he knows that the inner core of the city has escaped him, that place where a common blood pulsates and which, if discovered, could make the city his, too. Florence is the heart of the world, but closed and inaccessible.

I take another stroll through the Uffizi, a gallery which has succeeded in retaining a human dimension and, for this very reason, one of my favourite museums. What could I possibly write about those hundreds of paintings? List their names and titles? Copy out the catalogue word for word? I would never finish. Suffice it to say that the collection includes the magnificent portraits of Federico da Montefeltro and his wife Battista Sforza, painted by Piero della Francesca. In their presence I lose all sense of time, and I much prefer them to the *Venus and Primavera* of Sandro Botticelli, whose work I am probably not mature enough to appreciate for I concocted a whole episode of science fiction while contemplating the *Adoration of the Shepherds* by Hugo van der Goes (the Child Jesus lying on the ground was obviously put there by some celestial being from the planet Mars or Venus); I gaze once more with reverence at another *Adoration*, this time painted with religious aggression by Mantegna. In contrast, Rubens leaves me weary and bored. And if Rembrandt's paintings do not bring tears to my eyes, that is simply because I have never had the opportunity to study them on my own.

I decide to forgo a second visit to the Pitti Palace, a prodigy of museological teratology which never fails to irritate me (waste is always irritating), for there the paintings and sculptures are treated simply as decorative objects gathered within a sumptuous setting which only stops short of repelling the visitor because he finds himself constantly submerged amidst a seething multitude. I prefer simply to wander along this embankment and I shall only cross the Ponte Vecchio one evening to watch the Arno flow between the city walls and to recall that these gentle waters turned into a horizontal flood six years ago: they burst their banks and, erupting like a ground swell, inundated streets, houses and churches, leaving havoc and pollution in their wake and bringing Florence to its knees as if the end of the world were nigh.

I shall form a clearer impression of the damage when I later pay a visit to an exhibition about the restoration of Florence. There I shall examine a diagram showing the scale of the disaster, see photographs of the damaged paintings, wooden sculptures saturated with water and greasy mud, the interior of the church of Santa Croce like a cavern invaded by every imaginable wind and tide. I shall see, to my dismay, what remains of Cimabue's *Crucifixion*, and will finally come face to face, after so many frustrated attempts, with Donatello's *Mary Magdalene*, now stripped of the many layers of gesso and dirt which had been covering the original paint.

Once again I shall see Fra Angelico's frescoes in the Basilica di San Marco, the church of Santa Maria Novella and the Cappellone degli Spagnoli with its exquisite frescoes painted by Andrea di Bonaiuto; I shall stroll at my leisure through the Duomo, storing up memories to cherish after my departure; I shall seek out the sculptures of Donatello in the Bargello Museum like someone putting his lips to a glass of cool water; I shall discover (never having been there before) the Archaeological Museum and, after making a return visit to the Medici Chapel, indulge my admiration for Michelangelo in the Biblioteca Lorenziana, where architecture achieved a perfection which has never been surpassed.

Time to leave. Evening is drawing in. I gaze upon the Tuscan landscape, countryside beyond description, because to speak of 'hills, shades of blue and green, hedgerows, cypresses, peace, infinite horizons' would be meaningless. Better to contemplate this stretch of

JOSÉ SARAMAGO

landscape which appears in Botticelli's *tondo*, entitled *La Madonna del Magnificat*: this is Tuscany.

And now Siena, the beloved, the city which truly fills my heart with joy. Such a friendly place, where everyone appears to have drunk the milk of human kindness. Siena, I shall always prefer you to Florence. Built on three hills, the city has no two streets alike and not one of them observes any geometrical pattern. And then there is this wonderful colour in Siena, the bronzed tones of bodies exposed to the sun, of the crust on a loaf of bread. This wonderful colouring which can be found on stones and rooftops softens the light of the sun and erases all anxiety and fear from our faces. Nothing could be more captivating than this city.

Since this itinerary of mine also (or, above all) takes in famous museums and monuments (I shall never distinguish between men and their works), I look at the Duomo, built where there was once a temple dedicated to Minerva. Who was the first person to invent this blending of pink and dark green stone which covers the entire cathedral with horizontal bands and forces us to look closely at the architecture? Who was courageous enough to choose coloured stones and arrange them as if working on canvas?

Inside, the floor is like an enormous book of illustrations. There are forty-nine squares made of embedded or engraved stones, *sgraffiate* or inlaid with detailed designs which distract the visitor's attention from anything overhead. One travels within an art at once robust and delicate, and this aptly defines the spirit of Siena.

In the Museo del Duomo I take another look at Duccio di Buoninsegna's *Maestà* and the Scenes of *Christ's Passion* displayed, illuminated and protected with overwhelming affection. Impossible to enter this room in the museum without lowering one's voice to a whisper, as if the Delphic Sybil were present, alive and prophetic.

From here I go to the Pinacoteca. There Sienese paintings from the twelfth to the sixteenth century await me, the best work produced by this school over five hundred years. Numerous pictures by Guido da Siena, an entire room dedicated to Duccio di Buoninsegna and his pupils, and paintings by the Lorenzetti brothers (Pietro and

Ambrogio), by Sassetta and many others. In my opinion, the two landscapes by Ambrogio Lorenzetti are 'the most beautiful in the world', two miraculous pictures painted at a time when landscapes were not yet seen as themes exclusively for painters and were treated as something one associated with dreams: a castle, a city, an anchored boat resembling an olive branch, the odd tree here and there, in shades of grey, cool blues and greens, all bathed in a luminosity which comes from the eyes of the artist, overwhelmed by what confronts him.

I go into a café and order a coffee. The waiter serves me with the voice and smile of Siena. I feel I am outside this world. I go down to the Campo, a sloping square, curved like a shell, which the builders decided not to level and thus it remained, truly a masterpiece. As if cradled in the middle, I gaze upon the ancient buildings of Siena, old houses where I should be happy to live one day, where I could have a window all to myself and look out onto those rooftops the colour of terracotta, onto the green window-shutters, trying hard to decipher the secret Siena whispers into my ear and which, although I may never understand it, I shall go on hearing to the end of my days.

JOSÉ SARAMAGO

In my opinion, everything is biography. I insist with even greater reason, as someone in its pursuit, that everything is autobiography (autobiography? reason?). It (which of them?) enters into everything like a thin blade being inserted into a slit in a door in order to spring the lock and force entry. Only the complex diversity of languages in which this autobiography is being written and unfolded allows us, but with some discretion and considerable secrecy, to move among our disparate fellow-men. Yet I can see all too clearly that this last chapter of mine has little to do with biography. Between Florence and Siena there was no gap in which to insert a blade. Everything remained in those shadows projected by works of art, sometimes between the rough brushstrokes or the almost imperceptible grooves of polished stone, and I have obviously been much too pre-occupied with capturing vibrations which constantly elude me and, because of this preoccupation, rather than because of those elusive vibrations, nothing or almost nothing of me remained. Unless, and this possibility consoles me, I am finally revealing myself through the traditional methods of autobiography, concealing less than is customary, although I somehow see myself as the loser of the initial challenge which was to talk about myself without appearing to do so.

I have slept badly. And I am alone. The telephone has not rung for over a week. I have dismissed my cleaner. 'Only for a short while,' I told her. 'Right now I don't have much work and I shall manage somehow on my own.' Adelaide listened. Not a muscle moved in her face, but her right foot twisted slightly, became heavy, painful, afflicted. She left without saying a word, or simply muttering: 'Until you need me.' Until I need her? Until she needs me? How would one say this in a painting? I do not know, but the difference would certainly be (I am mentioning it for a second time) one of two shades of the same colour. Painting has no such ambiguities but it has others, not forgetting certain insoluble problems which led me to take up writing. To prove beyond any shadow of doubt that there is justice in this world, the ambiguities and insoluble problems of writing would have to drive me to painting. Or something in between. I have already invented the theory of the hundredth second which I do not know how to apply. I would now have to discover write-painting, this latest and universal esperanto which will transform all of us into writer-painters and, with any luck, into practitioners of those blessed artemages. In my sleep I go on searching: artemages, bartemages, barthes mage, cartemages, karl marx, dartemages, eartemages, and what about art?

I am so certain of this that I do not need to write it. But since I have decided to reveal almost everything which permits one in ordinary speech to eliminate the *almost*, I hereby swear on my heart that it is not Adelina's absence which robs me of sleep because, frankly, I do not even miss her. My problem is not absence but some sort of presence. Lying on my back in my attic room which has given pleasure (I am referring to the room, not to those sexual acts people usually perform behind closed doors) to certain women of good taste which does not mean that all of them slept here, I probe within myself, patient as an insect using its claws and feelers to remove the obstacles keeping it from its food: clean bread, excrement, motionless larvae, blood pulsating beneath the skin – I probe and try to define this tension inside me, or somewhere inside the room, or circling all around me whenever I move – this tension which is like a flexible back, arched and undulating, perhaps like a snake's, although this is much quicker in comparison, or an atmospheric ridge in the wake of a hurricane, which is why I speak of tension.

I could speak of premonitions again if I wanted to. But since I am the one who is writing and, at the same time, feeling, I have decided I do not want to, with the double power I exert in my dual role of seeing and being seen. However, something is surely about to happen. An earth tremor? A fire? Another woman on the horizon? Or is it simply, as I am inclined to think, this writing, all these pages piled one on top of another with considerable weight, pages which from line to line project curves and loops and chains – and all this is tugging between its extremity and some place within my body, the father/mother of this lengthy discourse. I repeat: another woman? I doubt it. At my age there might still be other women, but for the moment I am not looking for them. Not because of any aversion to love. Not because of love or any aversion. If I wished, and I do not, to stage a little romantic comedy – where would I find an audience? Where would I find people to applaud? None of my many friends is around. And here in my room there is no one. And if, as I once read, it is true that heroes in romantic novels give vent to their woes by mourning over the portrait of their ungrateful beloved, this is not likely in my case, even though I do have a photograph of her right here. Besides, I am the one who is grateful, as I have already explained, and let me take this opportunity to reaffirm that I am not writing a novel.

Meanwhile, something is approaching. I understand that glorious moments are heralded with trumpets we humble mortals cannot hear because such loud vibrations of sound escape our rudimentary organs of hearing. I have also been led to understand that dogs can hear them and that we humans should pay attention, for when hounds bay they are not simply baying at the moon, but are being sent into a trance by the sound of trumpets. They howl in desperation, incapable of telling us what these omens foretell. And so they pass unnoticed either because we were not present at the right moment or fast asleep when we should have been listening. All that reaches us (I speak of myself, without probing, for example, what might reach Adelaide, my cleaner) is this tension, this extended back of a snake, this sudden blast of wind, unleashed in a great flurry.

The distance is already quite considerable. The average lifespan of people is much more than these fifty years or so of mine, or those years still to come, ever less, however many we may count. I am not contradicting myself. However many years the future may have in store for each and every one of us, nothing is greater than our infinite pre-history. I am not referring to a collective pre-history but to one that is purely individual. Suffice it to say that each day has eighty-six thousand and four hundred seconds and each month almost two million and six hundred thousand, and that they are not launched on us all at once, but one by one, so that nothing may be lost and everything gained. (The words of Lavoisier, who lived for fifty-one years and no more because they sent him to the guillotine.)

I shall go to sleep, it will not be long now, it cannot delay much longer. Through the half-opened door of my room I notice that the studio window which looks onto the street is no longer black: the grey hours commence which will gradually pass from total darkness to the light of day. But for this it is still too early. Part of me is already asleep, while the other part writes. That is why I have before me, spread out like the map of the world, my entire pre-history, so close that all I should need to do would be to copy the names – graphic, hydro-, and oro-irregularities. Thus one can see that it was the sleeping married man or married man fast asleep, what does it matter, today simply asleep, while on top of the crumpled sheet (do not forget he dismissed the cleaner) his fingers unconsciously count the years, so many of them, that journey took across the map of the world. And that earlier pre-history when life got easier for his parents and there was no more talk of renting rooms. The old alcoholic women died and people began defecating in the privacy of their lavatories, without any beauty, that processional beauty of bygone days, which consisted of restoring to the earth what the living had extracted from it, until they were ready to offer themselves. Hosannah. There are so many ways, and the conditions of production are as varied as those of excretion. In my dream I see a huge woman pass by, tall, broad and strong, carrying a chamberpot covered with an embroidered cloth, while angels hover overhead. Hallelujah.

Sometimes parents can be extremely foolish. They know nothing, could scarcely be more ignorant, make wild gestures no-one understands and use words to be found in no dictionary. And since they no longer carry, or to be more precise, the wife no longer carries the fecal offering through the corridors of the universe, they both decide in a moment of mental crisis, gentle, invisible, even smiling, without the assistance of a doctor or strait-jacket, that their son should go to Art School. There are two (excellent) reasons for this decision: the boy has an eye for drawing and the neighbours will be green with envy. 'Green with envy,' said Mother. And Father, while appearing to dismiss this female pettiness, agreed, shaking his head paternally. How sleep weighs upon us. So heavy that there is no need to add an exclamation mark: it is enough to say so. While we are asleep, I wrote, the silent world of statues and paintings keeps vigil. Just as well. Otherwise what would become of us? These are the people who keep the world safe, transformed in sleep by the possibility of recovering pre-history, these mysterious sheets of paper, for example, not the map of the world, but these sheets of paper I see in my dream, covered in writing which I read as I dream, striving to wake up reading, because I know that those pages were not written by anyone, nor were they written by me. In what other country of some other world is Portuguese written? What forests gave these sheets of paper, rags or embroidered cloths? One part of me is asleep, the other writes, but only the part which is sleeping could read what is written on the sheets of paper, only in my dream does this gentle breeze exist which sends them fluttering past, one by one, allowing me just sufficient time to read each page. Morning will soon be here.

To climb the slope also means descending it, or falling down just as the foot stepped on the last stone and one's eye suddenly took in the hidden landscape. Let me remind you that the sleeping man was married, not because it is important but lest anyone should say they have forgotten just because it was mentioned only once. It is a question of climbing the slope once more, of fingers unconsciously counting the years of one's journey on top of a crumpled sheet, of putting one's foot on the final stone on reaching the summit before beginning the descent on the other side. Could landscapes be lives waiting to be painted? Could someone who has only painted faces, so badly and without any expression, learn anything from Lorenzetti (Ambrogio)? In one's dream certainly, but only therein, just as those prodigious sheets of paper can only be read in a dream, perhaps the sixth and true gospel, perhaps the lost writings of Plato, or all that is missing from the *Iliad*, perhaps what was written by those who died before their time? This landscape, however, is simultaneously outside and within the dream, the landscape itself is both dream and dreamer, the dream and the thing dreamed, a painting with two sides which shuns the thickness of the wood.

I am whispering in my dream and write down that whisper. I do not decipher it, I write it down. I seek phonetic symbols which I put down on paper. And so a language comes to be written which no one can read, let alone understand. The pre-history is so very, very long. Men and women go around there entering and leaving caverns, and the history which will count them (enumerate them, narrate them) remains to be written. Unconsciously those fingers are already counting in my dream. The numbers are letters. It is history.

Carmo came to visit me. However, before writing about his visit and our conversation, which will reveal little about me and a great deal about him, I feel it might be useful to turn back to the last pages, much too contrived for my taste, having foolishly allowed myself to indulge in virtuosity, which contradicts the firm rule I established to narrate the facts and nothing more. On earlier pages there might be other infractions of this rule, but they are minimal and stem from the author's incompetence rather than from any deliberate contrivance. That these last pages might be deliberately intricate I cannot swear, but it is clear that at some point I became fascinated by word games, playing my violin on a single string and using extravagant gestures to compensate for the absence and elimination of any other sounds. I recognize, notwithstanding, this self-criticism, that there is something ingenious about 'one part of me is asleep, the other writing'. This is only a tiny and by no means risky somersault in terms of style but I am pleased with the result.

Artifice has its merits: by means of artifice I was able to simulate the dream, to dream it, to live the situation and witness all this, while remembering things from the past with the expression of someone pretending to be asleep, who speaks in order to be heard while calculating the effect of what he is saying. I now see it as an expedient which gets me out of two lengthy explanations: how my parents managed to avoid having to rent out rooms, prospered somewhat and sent me to Art School, and how I came to get married, the reasons for my marriage and its eventual breakdown. These are obviously chapters of my story. But are they really necessary? Art School did not make me a painter, nor marriage and fatherhood (something I omitted to mention) make me any different. It is not the external facts which are important but those seen from within, the dead bird, the hard smack and many other facts, all of them external but having already passed inside. If that was artifice, I can justify it and by pursuing it make it legitimate, if not for the sake of truth, for the sake of verisimilitude. I should make it clear, however, that those last pages were written when I was wide awake, and anything described there about dreams is not simply one dream confined to one night but the loose fragments of recurring dreams, some invariably repeated and, for present purposes, deliberately organized here into coherent incoherence. I know a fair amount about painting and now know enough about calligraphy to perceive (and try to put into practice) that the expression of incoherence demands a great deal of organization. I am speaking of expression, not simply about revealing oneself.

Carmo came to visit me. He turned up after dinner. He had startled me when he rang up to say he was coming, I had become so unused to hearing the telephone ring. From the tone of his voice I could tell he had something to confide. My suspicions were soon confirmed. Being someone's friend is not easy. What I am trying to say is that we never really know to what extent we are genuinely someone's friend. My friendship with Carmo was casual and relaxed. People meet once or twice, chat, perhaps confide in each other, become a little more intimate, then find they have become friends, are surprised they did not become friends sooner and take it for granted they will be friends forevermore. This was the kind of friendship I had with Carmo: not much to it. That we are any closer now I cannot be sure, but there is undoubtedly a qualitative difference (a nice adjective) in this sameness, even though the friendship may not last long, even though it may only have existed in order to exist no more.

Carmo arrived at my flat in a terrible state. He sat down wearily and sounded utterly dejected. It was inevitable: Sandra had given him his marching orders. At first, hoping to comfort him, I thought of telling him that here, too, things had been going badly. But I remained silent, aware that Carmo would find it difficult to bear the contrast between my serenity and his despair. Or worse still for me, I would have to keep up this pretence of sharing his despondency. This promised to be quite an evening: two grown-up men, one of them well past his prime (forgive me, Carmo, but it happens to be true), weeping to the background music provided by Lalande's *De Profundis*, cursing all the daughters of Eve and swearing that never again will he fall into their clutches. I simply gave him to understand that my relationship with Adelina had soured, so that Carmo could have a consoling foretaste of my own imminent separation. We must not despise people because of their weaknesses: no one feels healthier than when comforting the sick, no one stronger than when confronted by a weakling, no one more intelligent than when speaking to an idiot. From this moment onwards Carmo began to calm down.

But things got off to a bad start. No sooner did I open the door than he collapsed dramatically into my arms, weeping his heart out. I pushed him towards the divan, poured him a drink and asked him: 'Now then, what's all this?' Bronzed by the sun, Carmo looked as if he were wearing a mask. I have never been one for summers by the seaside, for lolling about on the beach under a blazing sun. I reckoned Sandra must have worn him out: Sandra sunning herself on the beach, Sandra in the nightclub, Sandra in bed, and an exhausted Carmo pleading mercy for his weak heart and tired penis. I was guessing, but my guess proved to be right. 'I've had enough, old chap.' This was Carmo. 'It's finished between me and Sandra.' Now then, my friend, why so proud, what is this 'me and Sandra', this 'It's finished' when you're the one who's finished, perhaps for a short while, perhaps for longer, perhaps forever. This is what I was thinking as Carmo told me in his own words how he had managed to win over Sandra, her interest (interest? sheer lust). How good Carmo felt as he relived his moments of glory, erotic feats he refrained from describing in detail but hinted at, imploring me with his eyes to believe him, not to doubt him, smile ironically or, worse still, mock him. Nothing could have been further from my thoughts. Any man who has experienced life knows that middleage (and old-age even more so) recompenses any loss of sexual vigour with experience in the art of making love. Why should things be different for Carmo? One need only consider the passion young girls in the flower of youth (in shade and sun) show to the point of indecency for older men who could easily be taken for their uncles or fathers. 'It doesn't surprise me,' I told him gravely. 'Just think of Chaplin. Oona O'Neill was much, much younger, yet they fell in love. Lots of children, no fewer than nine of them.' Carmo became suspicious or, at least, looked suspicious, but my words did him some good. And he delivered a solemn declaration: 'No one could have been happier than we were.' He downed half the whisky as if he were drinking water and began brooding, his elbow resting on one knee, his fist to his forehead, his lips moist with drink as he sat there slouching in his usual manner. 'But tell me, how did you two come to quarrel?' Carmo awkwardly raised his head: 'There was no quarrel, we simply parted. Can't you understand? It's all over. Everything is over between us. Everything.' And, as one might have expected, Carmo broke down at this point. I tactfully left him on his own, passed quietly into the kitchen, washed my hands to give him time to pull himself together, then rejoined him in the room. Looking more composed, my ageing friend was removing (painful, I concede) one last tear from the corner of his eye. His glass was empty. I poured him another whisky, then sat on the floor resting my back against the divan. From there I could get a better view of my chaste St Antony with his sheepish expression of someone who is at a loss for something to do, once having lost his halo, book and Child Jesus. 'Tell me all about it.' 'Things couldn't have been going better. The sea air was doing me good, I loved the dancing and felt as fit as a fiddle. I hadn't felt so well in years.' Carmo felt what he had not felt in a long time, the resurgence of youth when one no longer expects it. I understand only too well, my friend. 'I understand. And then?' 'Then? What do you want me to say? Naturally, I began feeling weary, but didn't let it worry me. The hardest thing of all was that during those last few days she began to sulk, to look at me resentfully. One evening she had clearly made up her mind to pick a quarrel and refused to accompany me to a nightclub. We spent the

JOSÉ SARAMAGO

evening in the hotel. It was all very disagreeable. She sulked in silence. I was at a loss for words. At one point she got to her feet abruptly and, without waiting for a reply, announced she was going out to buy some cigarettes and left. I followed her out into the corridor, but I was wearing my slippers, I did not want to call after her or cause any embarrassing scenes. She returned at three in the morning in a state of great excitement. Of course I was awake and unable to get to sleep. She told me she had been walking on the beach all alone. I believed her. What else could I do? Next morning we were no sooner out of bed than she began packing her bags and told me she was going back to Lisbon. That I could stay if I wanted to. Naturally, I didn't stay, what was there to stay for? We travelled back in the car, with me trying to make conversation, to force some explanation out of her, but it was hopeless. When she dropped me at the door I invited her in to talk things over, but she refused.' Carmo stopped speaking, took another sip and sighed, then resumed his silence. 'And then?' I asked. 'Well. I was already on the pavement when I looked back, waiting to see what would happen, and suddenly she leaned out of the car window and told me it would be best to end our affair once and for all. As far as she was concerned we were finished and there was no point in my insisting. I felt stunned. She drove off while I just stood there like a fool, not knowing where I was. You can't imagine the state I was in when I got indoors. I tried ringing her number several times but there was no answer. Either she was still out or did not wish to speak to me. That was three days ago. Yesterday I managed to catch her on the telephone and she began joking, telling me to put everything behind me, that we had had some good times together, but these things happen and there was no reason why we should not still be friends, and so on and so forth. You know what she's like. The same old humbug.' The situation was clear and had been clear from the very beginning: another of Sandra's little whims, another of Carmo's little dreams fulfilled. Doomed from the outset, the dream would only last the duration of Sandra's whim. Why was Carmo complaining? 'And now? What do you want me to do?' 'I don't know, old chap. I can't bear it. I feel like doing away with myself.' 'Don't talk nonsense, you'll do no such thing. You know very well what Sandra is like.' Flying into a rage, Carmo interrupted: 'I won't allow you to say anything against her. You probably fancied her yourself and got nowhere.' 'I've already told you to stop being an ass. I've never fancied her or shown the slightest interest. I was only trying to help you.' Carmo suddenly felt ashamed: 'Forgive me, I'm afraid I lost my head and one thing leads to another.' He rattled the ice in his glass, took two quick gulps and, averting his eyes, said: 'You could do something for me. Ring her, say you're concerned, tell her you found me a bit low, that I took you into my confidence. You could telephone her right away while I'm still here.' 'But, Carmo, it won't do any good. I know Sandra and so do you. Once she has made up her mind there's nothing to be done.' 'I'm asking you a favour. Please help me.'

Carmo made this request with awesome simplicity, his tearful eyes staring at me with the expression of someone who is about to drown and knows it. At that moment I felt our friendship was worthwhile and sincere and I wanted it to continue. I got up, went to the telephone in the bedroom, looked up the number in my diary and dialled. I had heard Carmo follow me and I was aware he was lingering there in the doorway, clutching his glass with both hands, looking nervous and miserable. Poor Carmo! My heart went out to him and I fleetingly asked myself why Carmo's misfortunes should be so upsetting when my own situation left me unmoved. 'Is that you, Sandra?' Carmo made no attempt to move closer. 'Hello there. How are you? You never call me but I recognized your voice at once.' 'How are things?' 'Fine. Couldn't be better. And what about you? Is Adelina still away?' 'Yes, she is. And have you been on holiday yourself?' 'I'm back, as you can see.' 'I ran into Carmo yesterday.' 'Oh.' 'He told me you had broken up. He seemed very depressed.' 'You men dramatize everything. What's past is past. Okay, we slept together. But it's over and done with. What a bore.' 'I didn't mean to annoy you. I only rang because I'm worried about Carmo.' 'He's not the only one to have suffered. Aren't you concerned about me?' 'Of course, I'm concerned. But it's Carmo who's feeling depressed, not you.' 'Mark my words, he'll get over it. Men always do.' 'I suppose you're right.' 'Did he ask you to ring me?' 'Not exactly.' 'I see, in other words he did.' 'Well, goodbye for now.' 'Are you ringing off? Just when I wanted to have a chat.' 'Some other time, I have one or two things to attend to.' 'Don't worry, I'm not going to seduce you. Although I might have a go one of these days. You're such a pet.' 'Good night, Sandra.' 'Back to your painting, then, off you go.'

Carmo had drawn nearer without my noticing. He looked disheartened. 'Did I hear the word bore?' All of a sudden I felt my patience running out. A man with the perfect desert, so effectively depopulated, so well and truly deserted, and now this. I nodded affirmatively and walked through the studio. Carmo came after me like a bull (God help me). I turned on him: 'Will you never learn? I did warn you. There's nothing to be done.' Carmo emptied his glass with a gulp, whisky dribbling from the corners of his mouth and, wiping his mouth with the back of his hand, he grunted: 'Slut, whore.' I drew away and told him: 'Your behaviour is disgraceful. A few minutes ago you were weeping your heart out. And tell me: Was Sandra already a slut and whore when you went to bed with her? Or only after you slept together?'

The attack was brutal but produced results. Carmo sat down slowly, lit a cigarette (he usually smokes a cigar: cigarettes are reserved for moments of crisis, in private and at work) and said nothing more about Sandra. I went round the studio giving the impression that I was trying to tidy up the place and put my paints in order, wondering whether I should put these things in writing or pretend they had never happened. Carmo got up, excused himself and went into the other room. He returned, peeved but tranquil. I observed that he had washed his face and combed down the little hair he had left. The worst had passed.

'Would you care for another whisky? Help yourself.' Carmo's hands were trembling somewhat, but on the whole he was putting on a brave face. He tried to conceal the trembling by constantly shaking the ice in his glass. And, suddenly becoming very formal: 'To come back to what we were discussing the other day in the restaurant. Those travel notes describing your Italian tour. I spoke about publishing them.' 'I treated it as a joke. Don't imagine ... ' 'This type of book really isn't much in demand these days.' 'No need to explain. It was Adelina's idea.' 'Of course. How is she, by the way? Forgive me for not asking sooner.' 'As far as I know, she's fine. She must be back by now. Things have not been too good between us.' Carmo: 'You don't say? Anything serious?' 'Difficult to tell.' Carmo, the man of experience, rather bloated and sounding pompous: 'What do you expect? You know what women are.' 'I know. At least I think I know.' No more was said about affairs of the heart. No further mention of my trip to Italy. We spoke vaguely about politics, we called Marcelo Caetano a few choice names. Carmo told me Tomás' latest joke and then took himself off, much more composed, Sandra having been well and truly categorized and me prepared for the next separation.

I cannot see myself as an author. Now Sandra will no longer serve as an involuntary means of pressure, unconscious rather than involuntary. I am of the firm opinion that people should be judged by what they do, which explains why I have such a poor opinion of myself. But there are certain circumstances in which people are also what they say or have said. Once they speak, they compromise themselves more than they would care to in their own eyes as well as in the eyes of others. To speak is also to do or, at least, to make a public declaration. Without Sandra as witness and judge, and also without Adelina, as I now realize, my book will not be written. Which is obviously not an excuse for not finishing the task. Now I am about to write the fifth and final chapter.

JOSÉ SARAMAGO

Fifth and final exercise in autobiography in the form of a travel book. Title: Lights and shadows.

That one should go to Rome just to see the Pope is a gesture I have come to respect. After all, I went to Arezzo just to see Piero della Francesca. And I could kick myself for having yielded to the pressure of time which dissuaded me from making the detour through Borgo San Sepolcro, the artist's birthplace, where some of his other paintings were seeking my attention. I seek and find resignation in the frescoes of *The History of the True Cross* in Arezzo's church of St Francis, which signal one of the happiest moments in the entire evolution of painting. Anyone who is only familiar with Piero della Francesca's *St Agustine* in Lisbon's Museum of Ancient Art will find it difficult to imagine the monumental splendour of the figures of the *True Cross*. Although extensively damaged, what remains of the frescoes dominates the bare patches where the colour and design have disappeared, and they linger in one's memory like a musical note which continues to send out echoes and infinite modulations.

But Arezzo is also the city itself, luminous and tranquil, built around a hill with the Duomo on top which has two ceramic altarpieces, one by Andrea, the other by Giovanni della Robbia. And there I discovered a painter whom I had not come across before: Margaritone di Magnano, born in Arezzo in the thirteenth century, and whose paintings include an admirable St Francis in the Byzantine style. Arezzo remains one of my favourite Italian cities.

What can I say about Perugia, where I always arrive full of hope only to come away disenchanted, not because the city disappoints me in any way but because that essential spark of enthusiasm always fails to strike up between us? Yet here one finds the Fontana Maggiore in the centre of the old Piazza dei Priori, with its delicate thirteenth-century sculptures still intact as well as all the surrounding buildings: the Cathedral, the hall of the Palazzo Communale with its vaulted ceiling supported by massive columns, the Logge di Braccio Fortebraccio, the first example of Renaissance art to be executed in Perugia. No doubt the day will come (I owe it to myself) when this city becomes my second home. The rooms of the museum give me a sense of peace. There, I reencounter the great Piero, a magnificent altarpiece portraying *The Virgin with the Holy Infant and Saints*. Above the altar hangs a painting of *The Annunciation* which is unspoiled by the artificial surround added at a later date. On the predella I observe an almost nocturnal scene: St Francis receiving the stigmata while another friar looks up with an expression of dismay and scepticism.

I visit Rocca Paulina, shiver with cold and feel sorry for the watchman who is anxious to have a chat. The Rocca is an underground street with vaulted roof and houses on either side. There are shops which no longer function and ovens where bread is no longer baked. A gloomy place despite the lighting, and one emerges with a sigh of relief. Outside, in broad daylight, is the Corso Vanucci, swarming with boys and girls from the International University. Here you can hear all the languages of the world being spoken and perhaps it is these noisy hordes of foreign students who come between me and Perugia.

Heading south, I arrive at Todi. There I lunch in full view of the astonishing landscape of Umbria, which surpasses even that to be seen from Assisi, incredible as that may seem. It was in Todi that I spotted an enormous electoral poster with the bold headline: COR-AGGIO FASCISTI. I felt as if a sudden shadow had clouded my face. I looked around me and the tiny square of Todi was transformed into the whole of Italy. I feared for Italy and for myself. I recalled the outcome of the recent elections and the number of votes won by the neo-fascist Movimento Sociale Italiano, and this private pilgrimage through paths and belvederes, through the naves of churches and the rooms of museums, suddenly struck me as being futile and superfluous, without wishing to offend either myself or Italy. But Todi offers so much consolation.

Now it is time for Rome, the gigantic, the city whose doors and windows were made for men some ten feet tall, the city no visitor can hope to cover on foot, a city which tires one's limbs and bones (and if you will pardon the heresy) leaves one weary in spirit. I must confess in all humility: I do not understand Rome. Yet I shall never tire of visiting the Museum of the Villa Giulia, where the archaeological remains of Southern Etruria are ingeniously set out and offer a salutary lesson in art and history. I submissively return to the Museo delle Termi, although Roman sculpture nearly always leaves me feeling somewhat melancholy; and I use every hour at my disposal to tour the Vatican museums, a challenge which defeats me from the outset because an entire lifetime would not be enough to satisfy my curiosity.

There seems little point in going down to the Sistine Chapel. To seek out Michelangelo and come face to face with hundreds of tourists looking up into the air and craning their necks in order to glimpse amidst the shadows the creation of the world and of man, original sin, the great flood, the drunkenness of Noah – it is probably the greatest disappointment ever likely to be experienced by any serious art-lover, unless he is fortunate enough to be allowed into the chapel at dead of night which must be the only time the works of art in the Vatican are not on public view. So once having memorised the overwhelming impact of this titanic collection (a banal description, but I can think of no other), all one can do is to find a book with good illustrations and make a detailed study of the ceiling paintings and *The Last Judgement* on the rear wall, however poor a substitute it may be for the real thing.

I have no idea what Cairo has to offer by way of mummies, but I very much doubt whether any of them could be as impressive as the one kept here: the exposed head and face are swarthy, withered and wrinkled, but most distressing of all are the hands, also blackened, but terrifyingly well conserved with white nails in a state of perfect preservation.

There is no end to the Vatican museums. One progresses through dozens of enormous halls and galleries, rotundas and rooms, always afraid at having left behind, perhaps forever, some picture, fresco, sculpture, or illuminated manuscript which might easily help us to reach a better understanding of this world and of our earthly existence.

One finds here, for example, a Roman copy of a statue of Socrates, with round head, short neck, curved forehead, flattened nose, eyes which not even the emptiness of marble can erase – the most strikingly ugly man in history, he who exhorted other men to renew themselves, he who was accused of 'having honoured strange gods and trying to corrupt youth', charges which led to his untimely death. And these are the two eternal accusations against man. I take a quick look inside St Peter's. Behold the splendour and overpowering riches of a triumphant Church, but here, too, are the works of mankind, the crowning achievements of man's genius and manual skills. On the right once stood Michelangelo's *Pietà* which some suspicious madman vandalized. The tourists, however, show no real displeasure, nothing more than passing irritation that an item should be missing from their guide-book.

A rapid tour of Naples gave me the impression of one great traffic jam, of a gymkhana of placid madmen (where was that verbal exuberance of the Neapolitans?). I also carried away the memory of the bay all lit up which, seen from the balcony of the hotel, resembled a candlelight procession at a standstill all along the coast.

Naples is also the city where I came across the initials MSI scrawled across the walls and hoardings and on the park benches by the neo-fascists. It is also the city where street-vendors who feel nostalgia for Il Duce sell ashtrays which portray Benito Mussolini looking Caesarean in full uniform, with rousing slogans advocating the revival of fascism. It is also the city where I was twice warned 'in my own best interest' not to leave any valuables in the car.

But Naples, too, has its Museo Nazionale. I escape inside to take a look at what I missed in Pompeii or saw only fleetingly: the mosaics and wall paintings I only knew from well-meaning reproductions, which sadly lack that precious dimension achieved by means of deliberate irregularity in the case of mosaics and a rough finish in the case of wall paintings, which should be probed by one's eye rather than touched by human hand. And this wealth of sculptures: very few of Greek origin, but an infinite number of Roman and Hellenistic statues, enough of them to populate another civilization, a resuscitated Pompeii, a peaceful Naples. On leaving the city, I lost my way. It was inevitable.

And now I am resting in Positano on the coast of Salerno, a place I declared 'blessed' before discovering that this region of Italy is described in the official guidebook as *la divina costiera*. We are both right: the tranquillity here is divine and blessed. And whom do I see but Melina Mercouri, yes it is her, wearing a straw hat and long dress, pale and thin, and in the company of Jules Dassin. I rouse myself from my torpor in the heat of the sun and invent this imaginary dialogue between us: 'So, Melina, you are still exiled from Greece. So near, yet here you are, forbidden to enter your native land. How are things going there?' And back comes her reply: 'And how are things going in your country?'

I return to my spot, gaze on the stagnant waters of this inner sea which could tell so many ancient tales, and repeat the question to myself: 'And how are things going in your country?'

If the disastrous outcome of Carmo's affair had not deprived me of any hope of publication (if there ever was such hope and it was not simply a question of my complying with the decisions of others), what would I have done with these pages? Would I have submitted them for publication as a little booklet, pamphlet, notebook or brochure? To be frank, I think of them as exercises in autobiography for my personal use, worthless without the interpretation I put on them later. As travel memoirs, as an aesthetic or purely touristic guide, they are of no greater interest than the timid gesture of a Sunday painter, than that explanatory phrase which is so personal and intimate that it immediately arouses stolid hostility in the general listener. So blessed be Carmo, blessed be Sandra who, by pushing Carmo out of her bed (or to be more precise, out of the hotel bed paid for by Carmo), pushed me out of the publisher's catalogue before I ever got into it. They say God writes straight on crooked lines but I suspect that these are exactly the lines He prefers, firstly to show His divine virtuosity and conjuring skills and, secondly, because there are no others. All human lines are crooked, everything is a labyrinth. But the straight line is not so much an aspiration as a possibility. The labyrinth itself contains a straight line, broken and interrupted, I concede, but permanent and expectant. This geometrical god of whom I have been speaking must have become incarnate in Sandra, have prompted the decision, given Sandra's thighs their fill of Carmo, and so things obediently fall into their rightful place. Blessed be Sandra, blessed be Sandra, blessed be, blessed Sandra.

But these pages exist and my task remains unfinished. The exercises, yes, but not what came before. Certain things are now becoming clearer. I would even go so far as to say that they now seem quite obvious, whereas in the past there was only chaos and confusion. They represented another kind of labyrinth, undoubtedly reducible to a straight line, but resisting any such reduction, becoming entangled and compressing the spaces and making circulation impossible, Let us take the so-called carpenter's rule. This consists of ten units of ten centimetres (or is it five of twenty?), joined end to end and appearing to be folded over, so the plan is correct but the measurement wrong. It is necessary to unfold the rule and extend it to its full extent. In my opinion the same should be done to men or they should do it for themselves. We are already doubled up at birth; like rules simply juxtaposed we are compressed and confined. We have three metres inside us yet only move a hand's breadth.

I cannot say if this was in my mind when I recalled the head of Socrates I had seen in Naples. It was Socrates who obliged other men to be born from within, but knowing this is not enough to make birth occur by itself. And most likely his method of question-answer-question (which Plato himself recorded without the assistance of a shorthand typist or tape-recorder) would not be enough to extricate us from our own labyrinths, to free us from the defective position we take up within our own womb. Just as any pursuit through creative channels and works of art is not nor ever could be sufficient. I am not referring to my own work but to that of the great masters which sends me to my knees. This is purely subjective, as I believe I have more or less said before, and therefore should be treated with caution. If, for personal and aesthetic reasons, I speak of the regret with which I leave behind the illuminated manuscript, the statue, fresco or painting which might easily (I repeat: easily) help me to reach a better understanding of the world and our earthly existence – am I asking of art that tranquillity Socrates systematically takes away from men, or the peace Socrates would bring them once having destroyed that other one of conformity and habit? (This must be it, but there is a risk in saying certain things. All too often we utter nothing except words, and this is the great risk we take when discussing art. The same great risk we take when discussing anything.) Socrates, art, our understanding of this world and our earthly existence, joining stone to stone, combining colour with colour, the word recovered with the recovery of the word, adding what is missing in order to go on establishing the meaning of things, not necessarily in order to complete that meaning, but to adapt it, to attach the piston to the connecting rod, the hand to the wrist, and everything to the brain. And on arriving at this point, as was foreseen from the outset, I rise from my chair, take a book from the shelf (Karl Marx's Preface to a *Contribution to the Critique of Political Economy*) and being a diligent student, I copy out several pages, convinced that Marx needs to be added to Socrates and to art before trying to make sense of what follows: 'The mode of production of material life conditions the social, political and intellectual life process in general. It is not the consciousness of men that determines their being but, on the contrary, their social being that determines their consciousness. At a certain stage of their development the material productive forces of society come into conflict with the existing relations of production or – what is but a legal expression for the same thing – with the property relations within which they have been at work hitherto. From forms of development of the productive forces these relations become their fetters. Then begins an epoch of social revolution. With the change of the economic foundation the entire immense superstructure is more or less rapidly transformed. In considering such transformations, a distinction should always be made between the material transformation of the economic conditions of production, which can be determined with the precision of natural science, and the legal, political, religious, aesthetic or philosophic – in short, ideological forms, in which men become conscious of this conflict and fight it out. Just as our opinion of an individual is not based on what he thinks of himself, so we cannot judge such a period of transformation by its own consciousness; on the contrary, this consciousness must be explained from the contradictions of material life, from the existing conflict between the social productive forces and the relations of production. No social order ever perishes

JOSÉ SARAMAGO

before all its potential productive forces have developed; and new, higher relations of production cannot come about until the material conditions of their existence have matured in the womb of the old society itself. Therefore mankind only sets itself tasks it can accomplish; since, looking at the matter more closely, it will always be found that the task itself arises only when the material conditions for its completion already exist or are at least in the process of formation. In broad outlines Asiatic, ancient, feudal, and modern bourgeois modes of production can be designated as progressive epochs in the economic formation of society. The bourgeois relations of production are the last antagonistic form of the social process of production – antagonistic not in the sense of individual antagonism, but of one arising from the social conditions of life of the individuals; at the same time the productive forces developing in the womb of bourgeois society create the material conditions for the solution of that antagonism. This social formation brings, therefore, the prehistory of human society to a close.'

A somewhat lengthy pre-history. I have also spoken of pre-history in a muddled and indecisive way, one moment touching on the conscious, the next on the unconscious, but trying, above all, to express this peculiar state or human flux of life, which appears to be the constant product of a conscience and which at heart is a contradiction resolved, or whose resolution is attempted by spanning bridges between the conscious and the unconscious, if at all possible. To put it more clearly, or perhaps less clearly: consciousness carries the unconscious like a parasite, like a huge tapeworm betraying signs of life or existence only by the loose rings which have surfaced in excrement, not in material excrement, but in those traces we leave behind which are nearly always malignant, rings which later multiply, suffocate, strangle and diminish when compressed. Now that I have quoted Marx, I should like to get closer to this concept of mine about pre-history. There is the pre-history of human society, the pre-history of the individual as a part of human society and therefore of his own pre-history, and once more the pre-history of the individual which would be that period of time in his personal life when he becomes aware of having been turned into a parasite by his unconscious.

These things are really much too complicated for me but there is always something too complicated for someone, and notwithstanding, we must tackle them when there is no other solution. (Einstein was what we know or think we know he was, yet his life would have been much less fortunate had he been obliged to mend shoes or set up looms.) Meanwhile, I would be unable to go any further, but the sign of this incapacity, the scratch left by a nail, is already the first step, even though no others may follow. What distinguishes the one and only step from a first step is simply the patience shown or otherwise, while awaiting the second one. With Socrates, art and Marx, anyone can go far. Wearing one's father's boots is also a way of being a man, even though one's feet may be too small for them.

Besides, the best weapon against death is not our simple life, however unique or truly precious it may be to us. The best weapon is not this life of mine which is terrified of death, it is everything that was life before and has endured, from generation to generation, up to the present. I once held my father's skull in my hand and felt neither fear, repugnance nor sorrow: only a strange sense of power like that felt by the swimmer when he is carried along on the crest of a wave. Covered with earth, stripped of flesh, so different from what it looked like with flesh, so similar to all other skulls, just like a building block. When Hamlet speaks to Yorick's skull, it struck me, as I read the words (for the first time) that there is nothing more to be said between a corpse and a living man. Now I know better and through no merit of mine. Three hundred and seventy years have passed in the meantime, Marx was born, people have continued to write and paint, and Socrates has not been erased from history. All things in which I have personally played no part, either through deed or omission (and, in a manner of speaking, still play no part, for this is not writing, nor is this painting). But I believe I am doing my duty when I seize the opportunity and try to understand. No one can ask any more from an ordinary man.

I gaze, for example, at this mummy in the Vatican (another deathly image from which I cannot avert my eyes), its flesh preserved beyond putrefaction and uncomfortably close. All that separates us is that hundredth of a second in which I continue to believe. If the museum guide were to come and tell me that two or three thousand years have elapsed between this corpse and my body, I would believe him since one expects guides to know those things. But I am incapable of imagining what three thousand years might be when the body is there before me, the language barrier resolved by silence, and another dialogue already established. The hands, with their long, painted bones, covered with blackened flesh, without any trace of perspiration and seeking the contact of other hands. It would not take much to make them move, already half-way out of the coffin but not yet out of the glass case in which the corpse is enclosed. Those white nails, so very much alive, could soon be combing out the dandruff of the living with humility and humanity. Here is the lengthy history (not pre-history) of the material continuity of men. For millions of years, millions upon millions of men have been born from the earth and returned to earth. Terrestrial humus now consists much more of human debris than of the original crust, and the houses in which we live, made from what has come out of the soil, are human edifices in the strict meaning of the word human, made from men. For this reason I described my father's skull as a building block.

The world is full of probabilities. Let us imagine that the body was buried on some gentle mountain slope or on the extended curve of its ridge. No one can remember how long it has been there, perhaps for centuries, and this seems most likely. Winter rain and snow has fallen there four hundred times, autumn has made the grass green once more four hundred times, summer has dried it out four hundred times, and four hundred times spring has covered everything with flowers. This is a mountain where nothing has been planted other than a dead body, perhaps murdered and for this reason concealed there. But in this four hundredth and first year after its burial a living man climbs the mountain (as others have done before, but it is this man who concerns us), for no apparent reason, simply to inhale the air stirred by the wind, simply to look into the distance and gaze on other mountains to see if it is true that horizons are indeed always blue. He climbs the mountain, walks on grass, through the undergrowth, over stones, feels these things underfoot, as alive in these sensations as in all the others his senses transmit, and he stretches out on the ground in sheer bliss, lies there looking up at the sky, watching the clouds drift overhead, listening to the wind rustling amidst the branches of nearby trees. He has achieved that illusion of plenitude weak mortals experience when they suddenly imagine they know everything and need no further explanations. Only he does not know that beneath him, faithfully tracing the outline of his body, one body covering another with barely a metre between them, the man who has been dead for four hundred years can now see through the eyes of the man who is alive, skull upon skull, a sky which looks the same and a few clouds made from the same water. The living man gets up knowing nothing and the dead man begins waiting for another four hundred years.

I take my leave of the dead but will not forget them. To forget them, I believe, would be the first sign of death. Besides, after this journey through so many written pages I am convinced we must raise the dead from the ground, brush the loose earth from their faces now reduced to bones and cavities, and learn anew the fraternity out there. Contrary to the words written by Raul Brandão: 'Can you hear the cry? Do you hear it getting louder, increasingly louder and deeper? – It is necessary to kill the dead a second time.' Precisely (exactly; necessarily) the opposite. This is my honest opinion, despite what others have said.

And so I take my leave of the dead. This is a nice way of turning back to the living. Take a look at my closest friends: Carmo, Sandra, Ricardo and Concha, Ana and Francisco, Chico, Antonio (I wonder where he is?), Adelina (farewell). These are my friends. I know they are out there struggling, in and out of each other's company, or in mine, with no good reason for remaining friends, with no good reason for ceasing to be friends. Alive, each with his or her own life and,

JOSÉ SARAMAGO

on reflection, it is quite obvious why we know so little about each other, partly because they remain withdrawn, partly because I do the same, partly out of fear, partly out of pride. There is also a curious parasitism here. Within society we rotate like tiny globes with an invisible but almost insurmountable surface, or if not insurmountable, resistant, wherein we mutually trace complicated orbits, I and these living creatures, these living creatures and I, and all the others with each other. But there is a life common to all, that which embraces, as it were, all the globes. It is this life which is forever receiving the uninterrupted inheritance of corpses, while constantly launching new living beings into the world, all of them transforming and transformed, the agents of the minute changes to which they are subjected.

This explains why my conversation with Melina Mercouri in Positano, although only imagined, was quite feasible, and I was able to ask her how things were going in her country under fascism and for her to ask me how things were going in my country under a similar régime. We both refrained from making any reply. (I have no fascist friends unless someone is deceiving me. All of us, with all our faults and virtues, are anti-fascist. In so far as we have solemnly put our signatures to paper as if expecting this to bring a greater good to the world and to Portugal. All of us have contributed money at some time or other to worthy causes and through mysterious channels, without really knowing which of us delivered the message, or preferring not to notice. We already exchanged books and reading matter, opinions and prophesies. We longed for the death of Salazar. We now deplore the existence of this Américo Tomás and Marcelo Caetano. We dream of their disappearance without knowing or asking ourselves what will happen after they have gone or who will replace them. But nearly all of us become remarkably imaginative when the conversation turns to politics. For years now Ricardo, who is a doctor and seriously influenced by the methods and efficiency of commando operations, has been swearing that half a dozen well-trained men, ten at most, could attack São Bento there, a volley of gunfire here, a bomb over there, a stabbing yonder, and in no time at all capture Salazar (who was still in power then), stamp out fascism, in short, save the nation. Smiling sarcastically, Antonio replied there was no need for so many men, two would be enough. Ricardo, solemn as ever, entered into the game and defended his theory: No, two would be madness, ten, yes, or six as a last resort. Antonio insisted two men were enough. He could even name the two saviours he had in mind. Himself and Ricardo. Whereupon he asked provocatively: 'Will you join us? This is really what it boils down to. You'll see, the minute we decide to go all this will end, it won't last, it will go out like a flame. But we have to go, we can't stay here in comfort and safety, trying to tell ourselves it would take six or ten men to pull it off.' Ricardo could not control his temper. And Concha played the supportive little wife and agreed with him, to Antonio's annoyance. Antonio fell silent and refused to argue any further. Salazar continued to govern, then fell from his throne, rotted and died. And now we are stuck with Marcello with two 'll's just as Tomás signs his name Thomaz, the people are referred to as the congregation, the Fatherland called holy. Everything has changed for the better but only on the surface. That's how things stand here, Melina. And I presume they're not much different over there.)

It came as no surprise. Some days ago (I am referring, by the way, to an interruption of several weeks, from the moment the picture began to take on meaning and form), I began to feel that my clients from Lapa were becoming restless. I had dispensed with the wife's presence and had been working on the husband's portrait, but asked both of them to be present for the final stages of the portrait. That was yesterday. I arrived punctually, more of an obsession than a habit in my case, and was shown in by the maid (a withered old hag) who left me in a room which looked onto the garden and where, presumably because of the better light, my easel had been installed. There I found another maid waiting (this seemed to be the routine), who went immediately to summon the master and mistress. From the behaviour of the two maids (especially that of the old hag) I sensed there was something amiss. I went up to the easel, uncovered the canvas and examined my work. I felt pleased with the result. I had the feeling the tension in the air had something to do with the portrait. The background was white, not exactly white, light in colour, but worked in with that mixture of tints which evokes an unmistakable whiteness or the effect white has on the retina which we are constantly having to adapt (perhaps not the retina, yet it could be the retina after all) to our idea of white. The likeness to the models was undeniable, but, frankly, this portrait was not a worthy successor to those blotched and lifeless paintings I depended on for a living. Both the man and the woman had been painted (how can I put it?) in duplicate, that is to say, with those first essential touches to give the outline and shape of the face, the head, the neck, and then, over all of this, but in such a way that any excess is concealed, a second layer of paint was applied which did nothing other than accentuate what was already there. In the case of the wife, the effect was more obvious because there I had to introduce an intermediate layer of paint to cope with her make-up. The picture produced a sense of disquiet, like sudden laughter in an empty house.

As I was preparing my brushes the door opened. The master of the household arrived on his own, looking extremely nervous. He bade me good afternoon, biting on the words so as to remove any hint of warmth or intimacy which could only make things more difficult. I replied politely and gave him a questioning look which he was free to interpret in various ways: 'What's the matter?' 'Isn't your wife coming?' 'Have your shares gone down?' Gesturing with my hand, I pointed to the chair, but he shook his head with a violence which seemed inappropriate under the circumstances then went on the offensive. At least he tried: 'I've come to tell you. Forgive me, but I've only come to tell you that ... ' He broke off, cleared his throat twice. 'You can't sit for me today?' I asked him, trying to be helpful. 'No, it isn't that. I've come to tell you that we've decided not to go through with the portrait.' 'Not to go ahead with the portrait? I don't understand. Why this sudden decision when it's almost finished?' 'That can't be helped. We've decided we don't want it. If you can tell me how much I owe you, I'll settle your fee right away.' 'You know my fee. You've known since the moment you commissioned the painting.' 'Yes, I know, but the portrait isn't finished and I thought ... ' 'Then you thought wrongly. Do you think a hundred brushstrokes are worth more than thirty? That a painting is like a carpet, so much per metre, in other words, so much per brushstroke?' 'I don't want any arguments. If that's your attitude, then here's your cheque.' He took out his cheque-book and pen and scribbled rapidly, taking his time, however, over the flourishes of his signature before handing over the cheque. I remained quite still. 'Have you made this decision because you don't like the portrait?' 'Not exactly. My wife and daughter think ... Well, the portrait scarcely shows any likeness. Several friends of ours have commissioned portraits recently and they didn't turn out like this. Please take your cheque.' 'My dear fellow, let's see if we can get this straight. You're telling me you don't want the painting because you don't like it, or because your wife and daughter don't like it, and so you'd rather pay me off?' 'I'm in the habit of paying for anything I order whether it's a painting or whatever.' 'That's fortunate for those you deal with. There's nothing like having a clear conscience.' He gave his jacket a sharp tug and looked at me, trying to decide whether I was being ironic. Putting on a solemn face, I tried to look as formal and aggrieved as possible, every inch the painter from Lapa. But before he could open his mouth to answer his future son-in-law appeared. The somewhat theatrical manner in which he boldly made his entrance was intended to conceal the fact that he had been standing behind the door waiting to lend his support. A strategy they had clearly worked out beforehand. 'Now then?' he asked, dispensing with any formalities. 'He refuses to accept the cheque.' 'Excuse me, I said no such thing. I want to finish the portrait before accepting any payment.' The son-in-law broke in: 'Haven't you explained that we're no longer interested in the painting? That we don't like it?' His future father-in-law assured him: 'To avoid any argument I even made out the cheque for the original price agreed.' At which point I intervened: 'It's true. But if you're in the habit of paying for what you order, I'm also in the habit of not accepting any money until the job is finished.' The son-in-law: 'Interesting, but that's your affair. It's of no interest to us. This matter can be resolved very simply.' Just then the daughter or fiancée, according to one's point of view, came into the room. She stood aside looking at us, and never uttered a word until our conversation ended. She was looking in my direction for most of the time with a rather sardonic expression on her face. She was obviously much more astute than either of the two men and preferred to say nothing. I lifted down the painting and lowering it to the ground I rested it against the legs of the easel with the painted side facing them. They turned their eyes away. The girl could see their revulsion and smirked.

I adopted a conciliatory note. 'You don't like the portrait, therefore you don't want it. Very well. You can keep your cheque and I'll keep the painting.' The two men advanced on me: 'Oh no, you don't. The picture belongs to me and my fiancée, my father-in-law commissioned the portrait and here it remains.' 'I don't understand. Unless you pay for the picture how can you expect to keep it?' 'But we're prepared to pay for it, I've already offered to pay you.' 'So you did. But I also made it clear that I refuse to accept payment for a picture I've not yet finished.' 'But this is our portrait,' the father said in despair. 'True, but it belongs to me.' Whereupon the future son-in-law advanced several paces while the girl looked on in satisfaction. He stuck his hands in his trouser pockets as if he were not from Lapa or about to be married in Lapa: 'Look here, are you trying to make a fool of me? Let's settle this matter once and for all before I lose my temper.' I glanced at the girl: 'Do you mean to say you're threatening me here in your own house?' The father intervened: 'No one is threatening you, but can't you see you're being unreasonable.' 'I'm not being unreasonable. I'm simply being logical. Either I finish the portrait and receive my fee or I leave the portrait unfinished and take it away with me as unsold. Nothing could be simpler.' A deathly silence filled the room. The father nervously fingered the cheque. The son-in-law backed away and was looking at the girl as if pleading for help. And the girl was still smiling. I lifted the portrait carefully to avoid scraping the paint, wished them good afternoon, informed them I would send someone to collect the easel later and left. The two men came after me. 'You can't do this.' 'Oh yes, I can, I most certainly can. And now if you'll be so kind as to allow me to pass.' From the room looking onto the garden came a burst of laughter. The entire episode, in fact, had been ridiculous. And the farce continued, there at the top of the carpeted stairway where various things were happening at the same time: the son-in-law trying to grab me by the arm but unsure of succeeding, the father-in-law pointing his finger in silent fury at a maid who had been spying but was now scurrying away, while the mistress of the household finally made her appearance in the wide doorway with an expression of wounded pride. 'We ought to call the police,' suggested the son-in-law. But his father-in-law resisted the idea. There was little point in adding scandal to their humiliation. He shouted after me

JOSÉ SARAMAGO

threateningly: 'I shall be consulting my lawyer. Get out of here.' I was free at last under the spectre of justice.

I slowly made my way downstairs and, on reaching the bottom step, I looked back. Like generals on parade, the two men were glaring down at me with hatred in their eyes. I left quietly, taking care not to damage the canvas and, cautiously opening the boot of the car, gently eased the picture inside as if I were lowering a sleeping child into its cot. Before closing the boot, I momentarily glanced at the portrait. Two masked faces were staring up at me and I watched them there at my mercy, laid out flat and looking quite subdued. I slammed down the lid of the boot. As I got into the car, I caught a glimpse in the side-mirror of a curtain being drawn back. Who could it be? Those insolent, prying maids? The outraged males in that household? Their indignant women, or rather one of them, the other perhaps still amused? I felt sorry for the girl. She might be the same as the others, or end up being the same, but there was something different about her sameness, a crack in the porcelain, imperceptible to the naked eye but already sounding hollow. One finds this in certain wealthy families: things which can drive people to suicide. There was every reason to believe that history would repeat itself.

As for me, I knew perfectly well what had happened. In the boot I was carrying a bomb with a delayed fuse but none the less deadly. The mechanism already working. Whatever I might do, I was finished as a portrait painter hired by people who could afford to pay. Even if I were to turn back, to destroy the portrait in the presence of my victims and paint another according to their wishes and traditional criteria, my career was finished. Even if I were to apologize and take back everything I had said. The basket-weaver who makes one basket can just as easily make a hundred; let no man say from this water I shall not drink; the jug is carried to the well until the handle finally breaks: I had made one basket and could just as easily make a hundred, I had drunk from that water and upset my clients by leaving them with the handle of the jug in their hands. Within twenty-four hours (or forty-eight, or fifteen days, not to

The Manual of Painting and Calligraphy 167

exaggerate my importance) the Lisbon which exploited my talents will know not to use me again. It was a question of honour: a telephone call, a chance encounter during a game of golf or bridge, or during a pause at a board meeting, and with a few cautious words which scarcely gave a true account of what really happened, the matter would be settled. I have written this in the subjunctive, but it ought to be in the future tense, now that I find myself at home engaged in the inevitable task of writing these papers. In the future and present tense as well. I am finished as the painter of these shits I have been painting and who have provided me with a living. Within days my reputation as a painter will have been completely destroyed. What are those who own my paintings likely to do? Keep them because they like them, or out of stubbornness because they cost good money? Will my pictures be hidden in attics, be slashed down the middle with a knife, be banished to some country house, removed from frames worth keeping and the canvases destroyed? Any of these things might happen. *Esprit de corps* will demand this final act of my liquidation. No one will have the courage to oppose the general consensus. Some will perversely resist the idea, having grown accustomed to seeing the picture hanging in the boardroom, office or council chamber (what will the SPQR do? and what will S. do?), but my only real hope of survival will depend on how much love the living continue to show for the dead commemorated in these portraits. If the dead man was esteemed, out of affection, or for less sentimental reasons, then, perhaps, his portrait will escape this act of faith (or *auto-da-fé*); if he was not esteemed, the opportunity everyone longed for has come at last, and without further ado the owners of the firm will be rid of that hideous portrait and the unpleasant memories it evokes. There are always ways and means of achieving our secret ambitions: all we need is to find some pretext.

With the picture in the car boot, I drove aimlessly around the city thinking about some of the things I would come to write later, allowing other things to escape which were probably just as important (as unimportant or even more important). A justifiable note on the part of someone who is only now beginning to learn how to write: why

JOSÉ SARAMAGO

does one use one expression rather than another? The city, this one, or any other, is something strange. A city is erected for three reasons; it is inhabited by a thousand people (or thousands or millions) and survives even when those reasons no longer exist (other reasons which have surfaced in the meantime would lead to the creation of a different city). The city is inhabited, as I have just said, by a few thousand people more or a few thousand less and achieves the feat of holding together, globally speaking, this population and yet by various means does not allow it to unite. The joint wills of the inhabitants form, without their noticing, a different will which comes to govern and carefully watch over them. The city knows, the will knows, and the person who incarnates this will knows that if the unity of the inhabitants were to be restored, the final total, even if numerically the same, would be different in quality: the first and inevitable outcome would be the transformation of the city itself. For this reason it defends itself. It would appear to be true (although this warrants some discussion) that the body is directed by a central organ which is the brain (any such discussion would include an examination of the advantages and disadvantages of the existence of autonomous brains, even though not independent, which govern the different organs and limbs of the body, one's hand or penis, for example). But the city has no such certainty, or only in reverse, of the advantages of those completely functional brains, intact and precise, with which its inhabitants are endowed. What would become of a city with a million inhabitants if those million bodies were to correspond to a million brains?

Here are the houses, the people, the bustling streets, the shadows and sunlight, the trees, those mobile metallic forms, motor-cars, trams, buses, here are the shops with goods hanging up or arranged within confined spaces or displayed under glass; here is the stone, the asphalt, the cement beneath the coats of paint or tiles, here are the voices, the noise of traffic; here is the dust, the litter and the wind that blows it along, here is the scaffolding surrounding a new building and the scaffolding around another in the process of being demolished; here are the monuments, nearly all of them of men and a few allegorical women; others with heraldic, symbolic or functional animals such as lions, horses, several oxen, here is the city at close quarters, an image amongst countless others, and now seen from a distance, from the other side of the river, from the top of this bridge which is also part of the city; here is the living crust over the dead earth, or only alive in the waters and the irrepressible plants which sprout and flower between crevices; here is that undulation, so gentle when seen from afar, of houses and rooftops in colours which, no matter how vivid, fade in the distance and in this light which comes immediately before that other light we generally refer to as twilight. Neither of these descriptions tells us very much because the various gradations of light cannot be expressed in words, just as words cannot describe this city which is everything that has been said and been left unsaid, neither near nor distant, and probably as inaccessible as the brain that governs it and the men and women who inhabit it, even though absent. I gaze upon Lisbon from the esplanade, at this ridiculous monstrosity erected by the Catholic Church to honour Christ the King, I gaze upon the city and know it is an active organism, functioning simultaneously through intelligences, instincts and tropisms, but I see it, above all, as a plan which designs itself, attempting to co-ordinate the lines which curve from all sides or come out straight, resembling the inside of a muscle or giant nerve-cell, a dazzled retina, a pupil dilating and contracting in the daylight which is still bright. Locked in the boot of my car, two heads are immersed in total darkness. They keep their eyes open, will never be able to close them and are condemned to eternal vigil (an eternal painting?) and those pupils will not blink if light should suddenly enter but stare at me self-questioningly, now that they presume to have judged me. This city will be my witness. I am not guilty of what they accuse me, but probably of what they praise in me.

From this same spot, or from other vantage-points overlooking cities, other men and women have taken advantage of this romantic euphoria, vertigo or sense of wonder upon finding themselves physically towering above others in order to make an act of contrition. In traditional tales from Russia the hero would often kneel in the public square and confess his misdemeanours, crimes and faults in the presence of men and dogs. If novels speak of this, then some men in real life must have done it once upon a time or after reading about it. But in the novels written here in Western Europe, and in the experience of people like myself, it is much more common for men to take themselves off to some elevated spot and spout forth fine words or arrant nonsense, thus transforming this first act of contrition into final justification. I daresay this is precisely what I did. I keep reminding myself, however, that I am no longer on the first stages of my journey, that the distance covered gives me some rights, especially self-respect, and some consideration for myself. I bend down to examine the soles of my feet, however smooth or calloused, to test the resistance of the ground I tread, but then my head comes up: my eyes look straight ahead, deciding which direction to take. This is how one should proceed.

As I write, I glance at my wrist-watch which, as I explained, I usually place before me on the table. It is night, I have finished dinner and am now writing. I watch the second hand hopping along, going round and round, an image in miniature of human existence. Better than a portrait: a reassuring notion of time. One does not know what time might be. It is probably a continuous flow, invisible to the naked eye (a simple image of my own making to help me understand what I am saying), but the invention of watches which advance with tiny jerks has introduced into this flow minute stages, fleeting pauses which in succession and in the continuous sequence of tiny leaps into the void has given us some reassurance that time is an accumulation, an addition of infinite sequences of time which promise eternity. But modern clocks, electric or electronic, have brought back the anguish of the hour-glass: as with sand, time runs through them without pause or respite, without anywhere to rest, even for a second. These things, however banal, as no doubt others have said many times before, are of great importance to me at this stage. Like running water, my life has come up against a floodgate *en route*. During this enforced delay, it fills up, recedes, is disturbed by criss-crossing currents in opposition to each other. I am in the infinitesimal pause of the clock. But accumulated time pushes me forward. I look at the portrait of the couple from Lapa. Their eyes stare back at me, refuse to leave me as I move around the studio. And I feel their presence as I go up to the canvas on which I have finished painting that absurd tiled floor copied from Vitale da Bologna, and the prison narrowing in perspective almost to the point of vanishing. I am now painting the saint. On his side of the grille.

Adelina paid me a visit. She had telephoned me beforehand, somewhat withdrawn, and I thought she sounded a little nervous. She felt she ought to discuss the letter but I cut her short: No need to bother, there was nothing to discuss, no point in getting into an argument, something I had decided to avoid by not replying. I had the impression (was it simply a question of male pride?) that she was perplexed, perhaps repentant, anxious to talk things over. If this were so, then she must have cherished some hope (of what?) when I agreed she should come to collect her personal belongings, a few clothes, various tubes and jars of make-up, her photograph, those little feminine traces which remain (masculine, too, when the break is made on the other side, the woman staying while the man goes off), even when one thinks everything has been removed. One day, you unexpectedly come across a nail-file which isn't yours or you find yourself changing the position of some object, things return to their proper orbit, not the first one which has been lost for some time but to the one immediately before, slightly modified, needless to say, because forces once in equilibrium collided in this space when travelling in convoy, and then the equilibrium was disturbed, the journey interrupted and one might almost say life itself knocked off course. It would not be so in this case. Adelina came, collected her belongings while I deliberately set about tidying my books in the studio. She wasted no time, but when she emerged from the bedroom with a small suitcase in one hand, she looked at me in silence, making me responsible for these final moments. I was also looking at her but aware of the situation and, convinced it was in both our interests, I decided to break the silence. I had no wish to send her away nor did I want her to stay. I asked: 'Have you got everything?' as I went on pretending to arrange my books. I heard her take a few steps: she was now standing before the portrait of the couple from Lapa. I could tell she was curious. Had she made any comment I would probably have lost my temper and said something rude. Suddenly she seemed to be approaching a forbidden frontier. On the other side, I was prepared to open fire, to use heavy artillery (capable of causing death), non-recoiling cannon. She seemed to understand, who knows how, but she behaved as if she understood. She crossed the studio, left by the narrow passageway. I heard her open and close the door leading to the stairs, sounds covering a raised voice somewhere along the way, a voice which uttered sounds meant to convey some greeting, perhaps goodbye, perhaps farewell, perhaps good afternoon, perhaps see you soon, and then the rapid tapping of heels on the stairs, descending and diminishing down those four flights, the noise gradually dying away into the distance.

JOSÉ SARAMAGO

Having done my sums, I reckon I have enough money to live on for four to six weeks. There is no hope of any new commissions. I have already been through temporary crises, but this one has come to stay. There is only one solution: advertising. Here in Portugal, those who work in the arts (a frightful expression) whatever their worth, if they find their career interrupted by fate or collective misfortune, or if, as in my case, they cannot fall back on teaching (I did not finish my course at Art School and half of what I know I acquired later, however badly), they get out their diaries with addresses and telephone numbers and scan the pages in search of contacts in the advertising world, while inventing their past history in which they naturally appear in the best possible light, otherwise there would be no point in taking so much trouble. They very much doubt that anyone will believe them, but are forced into it for the sake of the firm's good name. My port of salvation will be Chico, at least I hope so. He has bailed me out on other occasions. Meanwhile, I have been working. The picture of the saint is finished. I hung it up in the studio with the postcard from which I made the copy pinned alongside. I also hung up the portrait of the couple from Lapa (so far no sign of any lawyer) and on a piece of paper attached below I neatly pinned the date of my expulsion from their villa. I spend little time at home during the day. I go out with my drawing pad and fill page after page with sketches and notes. I revisit old haunts, the coast where I used to go as a schoolboy to make drawings of boats, of men unloading crates of fish, the fishwives loading baskets onto their heads, to register those voices and expressions, to capture the light reflected in the oily water and choose from amongst countless scintillations to find the arithmetical means and laboriously transfer them onto the paper in black and white. Everything has changed but the river still flows between the same walls, unworthy of the name embankments because they are simply made of mud. Here, too, men and women are to be seen walking around or sitting, the men more than the women, staring for hours on end at the big boats on the river, at the oil-tankers which scarcely look like boats, the entrance to the Lisnave shipyard, the yellow smoke as dense and tumultuous as the heavy clouds rolling across the sky, the sails of the odd frigate and the frenzied flight of swallows, as relentless and incessant during the day as the chopping and lashing of waves against the ramp of the wall, the water extended like a towel or dishcloth and in circular motion as if the polluted river were intent upon washing those stones with murky water. I notice people looking at me inquisitively and can only surmise that the presence of an artist is rare in these parts. Human faces, gestures and hands are of little interest. Any well-programmed computer can produce a hundred paintings daily, each one different from the other. Any op-artist such as Victor de Vasarely can go on repeating the same design with endless variations on the inner and outer walls of today's intellectual bourgeoisie. I painted the portraits of the upper bourgeoisie and now I am nobody. I no longer count for anything and have no idea what will become of me. What I have kept, however, from my days as a painter, are faces, eyes, mouths, heads with or without hair, noses, chins, ears, shoulders, sometimes bare, formal attire for every imaginable occasion, uniforms, and when I get down as far as the hands, with or without rings – what I have kept or never entirely lost, was my enduring interest in the human face, in the delicate nature of skin, those faint or deep wrinkles, glistening beads of sweat on someone's temples or the forehead itself, the subterranean blue river of a vein. Not simply beauty, rare as it is, but ugliness, too, which is much more common amongst us humans because we are not by nature beautiful but accept our ugliness with a peculiar grace which perhaps stems from the soul. We go on moulding our face from within, but this fleeting existence of ours never allows us enough time to complete the task: that explains why the ugly remain ugly, or even grow uglier when they abandon this meticulous task of inner

JOSÉ SARAMAGO

moulding or make a complete mess of things. I should like to believe that if the human species were to live two or three times longer than these miserable seventy years biology permits (and to live for seventy years is my great ambition, if not the average lifespan), men and women would reach the end of their life in a state of radiant beauty, different because of the multiplication of features, colours and races, but one and unsurpassable. Nowadays, human beings begin (when they begin) with beauty and accumulate ugliness with each passing year and season, by day and by night, with every passing hour and second. A long life (I imagine) would make Helen of Troy and Socrates the same on the last day. Helen would not be more comely than Socrates, she would simply wait for him to catch up and together they would depart this life looking beautiful.

On returning home, I carefully examine the sketches, use them once more for further experiments, I bring the figures together, agonize over the space, not in the least concerned with the coast in the background. For me this sheet of paper continues to be man's location. The men and women who used to hire me have turned their backs on me, they have walked off the paper and left it blank. I now trace other figures who do not come of their own free will nor are they prepared to pay me, they are (or have been) accustomed to posing as models for students studying fine arts, or being photographed by tourists. Out of habit they have acquired a false indifference, composed of complacency, a hint of ingenuousness, patience and perhaps a certain disdain. And deep down I am convinced they are intangible. Seated on a packing-case, a coil of rope (cable, Mr Painter, cable) or on an upturned boat, I study them with my eye and draw them, but I have the feeling they are not defenceless. Each of them is independent and self-contained, and at the same time part of all the others and inside all the others. They are the whole and the part of some other totality. Running through them is an invisible (but sensitive) current which links them, which extends and holds (I guess) when they separate for hours or days. More than just the faces, I should like to reach that invisible current behind the faces. I believe that a certain kind of drawing, a certain manner of painting, if only I could master them, would allow me to capture that current through the faces and, once captured, I could then go back to the faces and transform each of them into a manifestation. Painting the bourgeoisie has not prepared me for this task, for this descent to the sun, nor has it robbed me (or could this simply be my intangibility?) of this sixth sense which permits me to capture, although incapable of deciphering it, the subterranean language, the seismal wave, the tremor beneath the epidermis of faces and bodies which are separate from me. And what were those other faces and bodies I painted like? All I can say is that they were just as detached from me. S. was detached from me (and this was how this writing or accounting started), the couple from Lapa were detached from me (and this is how this writing or accounting will end). What am I doing in space which, in its turn, separates people from each other? What does a painter do? When I pick up a pencil or brush and bring them to the paper or canvas, I notice there is a certain similarity in the way they both look at me. In comparing them, I find the same complacency, patience and contempt. And if there is any difference, I believe it to be cunning rather than ingenuousness, perhaps not even cunning but simply utter disdain.

Each and every one of them detached from me. And I from myself. Attention! I need your attention at this moment. I explained that I began writing when I realized I was remote from knowing S. Now I must tell you that I am about to interrupt or bring to an end what I am writing because I am just as remote or even more so from all those other bourgeois inhabitants of Lapa who belong to the same breed as S., although they are two quite different kinds of remoteness, the second being the logical outcome of knowledge and not its absence. Between the one and the other, it was in order to get closer to myself that I continued to write, when the first of these motives had already lost any importance. So what sum could I make, what total could I arrive at or firm conclusions draw? I continue to be as detached from others as before. And having rediscovered this separation from other men, I continue myself meanwhile with this new awareness. But what about this separation from myself? What finally resulted from this attempt to write an autobiography through different channels, combining fact and fiction in equal measure? What edifice or bridge was built? Of what resilient and lasting material? In reply, I can only say that I got close to myself. I adjusted my body to its shadow and tightened the loose screw.

I avert my eyes from the paper and watch my hand move under the light. With certain movements I can see how flaccid my skin has become in certain places, I can see the network of veins, the hairs, the pleated articulations of the fingers, I can feel in my eyes those curved nails, hard as any shield, and I know that I have never felt so little to be so truly mine. I move my hand and know that I am willing this movement, I am this will and this hand. I rest my forearms on the table and feel their pressure against the wood and its resistance. This well-being (to be well, well-being) is not physical or only becomes physical afterwards, it is not a point of departure, it is the point I have reached. I re-read these pages from the beginning. I look for the place, the situation, the word or space between the lines which might be that certainty which lurks around the corner: with each passing moment I remain the same, with each passing moment I feel myself to be someone different. What I need is a definite pause in time, that point which divides the distance covered from that still to be covered. I need the liquid intermediate state (in memory of those lessons I once received in elementary chemistry) during the transition from the gaseous to the solid, and to pause for a moment to study the process in detail.

The difference between the portraits of S. and the couple from Lapa is my difference: there one sees the difference. No one would ever suspect they had been painted by the same person, or at least would need time before making up their mind. What does the author's difference consist of? If this stroke is not the same as that one, what is the difference between them? The movement of the wrist, the tightening of the fingers around the charcoal or handle of the brush? Yet there is no difference in the way I shave although my hand is holding the brush. There is no difference in the way I hold my fork although it is my hand which is doing the holding. I have just paused to rub my eyes with the back of my hand (a gesture which has stayed with me since childhood) and both the movement and motive remain the same. Yet this same hand has sketched and painted similar things differently: there is no difference between S. and the couple from Lapa, but they were painted differently: the couple from Lapa are, after all, the second portrait of S. and my perception. I sketch and paint. Over the paper and canvas the hand traces out the same invisible network of movements but the moment it settles on the material the movement is transformed into material, the sign reproduces a different time-image, as if the nerves coming from the eye were about to join up with some new region of the brain, immediately contiguous, it is true, but the archive of some other experience and, therefore, the source of new information.

I finish with considerable effort. I now realize it has been much easier for me to say who I was than to affirm who I am today. This writing could go on to the end of my life with the same sense of purpose or futility there has been so far. I doubt, however, whether the narration of one's everyday existence without any plan (I mean the narration and not the day-to-day sequence of events) could interest me sufficiently to go beyond probing (if I ever used the word analysis then I was exaggerating). Meanwhile, alone as I find myself, without art or adequate training, a tension builds up inside me which I have already tried to express with words and this tension does not allow me to stop. The same tension fills my head with ideas and my sketch-pad with drawings; the same tension detains me here before the portrait of the couple from Lapa and the picture copied from Vitale da Bologna, just as it draws me to the easel where I have set up a canvas without being able to make a start. Because I do not know what to paint there. I have been painting for more than twenty years, but it would be wrong to suggest that I have anything like twenty years' experience: my experience is of repeating the same portrait for twenty years, a portrait painted in primary tones with a few basic gestures. No matter whether the model be male or female, young or old, plump or thin, fair or dark, intelligent or stupid, all it required of me was a somewhat imitative adaptation: the painter imitated the model. I used a different technique for the portrait of the couple from Lapa or perhaps not all that different after all. Habits do not change, whatever they may be. And a painter's technique, which is also a habit, cannot be changed at will from one minute to the next. There are no miracles in painting. The portrait I described as having a different technique is more truthful because it resulted from my sudden inability to react when confronted by new models with that mimetic process which had become second nature. I now realize that my first act of rebellion (how I love that extravagant word) was to attempt to paint a second portrait of S. I painted it in secret, allowing no one to see it, especially the model himself. There was much cowardice in that rebellion. Or timidity. In the presence of the couple from Lapa (reminiscent of certain characters in Portuguese novels: *Os Fidalgos da Casa Mourisca* by Júlio Dinis, *A Morgadinha de Val-flor* by Pinheiro Chagas, *Os Teles de Albergaria* by Carlos Malheiro Dias, *As Donas dos Tempos Idos* by Caetano Beirão, *O Barão de Lavos* by Arnaldo Gama, *Os Maias* by Eça de Queiroz and *O Senhor do Paço de Ninães* by Camilo Castelo Branco) the chameleon did not change its colour. If it was brown, brown it remained, and it was with brown eyes that he registered and transposed any colours which clashed or might have clashed with brown. (On taking a closer look at what I have just written I can find no reason for preferring the one tense to the other.) I doubt whether Goya was opposed to Carlos IV when he painted him surrounded by the Royal Family (were there any such opposition on his part, I believe this could be broken down into the three or four elements I mentioned earlier: complacency, patience and disdain, the last of these variable). Confronted by that gathering of degenerates, Goya looked at their faces dispassionately and, having decided there was nothing worth improving in his painting, he made everything uglier. This could be described as opposition, but it is only now we can say for certain, because in the meantime history has surpassed monarchial institutions in general, and this one in particular, and because we know what Goya did not yet know in the year 1800 (the date of the portrait of Carlos IV with the Royal Family): that in the year 1810 he would do a series of etchings entitled *The Disasters of War*, that in 1814 he would paint *The Second of May* and *The Executions of the Third of May*, and that towards the end of his life he would produce the so-called 'black paintings' and *Disparates*. Did I oppose the couple from Lapa? I do not think so. It would be truer to say they opposed me. To oppose can simply imply a change of mood, something which comes and goes and more often than not, in my experience, reflects a sense of dependence or subordination. This is where one begins to discover the relationship between inferior and superior. The next step is to rebel in order to get out of the situation, but if this can be done, then the opposition soon transforms itself into being opposed so that the first impulse is sustained and becomes permanent, a state of constant tension, one foot set firmly on the ground we claim as ours, the other foot forward. A thousand blows, one after the other, open a gap in the wall until the wall finally collapses under the constant pressure applied over a sufficiently wide area: the difference between the pick-axe and the bulldozer.

This is how I feel today within these four walls or when I stroll through the city: opposed to something. But to what? Firstly, to the portraits I painted and to myself for painting them, but not to what I was when I painted them: I cannot oppose what I was, now less than ever. I wanted to summon what I was (and do believe I succeeded) like someone conjuring up his own shadow which lingered behind and became soiled and ragged round the edges, barely recognizable in that jaded expression we know so well, but as much ours as sweat or sperm. And also opposed to everything around me. I am convinced this is where most of my tension stems from. I feel like the keen soldier who can no longer wait for the enemy to attack and begin to advance, or like the child whose excess energy has exhausted one game and immediately craves another. I liquidated (cleared out, examined, destroyed, annihilated) my past and my previous behaviour and now recognize that I did nothing other than prepare the ground. I threw stones, tore up plants, razed anything

JOSÉ SARAMAGO

which obstructed the view, and in this way (as I have already stated with different words and for other reasons) I created a desert. I now stand in the middle of it, knowing that this is where my house must be built (if it is to be a house) but knowing nothing else.

When Goya retired to his country estate (*La Quinta del Sordo* or Deaf Man's Farm), what desert had he created or had been created in him, deaf and therefore isolated, but not simply because of this infirmity? I have no intention of writing out Goya's biographical details or of providing a potted history of the Spain of his time. I am speaking about myself, not about Goya, and I should really speak about Portugal (were it not so painful) rather than about Spain. However, men who can be so very different are also very similar and individual countries are a combination of those differences and similarities, combined *ad infinitum*, at times coinciding beyond frontiers and ages, at other times mutually seeking out or rejecting each other. When, in 1814, Goya painted those two pictures describing the events of May 1808 and Ferdinand VII restored the Inquisition, what had any of this to do with me or Portugal then or subsequently? Although Portugal is a country which has found itself occupied ten times (by the Americans, Germans, English, French and Belgians and been dominated by five different monetary policies: monopolist, expansionist, colonial, speculative and fraudulent), we have no May to remember or commemorate in paint or prose, and while this painter may be present, Goya is no longer with us. But if I look back over events in Portugal during my own lifetime and list the names of prominent people: Salazar Cerejeira Santos Costa Carmona Agostinho Lourenço Teotónio Pereira Pais de Sousa Rafael Duque António Ferro Carneiro Pacheco Marcelo Caetano Tomás Moreira Baptista Rebelo de Sousa Adriano Moreira Silva Pais Rui Patrício Veiga Simão António Ribeiro, I am irresistibly tempted to pass Ferdinand VII's decree here without delay so that part of Portugal's history may also be explained in passing: 'The glorious title of Catholic with which the Kings of Spain were singled out from the other Princes of Christianity, as a reward for banishing from their kingdom anyone who refused to profess the Catholic, Apostolic and

Roman faith, has inspired me to strive with all the means God has put at my disposal to be worthy of those epithets. The grave disturbances and war which devastated every province in the Realm for six long years; the presence during all this time of foreign troops of different religious persuasions, nearly all of them contaminated with hatred and aversion to the Catholic Faith; the disorders which invariably come in the wake of such evils, as well as the lamentable failure during these years to nurture religion, gave these sinners complete licence to live as they pleased and the opportunity to introduce insidious beliefs which they disseminated amongst the people by the same methods used to propagate them in other countries. Bearing in mind, on the other hand, the need to remedy these grave evils and to preserve throughout our domain the holy religion of Jesus Christ, which we love and to which my people has pledged its life and happiness, and also taking into account the duties which the fundamental laws of the Realm impose on the reigning prince, and which I have sworn to protect and observe, and because it is the best means of safeguarding my subjects from internal dissension and ensuring their peace and tranquillity, I believe it is important under present circumstances to restore the jurisdiction of the Tribunal of the Holy Office. Wise and virtuous prelates and the major guilds and corporations, both ecclesiastical and secular, have reminded us that it is thanks to this Tribunal that Spain remained untouched by the heresies which provoked such trials and tribulations in other nations throughout the sixteenth century, while our country flourished in all the arts and produced great men of valour and virtue; that one of the principal methods used by the Oppressor of Europe to spread corruption and discord to his advantage, was the destruction of this Tribunal on the pretext of its being no longer compatible with the enlightenment of the age: and that the so-called Extraordinary General Courts were later to use the same pretext and invoke the Constitution in order to abolish the Inquisition and bring turmoil and sorrow to the nation. For these reasons, we have been loyally counselled to restore the Tribunal. In accordance with this advice and out of respect for the will of the people, whose deep concern for their religion has already led them to take the initiative and restore the functions of some of the important Tribunals, I have decided that henceforth the Council of the Inquisition and the other Tribunals of the Holy Office should be re-established and continue to exercise their powers of jurisdiction.' Fortunately (unfortunately) the people whose names I cited earlier have been inspired and go on being inspired by such mellifluous and hypocritical words, or fortunately (unfortunately) by those once uttered by our king, Dom João III (the Pious), when he implored the Pope to set up the Inquisition here in Portugal. Fortunately (unfortunately) by the words of more recent tyrants, Mussolini and Hitler, who are already dead. But Franco (the mighty general) was almost certainly inspired by Ferdinand III, Salazar by his masters from Coimbra, the disciples and legitimate sons or bastards of Dom João III and his disreputable lineage which has lasted for four centuries. As for Marcelo Caetano, a student all his life, he looks at the world around him and can find no one to follow. The hour of his putrefaction is nigh.

And I, what am I to do? I, Portuguese, once the portrait-painter of the bourgeoisie and now unemployed, I, the portrait-painter of the protégés and protectors of Salazar and Marcelo and their oppressive secret police. And for this same reason, I, too, find myself protected by those who protect them, thus protecting themselves and, therefore, in practice I am both protected and protector even though not in thought, what am I to do? All around me lies the desert waiting to be filled with what? Copy out, like anything else, a couple of pages by Marx and wholeheartedly believe in them, have enough knowledge and perception to confront them with history and recognize that they make sense? Herr Marx: in the restricted ambience of my profession, the relations of productivity have altered. Who is the painter going to work for now? And why? And for what? Does someone want or need this painter, is someone about to come to this desert and hire him? Nowadays (and not for the first time) abstraction is all the rage amongst painters: they imitate the illusion created by the kaleidoscope, they shake it gently every so often and carry on doing so, already aware that the human face will ever appear in this game with mirrors and coloured bits of paper. It may fill the desert but will never populate it. Although (and this my mind can grasp even if I am only a Portuguese painter who does portraits of the bourgeoisie) the topography of faces may not be enough to populate deserts and fill blank canvases. Deserts they remain. But let time take its course. Time only needs time. The popular rising in Madrid in 1808 only found Goya prepared in 1814. It is true that history goes faster than the men who paint and record it. This is probably inevitable. I ask myself: if I were to have some role to play tomorrow, what events of today would be waiting for me? (Unless this hope in a distributive justice turns out to be nothing other than a defensive front for the spirit of abnegation. May will-power assert itself. I should like to know what Goya would have thought about this. And Marx.)

Antonio was arrested three days ago. I found out this morning through Chico in the advertising agency where I have been working for almost a month. Chico came dashing into my office and blurted out the news, not that there was much to tell. Or perhaps his words only sounded jumbled, for I could scarcely believe my ears: 'Antonio under arrest?' Chico and I looked at each other. It seemed incredible but Chico was certain and we both asked ourselves the same thing: Antonio arrested? But why Antonio? What has he done? Or rather, what was he on the point of doing that they should have arrested him? As far as we knew, Antonio had done nothing wrong. But what did we know about Antonio? I know this is how we both felt because in the conversation that followed we touched on these things. Antonio had never shown any sign of being involved in politics. It is true that I had not seen him for many months but Chico, who had been with him only the week before, assured me he had noticed nothing unusual or different in his behaviour: they had talked vaguely about several things, as one did in our crowd, Antonio looking as distracted as ever, and they had even agreed to meet for lunch one day soon. 'So, as you can see, there was nothing to arouse my suspicions. Do you think Antonio could have been up to something?' I told him: 'I know as much as you do. Whenever we discussed politics Antonio never showed any more interest than the rest of us. Although he always seemed a bit too withdrawn, in my opinion. Perhaps he didn't trust us.' 'You must be joking. We've always trusted each other in the group.' 'But probably not enough for him to be able to take us into his confidence. Besides, what is this group of ours? For Antonio, clearly just like any other group and apparently not the most interesting as far as he was concerned.' Chico listened attentively, carefully pondering my words before making any reply: 'By Jove, I believe you're right.' 'How did you find out he'd been arrested?' 'Because of our luncheon engagement. I telephoned him at home yesterday and the day before yesterday on several occasions at different times and there was no answer. I thought he might have gone to Santarém to spend a few days with his family, but he's punctilious in these matters, as you know – one would never suspect he was an architect – and I refuse to believe he'd go off just like that without telling me our arrangement was cancelled. I went to his house this morning. I rang the bell for ages and nothing happened. I knocked at his neighbour's door and a rather attractive woman, as it happened, answered, but the minute I asked about Antonio a look of terror came into her face and I thought she was going to slam the door in my face. She must have been watching me through the peep-hole. All smiles, I managed to get the whole story out of her. Three days ago, about seven in the morning, the police arrived and got Antonio out of bed. They ransacked the house and took him away. He must be in Caxias.' Chico paused for breath, looked at me and murmured: 'Antonio.' The Antonio whom he had probably never shown enough esteem was now being discussed with affection, certainly with respect and perhaps even an indefinable note of admiration and envy. (That petit-bourgeois craving for martyrdom.) I got up from my bench, went to the window, looked outside without really noticing or taking in what I was seeing. I turned to Chico: 'What's going to happen to him now?' 'He'll come through. Antonio is tough.' 'And what about us, what are we going to do? We'd better warn his family.' 'Of course, but who's likely to know his parents' address or telephone number? I don't.' 'Nor me. Perhaps one of the others will know. We can only try.' Chico said anxiously: 'Leave this to me. I'll deal with it. I can contact the others.'

No one could tell us anything. From this detail and many others to which we had never really given much thought before, I began to realize just how little Antonio had confided in us. I don't feel I can blame him. If he were actively involved in politics, then he must have thought of us as being nothing but a fatuous bunch of

JOSÉ SARAMAGO

psychological and social misfits. In fact, everyone (or nearly everyone in the group, because I consider myself an exception) is forever being affectionate and sentimental with just enough cynicism to make it clear we are playing a game. As if we were constantly explaining to each other: Believe what I am about to tell you in such a way that it seems I do not want you to believe me. And besides: If you don't believe what I am telling you, even while appearing not to want you to believe me, I would know you don't value me, because if you were to value me you would also know that this is the manner in which intelligent people confide in each other nowadays. And besides, any reaction other than this one would be a sign of discourtesy, of backwardness and a lack of sensibility. Antonio looked on as we played out this farce and preferred to remain silent. I think back, see him with new eyes, try to feel his presence, to reconstitute certain words and phrases he used throughout all those years, only to discover someone who did more listening than speaking. But I clearly remember that it was he who advised me to read Marx's Preface to a *Contribution to the Critique of Political Economy* and who, when he asked me some time later if I had read it, went quite silent when I made the excuse that I still hadn't found the time. And I also remember that I could not bring myself to tell him when I eventually got round to reading the book, but not all of it. This must be said because it is the truth. I can still visualize that scene when he uncovered the painting in my storeroom, that second portrait of S. covered in black paint (how remote it all seems), and I ponder that episode in the light of the present situation. And in the light of what these pages have done for me. Everything now seems much clearer. Antonio must have been desperate and annoyed with all of us who were there commemorating the end and material outcome of the portrait, annoyed above all with me (and although I cannot explain it, I can understand his attitude). By provoking me, he had exposed my inferiority: things subsequently turned out in such a way that this supposed inferiority became clear to all, and all the more clear as the humiliating situation in which he had left me became more obvious. But if it was inferiority (this is an assumption rather than a statement of fact), then perhaps at the time he had no other outlet: his suppressed aggression finally surfaced. So, amongst the members of the group I was the most vulnerable and perhaps the most useful target. For different reasons both of us felt badly. Looking back, this is how I see it, and if this reflection serves no other purpose, it explains, and this is reassuring, why I never bore him any grudge or ill-will. I cannot say that I miss him: I find that unconsciously I was always aware of his absence. Now I feel it even more, and that is all.

Chico has just telephoned me to say that no one in the group knows where Antonio's parents live. We both agree that something must be done, but what? I propose we go to Caxias the following day to try to get some news and Chico agrees, but preferably not tomorrow when he expects to be very busy, appointments he cannot afford to cancel and several urgent visits to clients, that's business, and he cannot neglect his responsibilities at the agency. He suggests I go there with Ricardo who is a doctor, or with Sandra who is not easily intimidated and usually gets her way. 'More than can be said for me,' I think to myself. Yes, I shall go, but without Sandra because this is a matter I must resolve on my own. 'Unless we go there the day after tomorrow,' Chico suggested half-heartedly. 'No, there's no time to lose, it has to be tomorrow.'

I shall go. I am familiar with the walls of Caxias, which can be seen from the road. About the prison itself I know nothing. Or something, if seeing is enough. I can visualize the *Prigioni* of Piranesi, the photographs of Hitler's concentration camps, the various Sing Sings one sees in films. Images. Not really much help in this situation. By now Antonio has experienced the rest: the prison-cell, the interrogations, the guards, prison food, hard bunks. And perhaps even torture. Not just physical aggression but being deprived of sleep for days on end. No one is likely to give me any information, I am not a relative and can think of no persuasive arguments. While I am speaking (where? to whom?) they will take down the registration number of my car and bring it up at trial, every little detail or scrap of information might be useful, nothing is superfluous, nothing is discarded in case it turns out to be vital information. Antonio was of no interest to the police, then suddenly they pounced and put him under arrest. What did he do? What did he know? When and where did Antonio make some compromising move which warranted his arrest and detention in Caxias? For how long had he known he was in danger of being arrested because of subversive activities which had put him at risk? When Antonio conversed with us or went to the cinema or took a stroll, or right here in my apartment held up a portrait covered in black paint, what was he thinking about, mulling over, plotting, and where and when and how? And with whom? We all have certain things we allow or wish others to know, certain other things we hide from them, and this is the code of social conduct we observe, tolerated because harmless and normal, but Antonio had more to hide than the rest of us. He concealed the most important thing of all, his secret life. He was concerned about his safety and the safety of those who depended on him. And as we chatted and he listened, saying nothing, smoking, watching us attentively, what could he have been thinking? On a par with the audible reply he gave us, what other reply was he mentally construing in silence?

Enough of asking questions. On the territory of S.'s adversary I revive those questions I asked myself when I decided half-way through painting the second portrait to turn to writing to try and find out more about S. I went round in a circle and came back to where I had started from – after making my journey. I must refrain from asking myself any more questions, from interrogating Antonio who, like S., but for other reasons, might not want to answer me. Either I find out by myself or I shall never know. And today, within this circle, I have travelled in all directions, at least I know where the wall and boundaries are situated. No one can proceed further without this knowledge. The difference between the circle and the spiral.

Just as I expected. They turned me away from the northern gate and sent me to the southern entrance of the prison. I filled in a chit and waited for almost an hour. They summoned me at their leisure. I was not allowed beyond the corridor. A young smooth-faced policeman received me with chilling courtesy and indifference and confirmed that since I was not a relative I could not visit the prisoner. I enquired if Antonio was all right but he refused to answer me. I asked if his family had been notified and he told me curtly it was none of my business. Then added: 'Just because you turn up here claiming to be a friend of the prisoner is no proof that you even know him. I'm in no position to give you any information. Is there anything else I can do for you?' He accompanied me to the door. I left without so much as looking at him or saying another word. I climbed the rough path as far as the square in front of the northern entrance where I had parked my car. I opened the door, got in and clutched the wheel with all my might, shaking with rage and humiliation. Through the windscreen I could see the Republican guard in his sentry-box, and higher up on a low wall stood two more guards armed with rifles. This was Caxias. A tall, massive building with barred windows, cells I could only imagine, interrogations for hours on end, continuous beatings day and night, prisoners kept standing without sleep until their feet swelled up causing the laces of their shoes to snap – a form of torture I had heard people discuss and which Antonio must be familiar with by now. I turned the car round and slowly began descending the path until I reached the motorway. My mind was made up. Next day I would go to Santarém and would neither rest nor give up until I had found Antonio's parents. This was the least I could do.

There was no need to go. Around seven that same evening the telephone rang. I thought it must be Chico, although I had already told him about my fruitless trip to Caxias. I lifted the receiver and gave my number. I heard a woman's voice: 'This is Antonio's sister. I'd like to talk to you alone. Is that possible?' I immediately tried to recall if Antonio had ever told us about his sister. Perhaps he had mentioned her in passing a long time ago, just as he had spoken of his parents in passing. I replied: 'Certainly. Whenever you like. Where do you suggest we meet? I can see you right away. Or are you calling from Santarém?' Without a moment's hesitation she replied: 'I'm here in Lisbon. Could we meet at your place?' 'Of course. When do you want to come? At once?' 'Yes, if you don't mind.' 'I'll be here waiting.' I was about to put down the receiver when the thought occurred to me: 'Are you still there? Can your hear me? Take down my address.' She assured me: 'That won't be necessary, I know where you live.'

Feeling somewhat puzzled by this sudden call, I replaced the receiver. I was eager to have news of Antonio but discovered I was more nervous than pleased as I quickly began tidying up the room, putting away the clothes scattered over chairs and plumping up the cushions on the sofa. I wanted the place to look reasonably tidy. I put fresh towels in the bathroom, covered the unwashed dishes in the kitchen with a plastic cloth. This did not take long and I was soon sitting with a book and leafing through the pages. I seem to remember it was a book about Braque.

It is now two o'clock in the morning (night for those who go to bed late, morning for those who rise early) and I have just come in. I accompanied Antonio's sister to his apartment where she will spend the night. We were together for more than six hours and I think I ought to refer to her as M. Let us say it is a premonition, some vague desire or vow, the simple superstition of appeasing gestures. I am writing slowly, writing with enormous effort after six hour of dialogue and I am probably incapable of expressing vivid sentiments and emotions which are set out here with some sense of order, not exactly classified, but passed from hand to hand and arranged according to their weight, density and (since I have not given up painting) colour. This is what I have been doing while writing out some two hundred pages. I cannot write in any other way and, if I have thrown myself into this writing, it was precisely in order to give myself sufficient time to think, to think with time. To be born, live and die are universal truths which form a natural sequence. If we wish to transform them into a personal truth and natural sequence, then we shall have to write much more than the three verbs arranged in that order and concede that, between the two extremes of nothingness and nothingness, life may contain a number of births and deaths, not only those of others which may touch or distress us, but our own births and deaths. Like the cobra, we shed our skin when we no longer fit inside it, or we lose our strength and waste away, and this only happens to humans. A skin which has aged, turned dry and wrinkled, covers these pages with black and white pellicles, the words and the spaces between them. At this moment, I would describe myself as being flayed as St Bartholomew, the same image if not the pain. I am still holding bits of withered skin, but the fibres of my muscles and cords of my tendons are covered with a delicate membrane, the first metamorphosis of my personal silkworm which I assume will have continuous life rather than death inside its cocoon. The state of the chrysalis is not to be envied. Its very nature contradicts my perception of the continuous flow of life. (Nevertheless, the chrysalis is alive.)

A door is at once an opening and that which closes it. In novels as in life, people and characters spend much of their time going in and out of houses or other places. One thinks of it as being a somewhat banal act, a movement which is scarcely worth noticing or registering. As far as I can recall, only the most literary of painters

(Magritte) observed the door and the passage through with a look of amazement and even disquiet. The doors of Magritte, open or ajar, offer no guarantee that what we left behind is still on the other side. When we last entered, it was a bedroom; next time we enter we may find an empty and luminous space, with clouds slowly passing over a pale, serene blue sky. How strange that literature (if I have studied lots of paintings, I have also read many books) should not have paid more attention to doors, to these broad, wooden planks joined together, or mobile panels, lids standing upright and defying the law of gravity. And strangest of all, that no importance should be given to that unstable space between the doorposts. Yet that is where bodies pass through and pause to look.

This was how I first set eyes on Antonio's sister. I thought I was being alert but failed to hear her climbing the stairs. A sharp ping from the bell made me jump, put my book aside, childishly hoping its cover was facing upwards as I walked across the studio to open and pull back the door. A measured, uninterrupted movement. And now the briefest of pauses, just enough time to break that invisible membrane covering the gap in the doorway, just enough time for those feet to vacillate for a second on the threshold, enough time for our eyes to seek and meet as she arrives and I stand there waiting to greet her. A man and a woman. I repeat: I am writing this hours later and I am narrating our meeting in the light of what took place: I am not describing, I am remembering and reconstructing. Linking the last tactile sensation to the first, the latter now reconstituted on another plane: I said goodbye to M. a short time ago with a handshake, well not exactly, the handshake was when I first greeted her. I would say the two gestures were uniform. In as much as the time that elapsed between these gestures is taken as a mere instant and not as a juxtaposed succession of hours, full or otherwise, fluid or dense, slow or quite the opposite, flickering. That is why this narrative must appear to contain less and more. And one will never know how much the time compressed into these pages really contained.

Lingering in the doorway, M. stood there looking at me. The first thing I noticed were her eyes: bright, hazel, tawny, the colour of gold, big and open, staring at me like windows and who knows, perhaps more open inwardly than outwardly. The hair, short, the same colour as her eyes but then darker under the electric light. Her face triangular with a sharp chin. The faintest tremor on the lips because of an unexpected line of tiny stitches which successively change in tonality once she starts speaking. Her nose narrow and nicely shaped. A hand's breadth shorter than me. Her body agile. Her shoulders slender. A tiny girlish waist over a woman's hips. Forty years old, or thereabouts. Not a bad description for someone who claims to have seen all this in the time it takes to pass through a door, to enter the room, remain standing there and then sit down, a brief exchange of words distracting his observations which at that moment could not possibly have been very precise. But let me remind you that there have been six hours of eyes, words and pauses. It was only in the restaurant, for example, that I became aware of that curious tremor on her lips which the waning evening light in my apartment had prevented me from noticing sooner.

She repeated the words she had started to say to me over the telephone. 'I'm Antonio's sister.' And added: 'My name is M.' I opened the door wider to allow her to enter. I introduced myself. 'My brother spoke to me about you.' 'Did he really?' I was more surprised than I looked as I led her to my shabby and much-used sofa. 'Can I offer you anything?' She declined, explaining that she rarely drank. 'I suppose you must be wondering why I've come here but would rather not ask lest I take offence.' I made some vague gesture which could not be translated into words but was meant to say much the same or at least the first part. 'Antonio told me ages ago that if something were to happen to him, if he should be arrested, I was to contact you. That's why I've come.' How can I express what I felt? Let me put it like this: the lines of my relational diagram (does the term exist?) wavered and broke, tried to reconnect where they were broken, some succeeded, others went on vibrating, detached, seeking new moorings. 'I'm afraid I won't be of much help. This very day ... ' I broke off as I recalled the smooth complexion of the young policeman. 'This very day I went to Caxias and achieved nothing.' 'You went to Caxias?' 'Yes, I've been there myself. They wouldn't let me see Antonio. Not before Wednesday of next week. Perhaps, was the word they used.' 'Not before next Wednesday?' 'They told me they could give me no information whatsoever. Nor were they obliged to do so.' 'We all know they have no obligations. They do just as they please. It was only yesterday that they contacted us in Santarém. Yet Antonio has been under arrest for four days.' M. was not leaning back on the cushions of the sofa but she showed no signs of tension or nervousness. 'Antonio and I are friends, but we haven't seen much of each other recently. What you said just now rather surprised me, I must confess.' 'That I should contact you if anything were to happen?' 'Yes.' 'He must have had his reasons. But there is one hypothesis which I myself must eliminate. You said you haven't seen much of Antonio lately?' 'That's true.' 'So there were no political ties between you?' 'None whatsoever.' M. stared at me for some time as if examining an equation before trying to resolve it, or a model before tracing the first line. 'In that case, my brother was asking me to contact you simply as a human being.' I smiled: 'It would appear so, simply as a human being. Forgive my being so little.' She also smiled. (M. does not smile like most people, who slowly part their lips with some effort. M's smile opens up at once and is slow to fade: she smiles like a child startled by wonders which continue to be wonders even after that smile, which is why it is retained. Although as a mere spectator I do not include myself in this category.) 'I am grateful to you. You did more than your duty. You went to Caxias and did your best. I believe my brother was right.' 'If I can be useful in any way, you may count on me. I want to help Antonio clear his name.' This time it was perfect, we both smiled at the same time. Then I remembered the prison, tried to imagine what might be happening there and shuddered. 'How do you feel about Antonio's imprisonment?' I asked. She crossed her hands on her lap: 'Nothing in particular, obviously I'm worried, of course I am, but I'm trying to persuade myself that Antonio is spending a few days of his life in some other place, that those days, however few or many, are also part of his life and that the place itself is where any one of us might spend a part of our life.' She said this in a firm tone of voice, yet unemphatically, as if the very weight of the words excluded any affectation in the intonation. 'You said any one of us. I'm just an ordinary citizen of no political significance, so I doubt whether you could include me.' 'I mean all of us. You're Antonio's friend, you went to Caxias, even now the police must be checking up on any visitors. And if they haven't already started making inquiries, they won't be long in starting. I'm Antonio's sister, I've been to Caxias, I am sitting here in your apartment, they may even have had me followed.' M. now gave a wan smile: 'As you can see, between being free and under suspicion, between being under suspicion and in prison, there isn't much distance. But we mustn't let this worry us. The police can't throw everyone under suspicion into prison. Besides, the fascist régime has found an effective and simple manner of dealing with this problem. Caxias is merely a prison inside a much larger prison, the whole country. Very practical, don't you agree? Within the larger prison suspects can usually move about at will; once they become dangerous they are transferred to smaller prisons: Caxias, Peniche and other less notorious institutions. It's as simple as that.' What impressed me was her straightforward manner. I got up from my bench, switched on the lights and went to pour her a whisky and one for myself, I dropped in some ice from the bucket I'd prepared, distracted, and completely forgetting that M. had told me she rarely drank. It was only when I held out the glass that I became aware of my foolishness (I did not even know whether she liked whisky) but she accepted it quite naturally and raised it to her lips. I also drank. 'Have you ever been imprisoned?' I asked her. 'Yes, I have.' 'A long time ago?' 'Years ago. Twice. The first time for three months; the second, for eight.' 'How did you cope?' 'It wasn't very pleasant. But there were others who had a worse time than me.'

Then there was silence. My relational diagram recovered its stability, but with some of the lines arranged differently. In the middle a spiral became displaced, turning on itself, blindly swaying from one

JOSÉ SARAMAGO

side to the other, like a rotifer inside a drop of water. I once saw this in a painting and it startled me. The painting was abstract and it made a deep impression. I thought to myself: 'A rotifer is not abstract, much as I should like to think so when I swallow one in a sip of water.' I was torn between this triviality and the attentive expression I directed at M. This is a strategy I often practise but this time I sensed some disloyalty. The silence was beginning to seem endless and I wanted to break it, but she spoke first: 'Antonio told me you're a painter.' I told her: 'He was exaggerating. It's not enough to paint in order to become a painter. Simply by writing one doesn't become a writer. Antonio knows perfectly well the kind of painter I am. The kind of painter I have been. I paint portraits for people who can afford to pay handsome fees. That's not painting.' 'Because they're portraits or because they fetch a high fee?' I looked at her sternly. Now it was my turn: 'Because it's inferior.' M. looked around her. Apart from some old sketches, a few still-lifes and several good quality prints worth looking at, all I have on my walls is the portrait of the couple from Lapa and the picture copied from Vitale da Bologna. 'I'm no judge or expert. Did you paint that?' (It was the couple from Lapa.) 'Yes, I did.' 'It strikes me as being very good.' 'I would agree but it's unfinished. The clients didn't want it in the end.' Suddenly I remembered the scene of my expulsion from the villa in Lapa, carrying my portrait so as not to damage it – and I burst out laughing. M. also laughed out of sympathy. 'What are you laughing at? Am I allowed to know?' Of course I was hoping she would ask. I gave her a detailed account of the episode as I remembered it, not so much based on facts as from the version I gave earlier. 'They were the victims of their own greed. If only they had allowed me to finish the portrait, pay me my fee (but this is what they were anxious to avoid), and then destroy it. As things turned out, I came off best. I finished up owning a picture I really like.' We found ourselves laughing at the sheer absurdity of the whole affair. More silence followed but different this time. As if for the first time we seemed to discover (certainly in my case) that we were man and woman, each of us conscious of our own sex and of each other's. Sitting up straight on the sofa (she had leant back in the midst of our conversation), M. put down her glass and sat there staring at the ice-cube melting at the bottom. 'Another whisky?' I asked. She shook her head. Raising her eyes she spoke in a slow voice: 'Unless I'm mistaken, this picture is different from the others you've painted.' 'Quite different.' 'Why?' 'It's difficult to explain. These last few months have made me reflect on things. I've been thinking, making notes, and when this commission turned up, this was the result. They were justified in throwing me out, in my opinion.' 'And now, what are you going to do? Will you go back to your earlier style of painting?' I snapped back with an unseemly bluntness I could not avoid: 'Most certainly not.' The white cloud against a blue background had come and gone. Calm was restored. M. said: 'I think you're right. But you have to earn a living.' 'I've landed a job with an advertising agency. That's fairly normal. Chico works there. Antonio may have spoken about him.' 'No, I never heard him mention that name.' (Yet he had told her about me: sly Antonio.) 'Right now I have no idea what I should be painting. I prefer to wait and see what happens. Here's hoping.' 'And what's that picture over there?' 'One of my little jokes, based on a painting by a fourteenth-century Italian artist. The picture on the postcard.' Once more we fell silent. Then M. rose to her feet. She got up like a tiny furry animal, a cat, a squirrel or a poodle, as if coming out of herself: this was the strange impression she made on me. Slow to react, I just sat there watching her and feeling uneasy. Was she about to leave? 'Well, now that we've met, I must be going.' I then got up, realizing I knew nothing about her, wanting to hear more and reluctant to see her go. 'Are you returning to Santarém so soon? Without finding out something more about Antonio?' 'I'll travel back to Santarém tomorrow. Tonight I'll sleep in my brother's apartment. He gave us a key.' 'Then why leave so soon, now that we've got to know each other? It doesn't seem right for people to go their separate ways once they've met and got to know each other. You must admit, what I'm saying makes good sense. Why don't you have dinner with me?' The words came out before I could stop myself. Just like that. And it was not in my nature to be spontaneous. M.

hesitated for a moment, or paused for breath before replying: 'Why not?'

We both agreed it was time we had something to eat. Within two minutes we were walking downstairs. She descended ahead of me, leaning forward slightly to see where she was treading, and as I observed the nape of her neck, so slender, delicate and smooth, my heart missed a beat. The emotions I experienced were those of a child rather than of a grown man. I descended at my leisure with surprising agility. My heels (an old obsession of mine) tapped out a regular beat, not too loud, just right. In strict tempo is how I would describe it. At the bottom of the stairs we turned a dark corner and I extended my thumb and forefinger, in the direction of the nape of her neck. I was just out of reach and did not touch her, but my fingers measured the distance between us, so little and yet so great.

What follows is a brief summary. We dined and I accompanied her to the entrance to her brother's apartment. But the dinner was leisurely and animated, and afterwards we went for a long stroll around the city, chatting almost non-stop. I did not tell her I was doing some writing but dropped the odd hint. From her I learned that she had married early and divorced within four years. There are no children and she has been living in Santarém with her parents for the last twelve years. Her family had to move there from Lisbon because of her father's job. Antonio is two years older than M. She never finished her degree and works in a lawyer's office. Nowadays she rarely visits Lisbon. 'My work keeps me in Santarém,' she said in a tone of voice at once vague and quite distinctive. Apart from several comments about her brother's situation, we said nothing further about politics. She had paid her share of the bill with such nonchalance that I did not even attempt to argue. When she perceived that I was prepared to pay the bill on my own, she stared at me for two seconds (two seconds which seemed so brief yet somehow unending) and without changing her tone of voice she asked me: 'Why?' As I searched for an answer (and failed) she opened her bag and put the money on the table. We said goodbye to each other at the entrance to Antonio's apartment. I asked: 'When shall I see you again?' She replied: 'Next Wednesday. I'll ring you as soon as possible.' Ignoring the customary formalities, we held hands. But gently and not for too long. 'Goodnight,' I said. 'Good luck with your work,' she replied, smiling.

M. did not ring me from Lisbon but from Santarém. And not on the
Wednesday but on the Tuesday evening. I was taken by surprise,
thinking it might be Chico with instructions for the following day,
or Carmo having a relapse, or Sandra in one of her tantrums. Or a
commission from someone living on some other planet. When I
heard her voice I felt a sudden contraction (or expansion? or a simple discharge of nervous tension?) in my solar plexus, and my
heartbeat rose to a hundred and ten pulsations or so. M. informed
me she would be coming on Wednesday as arranged but she would
not be alone. She was coming with her parents in the hope that
Antonio might be allowed visitors. They wondered if I would mind
driving them to Caxias (from this I gathered that M. had mentioned
Antonio's trustworthy friend to her parents) unless this would inter-
fere with my work. She felt my presence would make all the
difference to her parents who were very worried about their son.
'They're now quite elderly and find it more difficult to cope.' I said
yes to everything with a smile, although scarcely appropriate
under the circumstances. We agreed on a place and time to meet.
They were travelling by train. 'And what about lunch?' I asked.
Lunch was not a problem. They would eat something before setting
out from Santarém. We chatted on until we had nothing more to say
to each other: 'I'm deeply grateful to you,' she said, her voice clear and
direct. I stood there with the receiver in my hand, smiling once more,
with a vague expression on my face, perhaps even happy.

I have not written anything for the last few days because I am
anxious not to turn these pages into a diary. If they had been meant
for a diary I should have jotted down that I spent every waking hour
thinking about my meeting with M. and re-reading what I wrote
about that meeting. Obviously I am exaggerating, but looking back,

I can think of no other mental activity which has occupied me more. I thought of developing what is merely a summary of our meeting, but it would be my first attempt at anything like this since I first began writing. I preferred not to alter a single line. But what I can say is that I am interested in M. What does a man mean when he says he is interested in a woman? As a rule, that he is interested in going to bed with her. But what do I mean? I shall be frank. I really would like to go to bed with M. Just because I am a man and she is a woman? No. Sandra is all woman yet I have never felt physically attracted to her in the slightest. M. interests me because I spent six hours conversing with her without ever feeling tired or praying for silence. M. interests me because she has a forthright way of addressing people, a manner of speaking which cuts no corners, penetrates walls, cuts through all physical and mental reservations. M. interests me because she is a beautiful woman and because she is intelligent or vice versa. In a word: I am interested in M. Twenty years ago I would have written the word love without a moment's hesitation, whereas I now speak of interest. With age and experience we learn to use words with caution. We misuse them, put them back to front without noticing, until one day we discover they are as threadbare as old clothes, we feel ashamed of them just as I can recall being ashamed of trousers I once wore with frayed bottoms which were meticulously trimmed every week to disguise the constant repairs. I believe that in writing these pages I have shown some concern for words and the way they are used. Before, I hardly ever used the word love and when I did, the word did not refer to me, or only to part of me. Now that it really concerns me why should I not be cautious? I would even go so far as to mask the word if necessary, use other words, as in those anagrams we composed in primary school to act as props so that the real word might emerge and flourish. However, having given this some thought, I prefer to invoke the word love loud and clear and see what happens.

At the appointed hour I was waiting in front of Santa Apolonia Station. I waited almost twenty minutes (the train was late) and finally saw M. arriving with her parents. I doubt if people are really capable of controlling their emotions, as the saying aptly goes. Having been anxious to meet M.'s parents, I only noticed them when parents and daughter were standing before me or I before them if I made the first move. M. introduced me as so-and-so, Antonio's friend. I shook their wrinkled hands, then looked at those two weary faces (solemn rather than sad) and allowed my eyes to follow their natural inclination. M. was standing beside me, her eyes bright in the harsh afternoon light, her lips trembling. I felt another jolt in my solar plexus. Naturally, we spoke. We all spoke, about Antonio, prison, the regime, the situation in the country (remarkable how both parents spoke with assurance and judgement), we chatted as I drove the car through the Baixa, along the Avenida da Liberdade, M. at my side, sitting back calmly in her seat and turning her head from time to time to address her parents. One couple in front, another behind. I took a deep breath, feeling an upsurge of strength in my arms and shoulders and a tension in my lower abdomen. I did not reproach myself, refused to be hypocritical and feel guilty because sitting behind me were two elderly people who were worried about their son. They were composed, just as their daughter was composed. At a red light, I looked back and listened more attentively to what the mother was saying, and found myself confronting the couple from Santarém, and by comparison the couple from Lapa were mere caricatures (I am referring to the real couple from Lapa, made of flesh and blood, for the couple in the portrait are already a caricature of the caricature itself). We got on the motorway and I increased my speed. We did not want to arrive late and give the guards at Caxias an excuse for refusing us admittance. We turned off in the direction of the prison, beneath the eucalyptus trees. Through the open window of the car came the warm scent of the trees, that musky scent of cinnamon and pepper which opens the lungs and makes one feel dizzy. I began climbing the ramp and heard M.'s father saying behind me: 'Nothing has changed.' I asked 'Have you also been detained here?' 'No, but we came to visit our daughter.' I glanced sideways at M. She was blushing. That girlish blush was all I needed. How I adored her at that moment.

We entered the forecourt facing the entrance. I parked the car and opened the doors. The mother asked: 'Can you wait for us? We don't want to take too much of your time.' 'I'll wait for as long as is necessary. I'm only sorry not to be able to do more.' They went off in the direction of the main gate, side by side, the mother in the middle. The Republican guard in the sentry-box questioned them and M. replied. I could not hear what they were saying. They stood there waiting. At one point M. turned in my direction and smiled. I waved, not to say goodbye but as if promising to join them. A few moments later the gate was opened and they disappeared inside. As I waited (forty minutes precisely by my watch) other people arrived. The same exchanges through the port-hole of the sentry-box, the same waiting and then admittance through the gate which opened reluctantly, barely enough for visitors to squeeze through. I strolled around the car, sat on the brick border of a flower-bed full of withered geraniums. A few minutes later I got up and went up to the sentry-box: the Republican guard was on the telephone, he would listen, then reply. He peered at me from out of the shadows, then came to the port-hole: 'Do you want something?' 'No, I'm waiting for some people who've gone inside.' 'You're not allowed to loiter at the gate. Move away.' I turned on my heel without as much as replying. Son of a bitch.

When M. and her parents re-emerged I was sitting in the car listening to the radio. I went to meet them. The mother's eyes were red and tearful but she had only just started weeping, perhaps only after coming through the gate. The father's expression was grim. M. looked pale. 'Well?' I asked. The question was pointless but what else could I say? We got into the car. 'Shall we go?' M. asked in a low voice. I slowly started up the engine, skirted the wall and began descending the path full of potholes (deliberately left there, no doubt, to prevent any vehicle from making a quick getaway before the sentries had time to open fire) with which I was becoming familiar. 'He's been beaten up,' said M. 'He indicated he'd been beaten up but not to say anything.' 'My poor son,' sighed the mother. 'Tell me more. How did you find him? Did he have any message for his friends?' I caught the flicker of a smile in the corner of M.'s eye. 'Messages for friends, no. But he told me not to forget to get the painter to white-wash the chicken coop. I told him I'd already sent for him and not to worry. The one person who did not appreciate the conversation was the guard. He obviously thought we were speaking in code.' This caused general amusement. 'Trust Antonio,' I muttered to myself. Don't forget to get the painter to come and whitewash the chicken coop. Could he have been thinking about me when he made that request? Was I the painter he had in mind, the one who had covered over a picture with black paint and who had long since been chosen for this moment should it ever arrive?

M. told me someone would call at my apartment the following evening, a railway worker with a parcel of clothes and personal belongings, in addition to some books Antonio was allowed to receive. She asked me if I would take them to Caxias the next day and hand them in at the gate. This time she did not ask me if it would be any trouble. It was an order rather than a request. I pre-ferred it so. When we reached the Baixa I made a suggestion: 'Wouldn't you all like to rest a little at my place?' M. looked at her watch: 'I don't think there's enough time.' She smiled: 'By the time we climb those four flights of stairs ...' Her parents obviously knew she had been to see me. This transparent relationship caused me some embarrassment. As a rule people keep quiet even about things they should confide, and between parents and children, as I recall, this secrecy is the accepted thing, disguised with a greater or lesser show of affection, destined to play a role I am almost tempted to describe as theatrical. Within this short period of time I became aware on a number of occasions, from what was said or implied, of this special relationship between M. and her parents: a detachment which might be seen as the final stage in the most intimate of rela-tionships, a kind of freedom notwithstanding extreme dependency, a tree born on the outer edge of the forest. I parked the car near the station and accompanied them to the entrance. I have always been struck by the absurdity of farewells on station platforms. Everything has already been said and there is no time to start all over again, no sign of the train leaving as the clock ticks out those last few seconds – then at last – sheer relief as it makes its departure even though there may be tears and remorse after the last carriage has disappeared from sight. The father thanked me for my help and said: 'We'll make our own way to the platform. No need for you to wait.' M. and I withdrew to a corner of the entrance hall to avoid the crowd. 'I've enjoyed your company,' I said looking into her eyes. 'And I've certainly enjoyed meeting you,' she replied. And with a serene but at the same time pensive expression she raised her head, stood on tiptoe and kissed me on the cheek. And without another word, a traveller who had made her farewell and was setting off on her journey, she crossed the concourse and went through the barrier without looking back. I returned slowly to the car and got in. There are such moments in life: one unexpectedly discovers that perfection exists, that it, too, is a tiny sphere travelling in time, empty, transparent, luminous, and which sometimes (rarely) comes in our direction and encircles us for a few brief moments before travelling on to other parts and other people. Yet I had the feeling that this sphere had not disengaged itself and that I was travelling inside. The hour of fear is nigh: I whispered to myself. New faces are appearing on the horizon of my desert. Who is this elderly couple, what is this composure they possess? And Antonio, now in prison, what freedom has he taken with him into his cell? And M., who smiles at me from afar, treading the sand with feet of wind, who uses words as if they were glass splinters and who suddenly approaches and kisses me? I repeat: the hour of fear is nigh. Perfection fleetingly exists. Not meant to linger. Much less stay. 'I've certainly enjoyed meeting you,' she said. Taking the utmost care with my lettering, I write these words over and over again. I travel slowly. Time is this paper on which I write.

JOSÉ SARAMAGO

There has been an abortive military uprising. Troops from the Fifth Infantry Regiment stationed at Caldas da Rainha have marched on Lisbon, but finally returned to their barracks. There is much disquiet everywhere. M. gave me a copy of the manifesto issued by the Officers' Movement. Here is the closing paragraph: 'We hereby declare our solidarity with our comrades who are under arrest and we shall continue to defend them, whatever the circumstances. Their cause is our cause, however much we may deplore their hasty action. The revolt they have staged has not been in vain. It has served to awaken the conscience of those who were perhaps still wavering. It has served to define the existing factions and provides valuable lessons for the immediate future. It has served to give us a sharp reminder of the glaring conflicts within the Army itself, and – since the Army is regarded as *the mirror of the Nation* – of the general turmoil throughout our Country. Finally, it has served to demonstrate the methods to which our "leaders" resort, their lack of any scruples and the alliances they form in their attempt to crush and paralyse a process which has already become irreversible. Under this last heading we must denounce the intervention of the Secret Police (directly instigated by the Minister and Under-secretary of State for Defence) arresting comrades and, at least in one case, forcing entry into a comrade's house at five o'clock in the morning, abusing his wife and children physically and mentally, and searching the house without a warrant. This intervention by the military police is repugnant and intolerable and constitutes a further violation of our civil rights. Such actions cannot be allowed to continue, otherwise they will become accepted practice and we shall lose forever any remnants of dignity and self-respect. Nor did our so-called *leaders* stop here. Summoning the National Guard, they despatched them against our comrades with an inadmissible and outrageous mandate authorising them to besiege the Military Academy! For its part, the Portuguese Legion, revealing the existence of an active military and police network, collaborated with the Security Forces and the National Guard by helping to pursue the men of the Fifth Infantry Regiment as they made their way back to Caldas da Rainha. Could it be that the Government and their "military chiefs" have finally found in the Portuguese Legion, the National Guard and Security Forces those valiant soldiers needed to carry out their overseas policy in Africa? Comrades from all three branches of the Armed Forces: the march of the Fifth Infantry Regiment on Lisbon, together with the events preceding it, have renewed our determination to promote our Movement with even greater confidence and resolve. We are relying on your spirit of comradeship and on your support for those imprisoned (nearly two hundred men in all, including officers, sergeants, corporals and conscripts), who gave the first real sign to the Country and the Armed Forces that we are not prepared to tolerate this state of affairs. Finally, we appeal to you to remain faithful to the declared objectives of the Movement. We must stand together and reinforce our organization, convinced that if we remain coherent and lucid we shall soon achieve our goal.'

JOSÉ SARAMAGO

M. could not remain in Lisbon. I took her to Caxias. (Antonio has been interrogated again and kept without sleep for four days. Could have been worse, commented M. He's received everything except the books which were confiscated.) We then took a drive around Sintra which she scarcely knew. We did not speak much. I have noticed that her moments of silence (and, therefore, *our* moments of silence) cause no embarrassment. They simply create a different time-scale during pauses in conversation. I believe it is possible (and even desirable) to remain silent for ages at her side and that silence becomes another way of continuing our conversation. I write the same thing in two different ways, to see if one of them gets it right. The thing is said, yet is somehow inadequate. It is not entirely true, however, that we have not spoken much. But to write (as I have learned) is a matter of choice just as with painting. One chooses words, phrases, snatches of dialogue just as one chooses colours or determines the length and direction of lines. The traced outline of a face can be interrupted without the face ceasing to exist: there is no danger that the matter contained within this arbitrary borderline will vanish through the opening. By the same token, when one writes, one eliminates the superfluous even though those words might have proved to be useful when spoken: the essence is preserved in this other interrupted line which is writing.

We dined in Sintra. It was already agreed that I would drive her to Santarém. We took a short stroll around the Palace Square. It was fairly cold and I instinctively put my arm around her shoulders. The gesture was meant to be fraternal and so it was, but I was conscious that the warmth I felt as our bodies made contact was anything but fraternal. With her left hand M. gripped mine as it came to rest on her right shoulder and like this we walked back to the car. Darkness had fallen. As we left the town under the tunnel of trees picked out leaf by leaf in the headlights, she repeated: 'I enjoy your company.' She could not have said anything nicer and those words were all I wanted to hear. What should I do? Park the car in some lay-by, switch off the headlights, pull her towards me, get her excited, pull up her skirt, open her blouse? A sad adventure. As if reading my thoughts and guessing my intentions, M. said: 'We mustn't rush things.' And I replied: 'I'm in no hurry.' The road was now straight all the way and I could drive faster, but we were not referring to the journey.

We went back to talking about her brother and parents. 'You said the other day that all your work is in Santarém. Such an odd way of putting it. What did you mean?' She smiled: 'You've a good memory.' 'It's not bad but in this instance it's even better because I wrote down the phrase word for word.' M. remained silent. We passed through a village. The streetlamps lit up our faces as we passed. And when we plunged once more into the darkness of the countryside M. began to speak: 'I work in a lawyer's office. We went to live in Santarém for the reasons I mentioned. It was there I met my husband. We married, didn't get on and separated. All this you already know. My parents like living in Santarém. I don't mind although the town is provincial and restricted. They built it on a hill, otherwise it might have been a fine city. House by house, street by street, those stones, it's more beautiful than one imagines. But not the people. There are exceptions everywhere, even in Santarém, I'm glad to say, but the horizon of the people who live in Santarém is not what you're likely to find in Portas do Sol. You've never seen a city appear to be so open while being so inward looking.' 'And are your horizons those of Portas do Sol?' 'Of course they are those of Portas do Sol.' 'I don't know what you mean.' Once more she fell silent. Then she examined me closely: I could see her eyes, tense, wide open and lit up by the indicators on the dashboard. I drove at a steady speed, neither slow nor fast. M. went back to staring at the road. And then began speaking again: 'Listen, we've only known each other for several weeks. All I knew was your name, address and telephone number.

A few reassuring words from my brother. I contacted you, visited you in your apartment, told you about myself, we spoke as friends, which is only natural, and you have been honest. I'm not referring to anything sexual when I say you've been honest: I mean something else, much more complicated and difficult to explain. The kind of honesty one has no difficulty in recognizing. I enjoy being in your company, as I've already said. And I'm likely to say it again because it's true. Unless I'm deceiving myself, I believe our friendship will last, become much more intimate. And I don't mean sex.' 'I know what you mean.' Resting her hand momentarily on my knee, she told me: 'I'm in charge of a political operation in the region of Santarém. That's why I said all my work is there. Santarém and district, as people used to say in the old days.' 'Are you a Party member?' 'Yes, I am.' 'And what about Antonio?' I could feel her retract: 'Antonio's in jail. There's nothing more to be said about him.'

For some minutes we did not speak. 'Thanks for telling me these things. You were under no obligation.' 'I was under no obligation but I wanted you to know. So there's nothing to thank me for.' 'What type of work do you do?' I could feel her stretch out on the seat, even smile: 'Oh, nothing special. I'm not important. I make contact with comrades in a number of villages, with various organizations, a job no one notices, but necessary just the same. Things blow hot and cold and I've had my troubles. But, believe me, as I look at these fields right now, I'm convinced I'm doing the right thing. Don't ask me to explain.' 'You don't have to explain anything. I've also read Marx.' She laughed: 'Don't tell me you're another one who claims to have read the whole of *Das Kapital*.' 'Not quite all of it.' We both laughed. She rested her arm on the back of my seat and I repeated the gesture she had made in Sintra. Holding the wheel with my left hand, I squeezed hers with my right hand. But a narrow bend in the road appeared and the steering wheel required my roaming hand. 'Were you imprisoned because of these activities?' 'No. For something much more obvious. But they couldn't prove anything.' 'If I'm asking questions you'd rather not answer, tell me.' 'Don't worry. You simply won't get an answer. I might even call the police.' We were laughing again like a couple of adolescents. This miraculous sphere travelling with me inside.

'Your job isn't easy.' 'No, at times it can be tough, but someone has to do it. The workers have an even harder time and they don't complain: they just go on struggling. In 1962, when workers were campaigning for an eight-hour day, I was twenty-seven years old and had just separated from my husband. At that time I wasn't even a Party member but I was no less committed. My father is a veteran militant. I know he was extremely active in those days, mainly in the region south of the river: Almeirim, Lamarosa, Coruche, as far as Couço. Have you ever been to Couço? Anyone reading the newspapers at that time must have thought it was on some other planet. But that planet was right here. Let me try to explain: the workers didn't go around pleading for eight hours, they didn't go begging the Government to release them from labour that lasted from dawn to dusk. There are Party documents to prove it. In Alcácer do Sol, for example (a story I read and will never forget) this is what happened: the workers decided to ignore their foreman's orders and began work at eight o'clock. At ten-thirty, the normal time for lunch, the siren went, but they played deaf and went on working. At noon they downed tools and went off to have their lunch. By five o'clock they had been working for eight hours. Work came to a halt and everyone went home. Sounds simple, wouldn't you say? But you have no idea how much effort went into making workers aware of their rights, organizing meetings and debates. One has to be involved to appreciate the problems. And I could quote other stories: such as that of the landowner at Montemor-o-Novo. When some men asked him for work, he told them: "If you've already eaten the food you earned in eight hours, then you can feed on straw!" Whereupon the workers went onto his land and stole a lamb, leaving behind a note which read: "So long as there's meat, why should we feed on straw?" The authorities retaliated with arrests, torture, shootings. People were killed. Anyone who was there knows what it was like. I've only heard or read about these things.' 'Has the situation improved?' I asked. 'We go on. It's rather like a river. It carries more or less water

JOSÉ SARAMAGO

but goes on flowing. We're much the same, we go on.' She looked very serious, her eyes fixed on the road. To the right the river shone. 'Besides,' she said, 'this regime can't last much longer. The coup at Caldas won't be the last. And we haven't been idle. Our work goes on. Fascism is on the way out.'

We were approaching the city. I said: 'You must trust me, telling me these things.' 'Yes. I trust you. And I like you. I like you a lot.' A hundred and ten kilometres from Sintra I finally stopped the car. I pulled in to the side of the road and parked under a tree, listening to the leaves crackling beneath the wheels, and then silence. I turned to M. She was looking at me. She repeated: 'Yes, I like you.' I pulled her towards me but did not open her blouse or pull up her skirt. We simply kissed until the world was full of constellations. And I told her: 'I like you.' And then with one voice we said, 'My love'.

'My love.' To repeat these two words on ten pages, to go on writing them uninterruptedly without any clarification, slowly to begin with, letter by letter, carefully tracing out the humps of the handwritten *m*, the loops of the *y* and the *l*, the startled cry over that *o*, the deep river-bed excavated by the *v* and slack knot of the *e*. And then to transform this slow operation into a single quivering thread, a sign on the seismograph as limbs shudder and collide, the page a white sea, luminous towel or extended linen sheet. 'My love', and I repeated the words throwing my door wide open to receive you as you walked in. Your eyes opened wide as you came towards me as if you were trying to get a better look at me and you put your bag on the floor. And before I could kiss you, I heard you say quite calmly: 'I've come to spend the night with you.' You arrived neither too early nor too late. You came at precisely the right moment onto that precise and precious platform of time where I could wait for you. Surrounded by mediocre pictures, by things painted and watching, we removed our clothes. Your body so fresh. Both of us eager but taking our time. And once naked, we looked at each other without shame because paradise is to be naked and to know. Slowly (it could only be slowly, very slowly) we drew closer and closer until we suddenly found ourselves in a tight embrace and trembling. Our bodies were pressed against each other, my sex against your belly, your arms around my neck, our mouths, tongues and teeth, breathing and drawing nourishment, speaking without uttering a word, an interminable moan like some vibration, unformed letters, an interval. We knelt, climbed the first step, and then slowly, as if supported by air, you fell onto your back with me on top of you, both of us naked, and then we rolled over, naked, you now on top of me, your breasts elastic, your hips covering me, your thighs spreading like wings. We became as one and as one we rolled over once more, with me back on top of you, your hair glistening, my hands now spread on the floor as if I were supporting the world on my shoulders, or the heavens, and in the space between us tense looks, then blurred, the noise of blood ebbing and flowing in our veins and arteries, beating in our temples, surging beneath our skin as our bodies came together. We are the sun. The walls go round, the books and pictures, Mars, Jupiter, Saturn, Venus, tiny Pluto, the Earth. And now here is the sea, not the great wide ocean, but the wave from the depths trapped between two coral reefs, rising up and up until it explodes in frothing spume. The quiet murmuring of waters spilling over mosses. The wave retreats into the mysterious recesses of submarine caves, and you whispered 'My love'. Around the sun, the planets resume their slow and solemn journey and here from afar we now see them at a standstill, once more there are pictures and books, and instead of that deep sky there are walls. Night has returned. I lift you naked from the floor. Resting on my shoulder, you tread the same ground as me. Look, these are our feet, a mysterious inheritance, soles which leave imprints as they claim the little space we occupy in the world. We are standing in the doorway. Can you feel the invisible veil which has to be penetrated, the hymen of houses, torn and renewed? Inside there is a room. I cannot promise you the clear sky and drifting clouds of Magritte. We are as wet as if we had just come out of the sea and entering a tiny cavern where you can feel the darkness on your face. The faintest of light. Just enough to see each other. I lay you on the bed and you open your arms and hover over the white sheet. I bend over you. It is your body that is breathing, the mountain ledge and source. Your eyes are open, forever open, wells of glistening honey. And your hair is shining, a golden harvest. I whisper 'My love' and your hands travel down from the nape of my neck to the small of my back. There is a fiery torch inside my body. Once again your thighs spread like wings. And you sigh. I know you, I recognize where I am: my mouth opens on your shoulder, my outstretched arms accompany yours until our fingers clasp with a superhuman strength. Like two hearts our bellies throb. You call out, my love. The entire heavens are calling out above us, everything seems to be dying. We have already unclasped our hands, they have lost and found each other on the nape of our neck, in our hair, and locked in embrace we now await approaching death. You are trembling. I am trembling. We shake from head to foot and cling to each other on the brink of the fall. It is inevitable. The sea has just swept in, rolls us onto this white shore or sheet and explodes over us. We call out, close to suffocation. And I whisper: 'My love.' You lie sleeping naked beneath the first light of dawn. I see your bosom outlined against the light of that intangible veil covering the door. I slowly rest my hand on your belly. And sigh peacefully.

JOSÉ SARAMAGO

I already know what I shall do with the canvas on the easel. It is still too early for the portrait of M. but my time has come. The canvas has matured (in the atmosphere and light of the studio), the mirror has matured if such a thing is possible (tarnished with time), I have matured (this lined face, this canvas, this other mirror). I look at myself in the polished surface, the tubes of paint unopened, the brushes dried out after weeks of gathering dust. I gaze at myself in the mirror, not distracted nor in haste, but attentive, appraising, measuring the depth of the cut I am about to make. A brush, gentlemen (I am not addressing anyone in particular, it is a somewhat rhetorical form of address I have adopted before in these pages), a brush resembles an engraver's scalpel. It is not a scalpel but something like a scalpel. It can be used, for example, to prise off and gently scrape away the skin of the couple from Lapa in order to find out what is underneath. It has helped me to graft skin onto skin, as I have explained at length elsewhere, and I can claim to have carried out this operation during the last twenty years of my life as an artist (there is no other way to define it) some eighty times. As a skilled practitioner of this other type of plastic surgery, I compare more than favourably with the specialists. There are never any seams, scars or marks showing after I have carried out this surgery. I fear that once they unhook me from the wall they will not find it easy to replace me. The Eduardo Maltas of this world are a dying breed of painters and I might well be the last in the line. I am working on designs for packaging, I slip the art supplement into publicity campaigns and tactfully ask the copy-editor, who is very jealous of his work, whether he would mind moving his phrase to the right to give one of my lines some breathing space. And so I find myself in the interval. It is time to put this entire face onto canvas, and what those eyes in the mirror see around them, all those lines and planes which in one way or another always converge to the pupils of the eyes which are the vanishing point. Besides, there is another reason. This narrative is about to end. It has lasted the time that was necessary to finish one man and start another. It was important that the face which still exists should be recorded and that the first traces of the one about to emerge should be sketched out. Jotting these things down provided a challenge. I am now facing up to another challenge, but on my own territory. Would that I might succeed in putting onto this canvas what has been written on these pages. Painting must at least achieve this much. I ask no more for I am asking a lot. (Piero della Francesca, Mantegna, Luca Signorelli, Paolo Uccello, Bosch, Pieter Bruegel, Michelangelo, Leonardo, Matthias Grünewald, Van Eyck, Goya, Velazquez, Rembrandt, Giotto, Picasso, Van Gogh, and so many others put everything into their painting.) Would that I (H.) might be able to put something, however modest, into mine. I cannot say how long it will take me to paint this self-portrait. I have learned at last not to rush things. Writing has taught me this first lesson. Will the portrait also reveal the face of this apprentice? But let us not anticipate. What concerns us here is the soil today and not tomorrow's wheat. Tomorrow this mirror will be broken, today is its time and mine.

And now for the portrait, self-portrait, autopsy, which means, above all, inspection, contemplation, self-examination. On this side, the mirror; on the other, the canvas. I am between the two, like the rotifer between two sheets of glass, hovering in its last drop of water and about to be observed under the microscope. All the light one can capture, but not so much as to blot out the traces, or so little as to conceal them. The brush is very firm, a hybrid, being both animal and vegetable, a hard, long stem with bristles instead of willow-leaves. The canvas is still white. The canvas itself another mirror covered in dust. I would say my own face is painted beneath this thick layer which must be removed. I repeat, the paintbrush is like a scalpel. Could it also be a penknife, a scraper, perhaps even a pickaxe? This, too, is akin to archaeological excavation.

I have certain clear ideas about the picture. There will be a black band below, vaguely resembling a parapet or wall. My left hand will be placed on this smooth uniform balcony, and my right hand resting on it and clutching some sheets of paper. On the top sheet, folded at an angle allowing one to read what is written there, are the first three words of this manuscript. This shows that the spiral can be represented by the letters of the alphabet. I decided my portrait should be down to the waist. Behind me, as if peering over the wall to see who is passing, there is a flat landscape on a lower level with trees and perhaps the meanderings of a river (the Meandra: a river in Turkey noted for its many bends. Nowadays known as Buyuck-Menderez). Above everything as well as me, as one might have expected, sky and clouds. This picture will bear a coat-of-arms. In the upper left-hand corner there will be a coat-of-arms in miniature of the couple from Lapa, and in the upper right-hand corner another reduced copy: that of the picture I copied and modified from a painting by Vitale da Bologna. As a continuation of the handwritten manuscript the portrait must imitate something. Like the manuscript, and contrary to custom, it will make no attempt to disguise the seams, joins and repairs carried out by another hand. Quite the opposite: it will accentuate everything. The copy will seek to express more than is actually expressed in the original. It may not succeed in the end but, however disappointing the outcome, at least it will express something new. The portrait of Paracelsus painted by Rubens is undoubtedly superior to the portrait I am about to produce, yet the Rubens portrait is my model and point of reference, and it is the very same that is in the portrait I have just described. In a word, this picture of mine (as in the case of the manuscript) will not reject the copy but make it explicit. Therefore it is verification. Every work of art, even if as modest as this one of mine, must provide verification. If we want to look for something, we must lift up the lid (stone or cloud, but let us call it the lid) which is concealing it. And I am convinced we shall have little value as artists (and needless to say as men, people and individuals) if after finding, through good fortune or our own efforts, what we were looking for, we do not go on lifting the rest of the lids, clearing away stones and pushing the clouds back, each and every one of them. We must never forget that the first thing might have been put there deliberately just to prevent us from noticing the second one. To verify, in my humble opinion, is the truly golden test.

I am starting to mix the first tint on my palette. It is not an intermediate colour I need to combine and harmonize, like the voices in Monteverdi's *Magnificat* which fill my studio as I write. I simply squeeze the paint out generously, making no effort to economize. Black. This time intent upon revelation rather than concealment. I mean to work all day.

The regime has fallen. As expected, there has been a military coup. The day's events are beyond description: soldiers, tanks, a sense of relief, people embracing, words of joy, excitement, sheer jubilation. At this moment I am all alone. M. has gone to meet up with a Party member somewhere or other. Her clandestine activities are about to end. My self-portrait is making rapid progress. M. and I were asleep in my apartment when Chico, a real night-bird if ever there was one, rang up shouting his head off and telling us to switch on the radio at once. We jumped out of bed (Are you crying, my love?): 'This broadcast is coming from the Headquarters of the Armed Forces. The Portuguese Armed Forces appeal to all the people of the city of Lisbon ... ' We embraced (My love, you are crying) and, wrapped in the same sheet, we opened the window: the city, ah city, the night sky still overhead but the first glimmerings of diffused light way in the distance. I said: 'Tomorrow we'll go and fetch Antonio.' M. snuggled up against me. 'And one of these days I'll give you some papers of mine I'd like you to read.' 'Secrets?' she asked smiling. 'No. Just papers. Things I've written.'